THE HOLIDAY HOME

THE
HOLIDAY HOME

FERN BRITTON

LARGE PRINT
Oxford

First published in Great Britain 2013
by
HarperCollins*Publishers*

Published in Large Print 2014 by ISIS Publishing Ltd.,
7 Centremead, Osney Mead, Oxford OX2 0ES
by arrangement with
HarperCollins*Publishers*

CIP data is available for this title from the British Library

ISBN 978–0–7531–9282–5 (hb)
ISBN 978–0–7531–9283–2 (pb)

Printed and bound in Great Britain by
T. J. International Ltd., Padstow, Cornwall

For Jack. May all your dreams come true.
I love you.
Mum xx

ACKNOWLEDGEMENTS

I cannot thank Kate Bradley my wonderful editor enough for all the encouragement and care she has given me during the writing of this book. When the going got tough she talked sense into me over poached eggs and coffee. My love and thanks also go to John Rush who thinks, erroneously, that he is to slip into a quieter life away from his desk. I have news for you, John — you can't get rid of me that easily! Also, I must thank Luigi Bonomi, legendary literary agent, for his encouragement and inspiring words and the adorable Liz Dawson: hey little sister! As always my family have been my sounding board and mainstay. My love too, to Karen, Carole, Caroline, Lisa and the cycling pandas. No woman has better friends. My biggest and most heartfelt thanks of all, though, is to you for picking this book up. I hope you enjoy it.

Much love, Fern.

January 2nd 2013

Atlantic House 1988

The husk of a dead fly lay dry and brittle on the sun-bleached oak window sill.

The house was silent and empty in the drowsiness of the bright spring morning. If its almost three-hundred-year-old walls harboured any memories of previous occupants, the weddings and wakes, conceptions and christenings that had taken place here, there was no sign. Where rich brocade curtains had once hung from the tall windows, there clung trailing cobwebs. The days when handsome young men in tight breeches and high-collared frock coats had wooed maidens in muslin dresses were a thing of the past. Maybe the rustle of petticoats along the top landing could still be heard, but only by the tattered moths. In the musty bedrooms, patches of insidious damp crept ever outward, their spread unobserved and unchecked. In the cellars, the dark, dank, seaweed-scented stone walls were covered in a glistening silvery scrawl, marking the passage of slugs and snails. The worn steps, hewn out of the rocky floor, descended into darkness and the sound of the waves lapping against the walls of a natural cave beneath the house. On moonless nights, two hundred years ago, smugglers would time their arrival for high tide, steering their vessels through the opening in the rocks on the beach where the waves surged in, on into the torchlit cavern where their cargo of contraband brandy, tobacco and lace would be unloaded, away from the prying eyes of the revenue men. Only the odd holidaymaker ventured into the cave nowadays, but a rockfall twenty metres from the beach entrance prevented them from reaching the forgotten cave. The sea, however, continued as it always had done, ebbing and flowing into the recesses below Atlantic House.

In the old days, the gentleman of the house would welcome his gang of smugglers and lead them up the stone steps into an innocent-looking outhouse. A fortified wooden door opened into the garden. To the left was the back door of the house, now stiff with salt and age, which led into the kitchen. In front of the old hearth and chimney, still blackened by the fires of countless cooks, smugglers would have their wounds attended to by the lady of the house. And if the revenue men whose guns had caused the wounds came knocking, the fugitive would stay hidden in the cool of the pantry while the gentleman and his lady entertained them.

Today the ancient range, once the beating heart of the house, was cold, its doors seized with rust and its hot plates covered in soot falls.

Out in the garden, wild with broom, tamarisk, escallonia and fuchsia, the lawn bore no resemblance to the croquet pitch it had been between the two world wars; these days it was a Cornish meadow giving on to a buckthorn and gorse hedge. The weathered wooden gate, which had once banged so gaily on its sprung hinge with the constant traffic of beach-bound children, now drooped sadly.

As he placed the heavy key in the lock, estate agent Trevor Castle took in the commanding elevated position overlooking the much-sought-after Treviscum Beach. The key refused to move. Trevor leaned against the studded oak front door, gave the key a twist, and tried again. Still nothing. Bending down, he laid his clipboard, camera and retractable tape measure on the worn flagstones. Using both hands now, he managed to get the reluctant key to turn. As he pushed open the heavy door, a horrible squeal of protest from the unoiled hinges gave him a little fright. He steadied himself and carried on pushing. Something was blocking the door. When he had created a big enough gap to squeeze his head through, he paused for a moment, bracing himself for the prospect of a rotting corpse on the other side of the door. To his relief, when his eyes adjusted to the darkness he made out a pile of faded circulars and junk mail wedged against it. Chuckling at his stupidity, Trevor bent his full weight against the door and heaved until the opening was wide enough for him to step into the house. He stooped to clear the blockage and then returned to the porch to collect his estate-agent tackle.

With the door now open wide, the sun poured in, lighting up the impressive oak-panelled hall and spilling into the open doorway of the grand drawing room ahead with its breathtaking view down to the ocean.

"Wow. Hello, House," Trevor said out loud. He stepped into the hall, stirring aged dust motes. He didn't feel any gust of wind, but the front door banged shut so loudly behind him, he gave an involuntary jump and a yelp of fright. Hand resting on his pounding heart, he exhaled with relief.

"Steady on, Trev, buddy. Only the wind."

This was his first solo trip since joining Trish Hawkes & Daughter Property Agents. After weeks of trailing around after Trish, she had finally deemed him ready to go out and measure and photograph a house by himself.

"Atlantic House will be a good one to start you off," she'd announced, reaching round to the key cabinet and unhooking a large, obviously antique key. "Empty. No bloody occupying owner to interfere."

"Has it been vacant long?" he'd asked.

Trish had smiled, but there had been an uncharacteristic reticence about her as she'd replied: "Erm, about ten years. I think."

"Ten years! But it says here it's a sea-front location, with its own private cliff path to the beach. Place like that shouldn't stay empty ten minutes."

"Oh, erm, there was a bit of sadness in the family. Child had an accident or something. Anyway, the surviving daughter has just inherited and wants to get rid."

"Okey-dokey." Trev had been full of confidence as he had collected the heavy key from Trish's hand. "Let's make money."

4

He'd sauntered out of the office, conscious of Trish's eyes following him as he made his way to the car park. He reckoned he created a favourable impression, smartly dressed in a grey suit with matching grey shoes, his hair carefully gelled and coiffed, aftershave strong but not unpleasantly so. Little did he know that Trish considered him the epitome of an eighties wide boy, complete with aspirations of an XR3i Ford Escort Cabriolet and a fortnight in Magaluf (or Shagaluf, as she'd overheard him say when she walked in as he was on the phone to one of his mates). But the frown wrinkling her brow as he disappeared round the corner of Trevay harbour had not been prompted by any doubt about his abilities. It was a pang of guilt that had Trish asking herself whether she'd done the right thing in sending him out to Atlantic House. But then, he was a strapping lad of twenty-three; he'd be fine . . . wouldn't he? Rather him than her.

Having decided to start at the top of the house and work his way down, Trevor strode across the hallway. His footsteps sounded heavy on the bare wooden treads as he climbed the wide staircase. On the landing he stopped and counted eight doors, all closed.

The door to his left opened into a good-sized bedroom with a view over the driveway and lane. He measured up, took a couple of photos and jotted down a brief description to be written up in more flowery prose later. He carried on to the next room. A huge lavatory with a cracked wooden square of a seat and a chain-handled flush. The iron cistern above had been painted in many layers of cream paint, but he could just make out the maker's name and a date: 1934. Next door was a bathroom with an enormous, deep bath in the corner. Brown stains marred the porcelain under the bulbous antique taps, but when he turned one on there was no water.

The adjacent door led to a bedroom at the side of the house with a pretty sea view. The middle door, bang opposite the stairs, opened on to a magnificent master bedroom with French windows leading out to a balcony offering a stunning view of Treviscum Beach and the Atlantic Ocean beyond. The key was still in the lock and turned reasonably easily. Trevor opened the door to the balcony and stepped out into the light sea breeze. Now this was more like it. He tested the hand rail. The wood seemed solid enough, apart from a few splinters pricking his palms. Holding on in order to steady himself, he bounced lightly on the wooden floor. It bounced back. This house was going to be a money pit, but it would surely be worth it.

Trevor stood basking in the breeze for a moment, fantasising that the house was his. He closed his eyes and breathed deeply of the warm fresh air. Opening his eyes, he leaned over the balcony to take a look at the garden and terrace below. Suddenly the wood beneath his hand gave way, tipping him into empty space. As he lunged forward his scrabbling hand somehow managed to grasp one of the supporting uprights. There was a clank from below as the broken rail hit the flagstone terrace.

"Bloody Nora!" Beads of sweat broke out on his tanned forehead. Trevor cleared the floorboards of the balcony and made it back to the safety of the master bedroom in a single stride, shutting the balcony door behind him. Relieved that no one had seen his brush with death, yet at the same time shuddering at the thought of how long it would have taken for anyone to come to his aid, he stood with his back against the window, waiting for his breathing to return to normal. "Get a grip, Trev," he told himself.

After carefully relocking the door he set about measuring the room, followed by a further three bedrooms, all with either a sea view, a garden view, or a view of the drive. When that was done he returned to the ground floor.

Even in its dilapidated state, the drawing room was impressive with its high ceiling and generous window seats either side of French windows opening on to the terrace. Looking out, Trevor saw the broken piece of handrail lying innocently on the stone. Feeling a frisson of fear, he immediately turned his back on it, trying to put it out of his mind.

After measuring the drawing room he turned his attention to the study, followed by a charming morning room with an inglenook fireplace, and an intimate dining room with a plaster frieze of grapes around the corniced ceiling.

At the far end of the kitchen, which surely hadn't been updated since Queen Victoria's coronation, a tongue-and-groove door with a wrought-iron latch stood ajar. He went to it and saw it led to an old pantry

7

or larder with original worktops made of slabs of marble. This, he imagined, was where butter, milk and meat would have been stored in hot weather. Again he set to work with his notebook and measuring tape, talking to himself as he recorded the details.

When he finished measuring and checked his watch, he was surprised to discover that almost three hours had passed since he had left the office. And he still had the garden to do.

Locking up the front door and pocketing the key, Trevor fought his way through the thicket of dead grass and brambles, round to the sea-facing side of the house. How wonderful it looked from this angle, with the setting sun reflected in the windows, making the house glow as if it were illuminated from within and full of life.

Never in his brief career had Trevor been asked to measure a garden of this size. His puny tape measure was clearly inadequate for the task, so he decided instead to stride round the perimeter, counting each step as a metre.

He hadn't gone far before he lost count, the number falling from his memory as soon as he saw the old fortified wooden door in the side of the house. Natural curiosity and the desire to faithfully record every room led him to descend the four stone steps to the door. Half hoping to find it locked, he was surprised when it opened easily, releasing an aroma of sea damp and age that seemed to envelop him. The interior was pitch-dark and he could hear the distant sound of the sea coming up from below. In the light of the setting sun he struggled to make out the odd-shaped room, which seemed almost cave-like. As he stepped over the threshold, he felt a prickling at the base of his spine. Not fear, quite, but a warning not to go any further. After his unnerving experience on the balcony, Trevor decided it might be wise to let the surveyor check this one out. Closing the door behind him, he scampered up the steps away from the gloom and into the daylight.

On the drive back to the office he rehearsed the story he would tell Trish. Best to leave out the brush with death and the dark forebodings, he decided. As far as Trish was concerned, the house was a gem. In need of renovation, but a unique opportunity to acquire a charming period home with stunning aspects. Yes, that should do nicely on the particulars.

CHAPTER
ONE

As the wind whipped at her silk scarf, Dorothy struggled to tighten the knot that secured it under her chin. Although it was a sunny day with clear blue skies, it was bitterly cold. Not the ideal weather for motoring in an open-topped car.

Henry took his eyes off the road for a moment to glance at her. "Not too cold?"

"A little." She shrugged herself further down into her sheepskin coat.

He smiled, not hearing her. "Jolly good."

They had set off from their house in the Home Counties that morning, en route for Cornwall and a property described in the *Country Life* advertisement as:

An unmissable and rare opportunity to purchase this perfect Cornish Holiday/Family house. Accommodation comprises six bedrooms, two bathrooms, drawing room, dining room, morning room and study. Spacious original Victorian family kitchen. The master bedroom, with dressing room and en-suite bathroom, has its own balcony offering panoramic ocean views. All rooms on the ocean-facing side of the house boast equally stunning aspects. Set in half an acre of mature cliff-top gardens with private access to the public beach of Treviscum Bay. The property is in need of some modernisation. Despite its age (built circa 1720) it is currently unlisted.

"Take the next left," Dorothy, fighting with the turning pages of her road map, shouted above the wind as her husband sat grinning at the wheel of his new Aston Martin Virage Volante.

"What?"

"Next left. To Bodmin."

"Left here?"

She nodded vigorously and pointed with her gloved hand at the signpost.

He smiled. "Righto, Number One." He slowed the V8 engine to a throaty rumble and took the exit.

Henry couldn't believe how wonderfully his life had turned out. Who'd have thought he'd rise to this, given the dire straits he'd found himself in a decade ago.

On the death of his father, Henry had inherited Carew Family Board Games. Unfortunately the firm that had been his father's pride and joy was by this time a dinosaur in a shrinking market. Nobody wanted to play board games any more, even if they did have beautifully handcrafted pieces and block-printed boards. Henry had been left an albatross, complete with a mountain of debt, a loyal workforce he couldn't afford, and a factory with outdated machinery making parlour-game staples such as Ludo, Snakes and Ladders and Draughts. Settling the death duties on his father's estate had left him with no means to pay his own mortgage, let alone bail out the firm. In despair, he invited his bank manager out to lunch, hoping that a sumptuous five-course meal would secure him an extension to his business loan. It took the manager less than fifteen minutes to turn down the request. Indeed, if the current overdraft wasn't reduced forthwith, Henry's factory and machines would be repossessed by the bank.

"But my father was with your bank for more than forty years. Please, if you just bear with me a while longer, I won't let you down," pleaded Henry.

The bank manager, a fat man who enjoyed golf and making his customers squirm, shook his head sadly.

"Henry, your father was a close friend and a good man, but he didn't move with the times. Unless you can give me a sound business plan, some reason why the bank should reinvest, my answer has to be no."

Henry took a deep breath and looked the smug slug in the eye. "I have an idea for a game that will knock Trivial Pursuit, Cluedo and Monopoly into a cocked hat. I can't say more because our competitors must not get wind of it."

"My dear boy, what is it?"

"I told you, I can't say. But if I were to offer you my house as collateral, would you let me have the money I need?"

The slug stirred an extra spoonful of sugar into his coffee, thinking.

"OK, I'll authorise the loan — but only for six months. After that . . ." he continued stirring, his lips curving upward in a smirk, ". . . the bank moves in."

The relief Henry had felt at securing the loan evaporated at the prospect of this odious man and his bank getting their hands on his home and Carew Family Board Games. Unfortunately there was a major flaw in his new business plan. The top secret game that was going to take the world by storm didn't exist.

Henry drove back to the factory and locked himself into his father's old office. How could he have been so rash and stupid? How the hell was he going to invent a blockbuster of a game in a year, let alone six months?

He pulled out the bottom drawer of his father's desk and found the bottle of Scotch Dad had always kept there. He opened it and put it to his lips with a silent prayer: *Dad, I need your help. I'm in the shit and some of it's your fault. Give me an idea, a way out of this mess.*

He sat back in the tilting revolving wooden chair and put his feet up on the desk.

What am I going to do, Dad? I'm going to lose the factory and my home. A hundred people will be out of a job. People who loved you and trusted you. They are expecting me to make everything all right, but I'm afraid I've cocked it up. He took another swig of Scotch.

It was some time later when Old Reg, the foreman and longest-serving member of staff, came to say good night. He found Henry, his eyes red from tears, sitting in his father's chair, the bottle of Scotch half-empty.

Reg saw it all and knew without asking that it was only a matter of time before Carew Family Board Games became a footnote in history. Murmuring, "Good night, Mr Henry," he closed the office door gently behind him.

Henry's brain was in turmoil. Had he committed fraud? Could making a false promise be construed as extorting money from the bank? Would he be arrested? Could he afford a lawyer? What would happen to Dorothy and the girls? Lawyers were expensive. He was only trying to do the best for his workforce, his family. Oh God, he'd go to jail. He'd better get a lawyer.

In a panic, he dug out his father's old address book and flipped to the "L" tab. His finger traced down the pages.

"Lawyer, lawyer," he muttered under his breath. He stopped for a moment and said the words again: "Lawyer, lawyer." Feverishly he picked up a pencil and began writing the words, followed by *DEFENDANT. JUDGE. JURY.* Then he drew two boxes and wrote *GUILTY* in one and *NOT GUILTY* in the other.

He phoned home and told Dorothy not to expect him back for supper.

The next morning he called a meeting on the shop floor for every member of staff. He hadn't slept all night, he reeked of body odour and alcohol. They expected the worst.

"Ladies and gentlemen, thank you for giving me your time today. Carew Family Board Games was my

15

father's proudest achievement. Many of you worked with him and loved him as I did. You miss him as I miss him. I am very grateful that you have remained so loyal to me as I try to fill his shoes. But the truth is, the world is changing and this company is struggling. When arcade games and the Rubik's Cube came on to the market, my father thought they would be a flash in the pan. 'Nothing can beat the fun of a family sitting round the table playing Ludo,' was his mantra." Some of the older employees laughed in remembrance of this. "He was wrong, though. We are on the brink of insolvency."

There was a subdued murmur from the group, and then Reg spoke up: "Are you shutting us down, Mr Carew?"

Henry swallowed the lump that was forming in his throat. "I hope not, Reg. I have an idea for a new game. A board game that I think could beat even Monopoly for world sales. The World Toy Fair is four months away: if we can have the new game ready by then, we'll secure the orders we need to turn this company round — but I need your help and your faith to pull it off. This is the promise I make to you: if I can't turn this company round in the next six months, I will sell everything I have — bar my house, which is promised to the bank . . ." He paused, gulping back the tears that threatened. "And I will split the proceeds between you. However, if we make this game a success, you will all become partners, sharing in the profit."

His workforce stood, incredulous. Some of the older women who remembered the boom years were sniffing into screwed-up tissues. The younger workers looked dumbstruck. In the end it was Reg who stepped forward and asked, "What do we have to do?"

It took Henry and the team just two weeks to produce the cardboard prototype of Lawyer, Lawyer. Four sets were made and taken home in turn by the Carew workers. Each day they would come in with suggestions, refinements and clearer rules. Finally everyone was in agreement that they had the definitive version. A game of cat and mouse between the law and the citizen. Reg oversaw the first factory-made prototype as it came off the production line.

It was beautiful. The box lid depicted Number One Court of the Old Bailey. In the dock stood a decent but anxious-looking man. On the bench sat a hideous gargoyle of a judge bearing an uncanny resemblance to Henry's bank manager. And taking the floor was a smart lawyer, thumbs in his lapels and smiling wolfishly at the jury.

Reg carried it with pride to the boardroom and placed it on the elliptical table. The workers came and filed past it as it lay in state.

That afternoon, Dorothy dialled the local Chinese takeaway and ordered a supper for everyone. It was a party not one of them would forget.

On the eve of the World Toy Fair, Henry carefully packed the newly manufactured boxes of Lawyer, Lawyer into the back of his rented Rascal van. Dorothy was already settled in the passenger seat. The entire workforce gathered in the car park to wave them off.

Old Reg leaned in and put his hand on Henry's shoulder. "Good luck, Mr Henry. Your father would be proud of you."

Henry put the car in gear and drove carefully out of the factory car park, Dorothy waving from the window while he tooted the horn until they were all out of sight.

The World Toy Fair at Olympia was very familiar to Henry. He'd worked a stand there with his father from the time he was a boy. Only when his father fell ill did they stop attending. His death had left Henry without the cash or wherewithal to organise a stand. Now, he found himself looking forward to it. But at the same time he was consumed with nerves.

He glanced at Dorothy and said, "What if this doesn't work?"

She smiled back at him. "It'll work."

"We could lose every —"

"We could, but we won't."

Most exhibitors had booked a year in advance. When Dorothy had called to make a reservation four months previously, there were few slots remaining. They were allocated a stand on an outside corner.

"You wouldn't put a hen in a space as small as this," complained Henry when he saw it.

Dorothy, who was staggering under several boxes of order forms and fliers, ignored his pessimism. "Help me with these, will you?" she said, thrusting the surprisingly heavy boxes towards him. Then she looked around, hands resting on her slender hips. "Small but perfect. We're handy for the loo and the café — think of the footfall we'll have. Couldn't be better."

He grudgingly nodded. "Suppose so."

"Come on, Prince Charming — two more trips and the van will be unloaded."

Dorothy was a good organiser. By midnight, their little stall looked inviting and ready for the official opening in the morning. Several other exhibitors broke off setting up their own stands and dropped by to chat and reminisce about Henry's father. One or two were desperate to get a look inside the Lawyer, Lawyer boxes, but Dorothy was having none of it. "The premiere is tomorrow, boys! No peeking till then."

The four days that followed were the busiest they'd ever known. The opening morning was slow, but that afternoon the buyer for Hamleys came by. After Henry talked him through the rules, he couldn't resist playing a round. Henry let him win, obviously, and the buyer put an order in for such a large amount that Dorothy thought she'd misheard and left a zero off the end. When the buyer leaned over and corrected her, she couldn't stop herself from kissing him. After that, word of mouth spread quickly. Every toyshop chain and department store was clamouring to place an order for the exciting new game.

As soon as they returned to the factory, the production line got into gear. For the first time in the history of the company, the machines were rolling twenty-four hours a day, five days a week. Extra night-shift staff were taken on to meet the orders, which were coming in from as far afield as Australia and Japan.

Within months Lawyer, Lawyer was the game on every family's Christmas list. The fat bank manager invited Henry out for lunch. Henry accepted the invitation and was delighted when he heard the name of the restaurant: very expensive and excellent reviews. Henry selected the most extravagantly priced dishes and wine, enjoying the wincing expression of the slug sitting opposite.

Over coffee, and the finest brandy, the bank manager offered Henry as much money as he needed to expand the business. Henry thanked him, but declined to commit himself immediately.

On his return to the office, Henry immediately set about transferring all his company and personal accounts to a rival bank. Then he dictated a fax to his former bank manager, telling him to get stuffed.

A few days later, an order came through from Buckingham Palace. Henry made sure his Press Office (Dorothy) leaked the news to the Nigel Dempster column in the *Daily Mail*.

The company was now safer than it had been for twenty years, but there was no sitting back on their laurels. It was Old Reg who came up with the next idea. Tapping on Henry's office door, he came in and explained that his son, who had a degree in electronics and computer science, wanted to devise an electronic version of Lawyer, Lawyer. After discussing the proposal with Dorothy and his new bank manager, Henry began investing in the technology that would produce the first hand-held Carew Family game.

The resulting worldwide sales paid off the mortgage of every Carew employee.

And that was how Henry and his beloved Dorothy came to be sitting in an open-topped Aston Martin on their way to buy Atlantic House, the Cornish holiday home of their dreams.

CHAPTER
TWO

On the other side of Bodmin, past the wildness of the moor, the scenery grew gentler. Now they were travelling through a verdant countryside of fields and farms.

The Aston got stuck behind a tractor dripping slurry from its huge wheels. The smell of ammonia made Dorothy's eyes water. Henry started to get frustrated. He accelerated and braked and weaved in and out of his side of the road, banging the steering wheel with his string-gloved hand. "Pull over, you village idiot!" he snarled.

Dorothy saw the time had come to have words. "Henry! Do you want me to be sick on the cream leather? Besides, shouldn't you be trying to make friends with the locals?"

Grumbling, he attempted patience. By the time the old farmer pulled into a small lay-by, waving them through, Henry was almost amiable.

He had barely finished waving a gracious acknowledgement when he found himself stuck behind a bus.

"What do they want to bring bloody buses down these lanes for?" he growled.

Dorothy laid a hand on his knee. "If we're going to live here, we have to accept this pace of life."

Eventually the bus stopped and Henry throttled past.

The roads narrowed into lanes the closer they got to the coast. The hedges, studded with primroses, rose high above them. Signposts boldly announced TREVAY 5 MILES. But as anyone knows, five Cornish miles can mean anything between two and ten.

Dorothy consulted her map and raised her voice to be heard above the wind. "We don't want to get into Trevay itself. There'll be a turning on the left to Lower Barton first."

The Aston, stroking the vegetation between the narrow hedgerows, navigated the route to Lower Barton with its beautiful church and pub, then on to Higher Barton with its small supermarket, post office, pasty shop and garage, and finally down the unmade stony road to Treviscum Bay. And there, gleaming in the afternoon sun, stood the most wonderful house Dorothy and Henry had ever set eyes on.

Its large sash windows and porticoed front door seduced them immediately. Yes, the roofline was sagging, several slates were missing and the garden was badly overgrown, but they knew even before setting foot inside the door that they had to have it.

The front door opened and a young man stepped out to greet them.

"Mr and Mrs Carew? Hello, I'm Trevor from Hawkes Property Agents. Come in, and welcome."

Inside, the house was cool. There was a faint smell of damp, but the rooms were spacious and filled with sunlight. Henry and Dorothy took in the grandeur of the panelled hall, then followed Trevor into the

23

high-ceilinged drawing room. If they weren't hopelessly in love with Atlantic House already, the breathtaking view of the ocean from the French windows sealed the deal.

Careful not to sound too enthusiastic, they let Trevor escort them through the downstairs rooms and up to the bedrooms and ancient bathrooms. No words passed between Henry and Dorothy. They didn't need to discuss it. They knew this house was for them.

Back in the hall, Trevor asked, "Shall I leave you to have a walk round on your own?"

"Oh, I think we've seen enough," Henry said in a weary voice. "There's a hell of a lot that needs doing. What can be done on the asking price?"

"This is a highly desirable property that's attracting a great deal of interest." Both men knew this was a lie, but it was the expected opening gambit of the duel. "I think it very unlikely the vendor will drop the price," parried Trevor, before delivering a clumsy blow: "In fact, I think it's fair to say that a bidding war has already started."

Dorothy looked pleadingly at Henry, who had begun to reach into his pocket for the car keys. "I haven't come all this way to be held over a barrel. I'm a serious buyer, prepared to pay cash. Take it or leave it."

"Mr Carew," the agent stopped him, "I'm sure that if you were to make a hard-and-fast offer this afternoon, the vendor could be persuaded to come to some arrangement. Especially when I tell her you are a cash buyer."

"OK, let's do that."

24

"Why don't you follow me back to my office in Trevay and I'll see if we can't have the deal done by tonight."

In the car, Dorothy had time to air her thoughts.

"Please, please don't let this house get away," she beseeched.

"It'll cost a fortune to bring the place up to scratch. Besides, I am not about to be made a monkey of by some venal estate agent who takes me for a wealthy Londoner."

"But you are a wealthy Londoner."

"Yes, dear — but he doesn't know that."

"What do you suppose he thinks this car is then? A Reliant Robin? Henry Carew, your cover is already blown."

Subject to a surveyor's report and the usual searches, the deal was concluded that afternoon. Trevor, glowing with satisfaction and looking forward to working out his commission as soon as the buyers were out of the way, stood up to shake hands.

"Congratulations," he said. "If there's anything you need, don't hesitate to ask."

Dorothy, who was putting her scarf on, paused. "Actually, there is something: I'd love to know more about the history of the house."

Trevor looked over at his boss. "Trish, where would Mrs Carew be able to find out all about the history of the house?"

Trish, who had suddenly developed a keen interest in the contents of her desk drawer, seemed a little flustered as she replied: "Well, erm, the library would be the place to start. And, er, we have a very good local museum . . ." Then she looked up and met their gaze. "Actually, there is something . . . something you should know. A young girl died in the house. It happened about ten years ago. It's her sister who is selling the house."

Dorothy stopped fiddling with her scarf. "Died? How? Illness? Accident? Murder?"

"Oh, nothing sinister! No, no, it was a drowning. Poor thing." Trish turned to Trevor. "Did you show Mr and Mrs Carew the smugglers' cave?"

Trevor blushed. "I thought I'd leave that to the surveyor."

"Smugglers' cave?" questioned Henry "Sounds fascinating. Where is it?"

"The entrance is in the garden. There are steps leading under the house into a cave. At one time there was a passage or cavern that led out on to the beach somewhere. But I think it's blocked off now," said Trish.

Dorothy wanted to know more about the dead girl. "Did she die in the cave?"

"I can't remember all the details. I believe she'd been playing in the cave when it happened. Either the tide came up or she slipped . . . I'm not sure. It was in the papers at the time. The library will have copies."

Henry saw that this news had upset Dorothy. He put his arm round her. "Come on, old girl. We'll make Atlantic House a happy home again." He turned back to Trish and Trevor. "Right. I think my wife deserves a

26

slap-up meal to celebrate. Where's the best place to have dinner and stay the night?"

Over the following weeks, Dorothy threw herself into researching the history of the house. The coroner's inquest into the death of fourteen-year-old Claire Clovelly returned a verdict of misadventure. She had apparently hidden in the cave following a row with her family. Nobody was sure exactly what had happened, but the most likely explanation was that she had slipped on the slimy rocks, banged her head and drowned.

"I think we'd better block the cave up, Henry," said Dorothy, fearful. "I don't want Constance or Prudence going down there."

"The girls will be fine! They're far too sensible to mess about down there."

Dorothy was adamant: "Block it up."

Henry gave no answer. He'd already instructed the builders to open the cave up. With high tide access for a small vessel to sail in and out, it would be the perfect place to put a boat.

It took all that summer and autumn for the builders to do their stuff, but by the following Easter the house was reborn. Upstairs had been remodelled so that each of the six bedrooms had its own bathroom. Henry and Dorothy's room was the grandest, commanding a stunning view from its brand-new balcony.

The next-best was the blue room, which was cool and sophisticated, with double-aspect windows overlooking the beach and the bay.

The yellow room was bright and sunny, but slightly smaller. It had only one sash window that looked out on to the garden and the gate to the cliff path.

The remaining bedrooms were smaller still and looked on to farm buildings and the driveway.

Downstairs, the huge kitchen was once again the heart of the house. Simply done with a scrubbed wooden dresser and enormous table, it was dominated by the scarlet four-oven Aga, which had replaced the rusty old range. The roomy walk-in larder had been retained, along with the original flagstones, which had cleaned up a treat. New French windows had been installed in the sea-facing wall of the kitchen, opening on to the terrace.

They had also knocked through the old walls separating the kitchen from the dining room, which had in turn been merged with the drawing room, creating a glorious flow of light and space.

The study now doubled as a rumpus room for the girls and their school friends, who would join them for summer holidays.

It was the very epitome of eighties chic.

Outside, the ancient back door led to a newly planted herb garden and, Henry's pride and joy, the renovated smugglers' cave.

The curious room above ground was cool enough to house his wine cellar and the steep stone steps leading down to the cavern had been made safe.

"Mind your head," he told Dorothy as he led her by the hand, the light from his torch bouncing off the dimpled walls. "The electrician is putting lights in next week."

"I still don't like it, Henry. You shouldn't have wasted time and money on this. It would have been better blocked up. It scares me."

"Don't be silly, old thing. It's exciting — smugglers and redcoats and all that stuff — a slice of Cornish history, right in our own backyard."

Dorothy's concern was writ large across her furrowed brow. "I don't want to be proved right on this, Henry. It's an accident waiting to happen."

Henry patted her arm reassuringly. "I promise you, there's nothing to fear, darling. Besides, the children aren't little any more, so stop worrying!"

The steps took a twist and a turn and then opened out into the natural boathouse under the cliffs.

"Ta-dah!!"

Henry stretched out his right hand and Dorothy saw something bobbing on the water.

"What the hell is that?"

"A 1967 Riva. The best speedboat money can buy. And you see?" He pointed at the floor. "I had the lads concrete a level jetty on the old rock ledge so we can tie her up and get on and off easily." The torchlight picked out the jetty and the polished wooden hull. Dorothy could make out cream leather seats and a shiny wooden steering wheel.

"How much?" she said in an angry voice.

"It's a present to us from the company. We deserve a little toy."

"You and your bloody toys! That's *not* a board game. That's a monstrous waste of money."

Henry was crestfallen. "I thought you'd be pleased. I can take you and the girls out for trips around the coast and picnics on secluded beaches."

"That's another thing." She rounded on him. "Can you even drive the bloody thing?"

Henry smiled. "Ah well, yes, you see, I've booked the whole family on a seamanship course."

Dorothy pursed her lips.

"Don't you want to know what she's called?" he asked.

"No."

"Look, darling," he urged, pointing towards the boat.

She shook her head in disbelief as she picked out the golden letters painted on the stern: *Dorothy*.

Dorothy scowled. Henry kissed her. She frowned. He hugged her. Finally the beginnings of a smile reached her lips.

"You're mad and bad but lovely to know, Henry Carew."

"No greater compliment was ever received — thank you."

Henry and Dorothy were very pleased with their newly restored home and loved inviting the locals in to marvel at how the old house was being reborn.

Prudence and Constance had come down to see it during the Christmas holidays and had been less than impressed. Still in the throes of being renovated, the house was barely habitable. The girls were billeted at a local hotel while the damp and mould in the bedrooms was being dealt with.

"It's so cold," shivered Pru, clad in her new striped dungarees and red ankle boots.

"And spooky," added Connie, shaking her wash-and-wear perm so the corkscrew curls bounced.

Dorothy looked at them sternly. "There are no spooks here. And it's cold because the central heating hasn't been installed yet. Want to see your bedrooms?"

"Do we get to choose?" asked Pru.

"Well, let's see."

Sighing inwardly, knowing that a jealous spat between the siblings was bound to ensue, Dorothy led the way upstairs. The three of them picked their way over the dust sheets, abandoned tools and other builders' detritus cluttering the landing to the first door.

"Look at the view, girls!" Dorothy threw open the door leading to the yellow room. "Who wants this one, overlooking the garden and the cliff?"

Assuming their mother was showing them the best room in the hope of winning them over, Pru, who was always quickest off the mark when it came to getting what she wanted, jumped in: "I do!"

Connie's shoulders slumped dramatically. "I knew *she'd* get the first choice. It's not fair. I really like this room. Pru gets the best of everything."

Fighting the urge to scream, Dorothy forced a bright smile and kept her voice tone jolly as she told them, "Prudence, wipe that conceited look off your face.

Connie, please refrain from sulking. I have a super room for you — follow me."

Pru pushed past Connie, who whispered, "You *always* get the best."

And Pru replied *sotto voce*: "Tough shit, little sister."

When their mother opened the door of the blue room, Connie's mouth dropped open as she took in the double-aspect windows with views of the beach and the bay. "Yes!" she cried, fist punching the air. "Yes! This has to be the best room. I love it! Thanks, Mum."

Pru was now the one who was in a sulk. "I thought you said you wanted the other room."

"Nope. This is mine and that is yours. Fair's fair, eh, Mum?"

Dorothy, distracted by the screech of the plumber drilling in the en-suite, answered vaguely, "Yes, of course, darling. Sort it out between the pair of you. Off you go." Moments later she was lost in a discussion about power showers and hot-water tanks.

Pru glared at Connie. "Give me this room."

"No. You chose yours. This is mine."

"It's too big for you."

"No it isn't."

"The other room suits you much better."

"Why?"

"Yellow is your favourite colour."

"No it isn't. I like blue."

"You're spoilt."

"You're jealous."

Dorothy wandered back in from the bathroom.

"All settled, girls?" Registering the sulky expressions on the girls' faces, she promptly abandoned all efforts to placate them. "Oh, for Heaven's sake — why don't you two go and explore the beach before I banish the pair of you to the box room — you'll have plenty to mope about then, won't you?"

Nothing more had been said about the bedrooms. Not because Pru had given up; she was just biding her time.

The family didn't visit Cornwall again until the Easter holidays. That first day, both sisters were squashed into the back of their father's new Range Rover, surrounded by the bedding, kitchenware and other household bits and pieces their mother had packed around them after they'd got in.

Henry insisted on having Radio 4 on for the entire journey, so the girls plugged themselves into their Sony Walkmans, staring glumly out of the windows at the passing traffic.

At Bristol they stopped for elevenses. Moody as hell, Pru and Connie trooped in behind their parents, scowling at the food on offer in the cafeteria.

Dorothy tried to adopt a light, cheery tone: "OK, girls, what do you want?"

"A doughnut," said Connie.

"That's very fattening," said Dorothy, looking pointedly at Connie's rounded tummy. "Have an orange juice and a banana. Pru?"

Connie's lip wobbled, stung by the suggestion she was overweight.

Pru, still plugged into her Walkman, didn't respond. "Pru!" her mother asked again. No response. Henry took the headphones off his elder daughter's ears and shouted, "Take those bloody things off and answer your mother!"

Pru stared blankly. "What?"

"Your mother has asked you three times: what do you want to eat?"

"Nothing. And she only asked me twice."

Henry took the Walkman and headphones from Pru's hands and stuffed them in his pocket. "Right. I'm confiscating these."

"But, Dad!"

"What do you want to eat?" he barked again.

"Nothing," she shouted, and stalked off to W H Smith, throwing over her shoulder: "This is SO unfair."

Henry nearly went after her, but Dorothy laid a hand on his arm. "Let her go. I'll be glad of the peace."

Back in the car, Pru glowered and sulked without her Walkman. Connie smugly and irritatingly listened to hers, flicking her sister the occasional two-fingered salute.

After a while, Pru waved her hand in front of her sister's face in order to attract her attention.

"Hello," she said exaggeratedly. "Earth to Constance! Let me have a listen to yours, Con."

Connie was indignant. "Why should I? It's your own fault Dad took them off you, not mine!"

"Oh, come on, Connie," Pru wheedled, going for the sympathy vote — a tactic Connie was always a sucker for. "You know I've been desperate to listen to that new Madonna tape for weeks, and you did promise to swap when we left London. I was going to let you have the Kylie one, remember?"

"But Dad's confiscated it."

"Exactly — not fair! Come on, you know I'd do the same for you."

"You would not!"

And so it went on, with Pru eventually breaking her gentler sister down.

Connie managed to tune out the tinny strains of Madonna's "Express Yourself", and stared out of the window, drinking in the Cornish scenery as it sped by. She hoped that Pru wouldn't be a complete cow over the whole bedroom business, but she had a horrible suspicion that her sister would outwit her again, same as she always did. She sighed loudly, attracting a quizzical look from her father through the rear-view mirror.

At last the Range Rover crunched slowly down the lane and into the driveway of Atlantic House. Pru got out quickly and, with suspicious brightness, told her father: "I'll help you take the luggage upstairs."

He raised an eyebrow in surprise and disbelief, but handed her a suitcase and a couple of pillows and opened the front door for her.

A couple of minutes later, Connie climbed the stairs, lugging her bags behind her, and threw open the door of her bedroom, the big and beautiful blue room.

"Surprise!" sang Pru from the depths of the pretty four-poster bed. "Your room is down the hall, little sister."

"Very funny, Pru," laughed Connie, before turning to her mother. "Mummy, thank you. This is the best room *ever*."

"Which is why I am having it," said Pru. "The yellow room is so pretty and just right for you, Connie. Much more suitable for a fourteen-year-old."

Connie's face darkened. "And why should this room be suitable for a horrible sixteen-year-old?"

"Because," Pru said reasonably, "I am studying for my O-levels and I need this room to study in. It'll be quieter for me."

"Mummy!" Connie turned to her mother for justice. "You said this was my room."

Dorothy, staggering up the stairs with her own luggage, heaved a sigh. She was tired of constantly having to adjudicate in her daughters' petty squabbles. Opting for the path of least resistance, she turned to Connie. "Darling, be a sweetheart. Pru needs to do lots of studying to get good grades, or else she won't get a place at university. As soon as she's through with all that you can swap rooms — OK? Hmm? For my sake?"

Connie knew she was defeated before she'd even started. It was typical of Pru to resort to these guerrilla tactics. Mum always said she loved them both equally, but somehow she always ended up twisted around Pru's little finger. She was so manipulative!

Nonetheless, Connie acquiesced. She had no appetite for a fight she was bound to lose.

"OK, Mum — but I'm only doing this for you, not *her*." Connie cast a filthy look in her smirking sister's direction.

"Good girl. Right, girls — let's give Daddy a hand with the rest of the luggage."

Pru got off the bed and put her arm round Connie.

"Your room is lovely. It's perfect for you. I'll help you settle in."

Connie looked at her sister and silently swore that she would get her sister back for this. Never mind how long it took.

CHAPTER
THREE

Some decades later

"What on earth is your father doing now?" Connie Wilson could feel her temper starting to rise. "Greg?" she shouted up the stairs. "Come on — we've got to go."

Calm down, she told herself, *you've got the whole summer ahead of you. Don't let the holiday get off to a bad start, don't let it get to you!*

Abigail, sitting quietly on the sofa, bags packed and at her feet, looked up from her book. Though only sixteen, she had endured enough family holidays to realise how stressful her mother found the whole business. With an expressive shrug of the shoulders, she returned to her place on the page.

Connie tossed her expensively highlighted hair back and put a hand over her eyes.

"God, we're going to be late *again*. Why does everybody leave it all to me?"

Abigail sat unmoving, peering over the top of her book as her mother pulled the specs from her blonde head and checked for the umpteenth time the long list of notes she'd made in her Smythson diary.

"Well?" She looked at Abi pointedly.

Abi indicated the bags at her feet. "Mum, I'm all packed and ready to go."

"Sorry, darling. I don't mean to be a grouch, it's just that I hate the thought of Pru getting there before us." Connie glanced towards the stairs. "What on earth is your father doing? Why is he taking so long?" Rolling up the sleeves of her stripy sweatshirt, she marched to the foot of the stairs and bellowed, "Greg! Please can you turn your computer off. Surely work can wait for a few hours? We need to get a move on."

Upstairs, Greg had his feet propped up on the wide and empty expanse of his ultra-cool desk, or "work space" as he preferred to call it. This was his oasis. A place of sanctuary from the bedlam of his wife's domain. A place of privacy. He slowly rocked himself on the ergonomically designed kid leather chair, sighing as he ran his hand through his wavy dark hair, now speckled with grey — much to his annoyance.

Raising his voice he shouted back, "Darling, won't be a minute. Just got some loose ends to tie up at the office. Your father will want to have a full report as soon as we get there." He listened for a response from below, but none came. "Sorry about that, Janie," he murmured into the receiver of his agonisingly trendy and sleek steel handset.

"That's all right, Greggy," returned the voice of a well-educated young woman. "I'm so going to miss you."

"And I shall miss you. But I shall be thinking of you every moment of every day and every night, Janie darling."

"You will call me when you get there won't you, Greggy?"

Irritation flared in him. Janie was getting too clingy.

"Greg!" Connie was shouting again. "Please hurry up!"

"Greg, beginning to lose interest, was eager to end the call. "Yes, Con, I'm coming," he shouted. Then, speaking softly into the phone: "I'll try. I've got to go. If only for Abigail's sake." He started to tidy his desk, closing the lid of his laptop and looking round for its leather case. Lately he'd found himself wondering whether the time had come to kick Janie into touch. Lovely girl and all that, but it was asking for trouble, having an affair with your secretary. Especially when your father-in-law owned the company. Maybe he could pay her off, get her another job in a friend's company. He'd write her an excellent letter of recommendation. After all, she was very good at her job. And *very, very* sexy.

Greg Wilson considered himself a reasonable man. A man who was satisfactorily married while indulging in a slice of illicit cake. Surely it was expected that a man in his position would have a mistress? Then again, mixing business with pleasure . . . that was where he'd made a mistake. He'd have to give some thought to the Janie problem over the summer hols.

"Janie, I really have to go. I'm only off to Cornwall. Not to the other side of the world. I'll call when I can."

"Promise, Greggy?" she purred.

"Promise." Greg was now standing up with the phone sandwiched between shoulder and ear, shovelling things into his briefcase.

"Bye bye, baby cakes."

"Bye, sexy." And he hung up. He'd added the "sexy" to keep her sweet. She did the "sexy secretary" look very well. Business suits with tight pencil skirts and high heels. And beautiful underwear that encased her twenty-six-year-old derrière to perfection.

He could hear the sound of a heavy suitcase being dragged across the hallway below.

Taking one last look around the room to see if he'd forgotten anything, he gathered up his laptop and went downstairs to inspect the damage.

His wife frowned up at him, "Greg, you know I want to leave as early as possible. We must get there before Pru."

"Oh, for God's sake, Connie. Why you and that sister of yours insist on this ridiculous battle of wits each year is beyond me. And watch what you're doing to the floor. It costs a fortune to polish those marks out."

Connie was at the front door with the largest of three suitcases. She turned very slowly, took a deep breath, was on the verge of saying something unkind but thought better of it. Instead she continued towards the front door.

"Here, let me help you. Before you scuff the paintwork as well."

"It would have been nice if you'd spared the time to do your own packing as well," Connie muttered, then, more loudly: "I think I can manage, thank you."

Greg moved towards her just as she got the front door open. There ensued an unseemly scuffle as he tried to wrench the case from her hand and she held fast. It was Abigail who stepped in.

"Mum! Dad! Why do we have to start every summer holiday with all this aggro? It will be brilliant once we get there and we're going to have a LOVELY time! Let's get on the freakin' road."

Fifty miles away, in an expensive corner of South-East London, Connie's sister Pru was waiting for her pedicure to dry. She'd been up since four, tying up a few overnight loose ends that her overseas office had thrown up. These commercial surveyors could be such a bore. Now, she was lying on the bed in her extremely white and bright but sparsely furnished bedroom — a room so desperately tasteful it wouldn't have looked out of place between the covers of *Elle Decoration*. She watched as her beauty therapist packed away the many pots of nail polish and lotions she had used on her client.

"Thank you so much, Esther. I love this colour. What's it called again?"

"Pantie Glimmer," said Esther, a tall slender girl with a violent fake tan.

"Pantie Glimmer? Where do they get these names from? I should think taupe was a perfectly adequate description."

"Yeah," deadpanned Esther. "But not very sexy, is it?"

Pru was about to argue the merits of taupe, one of her favourite shades in décor and clothing, but was stopped by a gentle knock on the door.

"Enter," Pru called.

The door opened quietly and the slightly anxious face of her husband, Francis, appeared.

"Hello, darling. You look marvellous." He took an appreciative sniff of the room. "Lovely smell. What is it, Esther?"

"Ylang-ylang, geranium and sandalwood. It's very good on ageing skin."

Beneath her perfectly styled, short and sleek brown hair, Pru's face stiffened, and her blue eyes took on a look that could only be described as icy. Francis hurriedly said, "Well, that'll be lovely when my wife needs it." He turned to Pru: "Jeremy and I are ready when you are. I've packed the car and I've got some sushi for the journey."

"In the cool box?"

"Yes."

"Is there fuel in the tank?"

"Yes."

"Give me ten minutes. Oh, and remind Jeremy that once we start there's no stopping. I want to be there in under four hours."

"Righto."

Francis went downstairs, confident that he hadn't forgotten anything.

Exactly ten minutes later, having sent the Aveda beautician packing, Pru swept out of the house to find her sixteen-year-old son already in the back seat, iPod headphones stuffed in his ears, and her husband waiting to shut the front door.

"Is the alarm primed?"

"Yes." Francis nodded.

"Are the window locks checked?"

"Yes, Pru. All sorted."

"Good. Let's go."

Pru walked to the driver's side and got in. The keys were not in the ignition. Francis heard her tut of annoyance and, realising his mistake, hurriedly pulled the keys from his pocket and handed them over. "Sorry, darling."

Pru checked her face in the wing mirror and started the engine.

"My skin isn't getting old, is it, Francis?"

"Good lord, no." Francis smiled at her.

"I didn't think so."

She slammed the gear stick into drive and pulled away in a spray of gravel before either son or husband had done their seat belts up.

Connie was aware that she was clenching her jaw. Her shoulders were up round her neck and her hands were in tight fists on her lap.

"Can't you drive any faster? This is a motorway. You can do eighty without getting stopped. The police accept that."

"No, Connie. The limit is seventy and that's what I shall stick to. I've got nine points already. If I get stopped again, they'll throw the book at me. Can you imagine what your father would say? The expenses I put in for chauffeured cars last time I got banned were horrendous."

Connie bit her lip and looked out of the window to distract herself. They were passing the exit for Bristol Parkway station. The junction for the M5 wasn't far. Another half an hour and they'd be at Taunton Deane Services. She could have done with a loo stop and a Costa coffee, but she was determined to arrive at Atlantic House ahead of Pru. This year the best bedroom was going to be hers.

She knew that she was behaving stupidly. This happened every year, and every year she got angry with herself for getting sucked into yet another silly, juvenile spat with Pru. Most of the time, Connie was a normal person: loving mum, good wife, someone who knew how to enjoy herself with friends and who appreciated her luck in life. But at the prospect of getting within ten feet of Pru, Connie started acting like a whiney, jealous teenager. It was infuriating that after all these years she was still letting Pru get to her, but her sister's competitive streak, combined with her superior attitude, was too much to bear. God only knew how Francis and dear Jeremy managed to put up with the woman. Connie was convinced that it was only thanks to Francis that Jem had turned out to be such a well-adjusted kid. Mind you, neither he nor Abi were kids any more; Abi's seventeenth birthday was fast approaching, and she would be taking her A-levels next year and choosing a university. For a moment Connie allowed herself to wonder what Archie would have been doing now. Even after all these years it was hard to think about the little boy she had miscarried four months before she fell pregnant with Abi. Pru hadn't attended his funeral; she'd been in New York on business. And she'd changed the subject whenever Connie mentioned him, closing the door on that heartbreaking grief.

Connie looked at her watch and was horrified to see the time.

Hearing her muttering under her breath, Greg glanced her way. "Can't you just let your sister have the room she wants? She inevitably gets it anyway."

"Exactly my point. She *always* gets Mummy and Daddy's old bedroom. It's warmer, bigger and has the best view from upstairs. She knows it's my turn this year yet she always wangles her way in. You and I deserve that room for a change."

"Does it really matter? You'll be asleep anyway — you won't see the view. Besides, we get her old bedroom, the blue room."

"The blue room that was meant for me and that she took!"

"Darling, that was almost a quarter of a century ago."

"Quite! She had the best room all those years, now I want Mummy and Daddy's room. I like to go to sleep to the sound of the sea, and wake up to the sunshine. And anyway, the blue room is so dated and dingy. Why should I have Pru's cast-offs?"

Greg, who'd speeded up to overtake a horse box, pulled back into the inside lane and slowed down. An elderly Vauxhall with several young lads in it overtook him.

"What did you do that for?"

"What?"

"Let those yobs through."

"They weren't yobs. And if they had been, what would be the point of upsetting them and risking them ramming me off the road?"

Connie sighed in frustration and looked again at her watch.

Francis tried to look as relaxed as possible, though he couldn't stop himself casting nervous glances at the speedometer as the needle hovered over 110 mph. His legs were getting numb where they were jammed in the footwell against the cool box.

It made him nervous when Pru drove this way. Understandably. He tried to comfort himself with the thought that at least they would all die together.

This annual race between the sisters for the best room in Atlantic House was a mystery to him. All the rooms were lovely. A bit dated and faded perhaps, but that was part of the charm of the place.

He resisted the desire to brace himself and grip the armrests as Pru advanced aggressively, then braked hard, a few feet from the rear wheels of an innocent Renault Scenic with three bicycles strapped to its roof and a back window full of teddies and a potty.

"Get out of the way, you moron!" she hissed, rapidly tugging the stalk that flashed her headlights. "Use your mirrors and you'll see me."

The Renault resolutely stayed where it was: in the outside lane and pottering along at a reasonable seventy-five miles per hour.

"Right," said Pru, and suddenly swerved to the left then accelerated hard, undertaking the smaller car and blasting her horn as she did so.

The driver and wife stared in astonishment at this madwoman rushing past them in a blur. She swung the steering wheel to the right and, causing them to brake, pulled out in front of them.

"Ha! That's better."

Francis was aware he hadn't taken a breath for a few seconds and took a quick gasp.

Pru looked over at him.

"What's the matter?"

"Nothing, my love."

"Good. I think we're going to do this journey in record time."

Francis paled. "Great."

Jeremy's voice came from the back. "Are we stopping to eat?"

"No," said Pru.

Francis rustled around in the cool box at his feet. "Would you like me to feed you a bite-sized sushi, Pru?"

Pru didn't take her eyes from the bumper of the Porsche in front of her. "I'm driving."

"Righty-ho."

One hundred and fifteen, one hundred and seventeen . . .

"I'll have one." Jeremy's hand came over the back of his father's seat. "Is there anything to drink?"

His mother cut in. "Don't give him anything to drink. I told you I am not stopping. I want to get to

Atlantic House before my idiot sister and her husband stake a claim on our room. When I inherit the house, as eldest child, we shan't ever have this ridiculous argument again."

To emphasise her point she rammed her foot on the accelerator.

That was when they heard the wail of a police siren.

"Look — some silly fool has been caught by the cops." Greg pointed with delight at the car pulled over on the hard shoulder, an unmarked police car behind it with its blue lights twinkling cheerily across the back window.

"Oh my God!" cried Connie. "It's Pru and Francis!"

Abigail reached for her mobile phone and texted her cousin:

Hi! Just passed you. What room do you want? I'll make sure you get it. Love Abi xx

Connie could now relax. The police would hold Pru up for at least half an hour. Served her right.

"Anybody want a crisp or a prawn sandwich? They're next to you in the M and S bag, Abi love."

As the small picnic was shared out between them, the atmosphere in the car lightened.

Greg upped his speed to just under eighty, Connie sang along to her Michael Bublé CD and Abi had a little snooze. By early afternoon they were in Cornwall.

Another eighty miles and Connie called out, "Get your pointy fingers ready!" This was a family tradition.

The first person to spot the sea and point was the winner.

"I'm sharpening mine!" said Abi, miming a sharpening movement. Connie laughed. Abi had completed the family ritual.

Up a small hill, past an old coaching pub, and there, at the crest of the road, they saw ahead of them the sparkling Atlantic. All three of them pointed their sharp fingers at the sea and shouted in unison: "I see the sea!"

Within minutes they had turned on to the familiar lane, through Lower Barton, on to Higher Barton and along the narrowing and sandy lane that led to Treviscum Bay.

Holidaymakers were carrying surfboards and shepherding children and dogs down to the beach. The tide was low and a warm afternoon sun had made a welcome appearance. Greg drove slowly past them all and then turned right into the tamarisk-lined driveway of Atlantic House. Parking in the shade of a handsome blue hydrangea he pulled on the handbrake and switched the engine off. "We're here." He smiled at Connie.

She leaned over and kissed him. Pulling away, she said with a laugh, "Quick, let's nab the main bedroom."

As they got out of the car and stretched, an attractive older woman with implausibly chestnut hair, red lipstick and tight white jeans, topped off with a jaunty blue-and-white striped T-shirt, came walking round the side of the house. She stood with her arms open wide and a beaming smile.

"There you are!"

"Mummy!" Connie ran to her mother and hugged her.

"Hello, Dolly!" said Greg, who knew that his mother-in-law hated this abbreviation of her name. She ignored him and his pathetically tedious joke.

"Connie, darling! Welcome. Daddy and I have been on tenterhooks all day." She kissed her younger daughter.

"Where is Daddy?"

"At home, watching the wretched cricket highlights," Dorothy replied, turning to Abigail. "Abi darling." They embraced for a moment, then Dorothy stood back and appraised her granddaughter's figure. "So pretty despite the puppy fat. Never mind — I'll get that off you. I'll tell Poppa he's not to let you eat any of his chocolates."

"Mummy —" started Connie, about to chastise her mother for picking on Abi's weight, but she was cut off by Dorothy.

"Come on, Connie, I want to hear all your news. Let's put the kettle on. Greg — bring in the bags, will you?"

Dorothy swept Connie into the house, leaving Greg and a wounded Abigail to carry the luggage. Abigail kept her head down to hide the hot tears she could feel pricking her eyes. Greg put his arm round her. "Abi, she's a silly, jealous old woman. Forget it. There's nothing wrong with you. If anything, I reckon you need fattening up — and I shall make it my business to take you out for a cream tea every day."

"Thanks, Daddy," said Abigail, managing a smile.

★ ★ ★

Pru, still on the Okehampton bypass but driving at only ninety miles an hour now, was seething.

"These jumped-up nobodies in their little blue uniforms, doing no good to anyone. Why aren't they out catching criminals instead of hassling innocent motorists? It's appalling. I shall get on to the solicitor and demand an apology from the chief constable. They're not getting away with this."

Francis kept quiet, merely nodding when he felt it appropriate to do so.

On and on she went. Past the sign to Jamaica Inn and St Breward, through Bodmin, Wadebridge and Padstow, until finally they arrived at Atlantic House.

As soon as he saw that Greg and Connie had got there before them, Francis knew what was coming.

"Mummy, how well you look!" Pru limped slowly round to the front of the car and towards her mother, who was standing on the doorstep with a mug of tea in her hand.

"Prudence! Connie and I have been waiting ages. How long did the police stop you for? Connie saw you."

Connie came to the front door too. "Yes. Poor things. We saw you, but there was nothing we could do to help so we just pushed on. We made good time actually."

Pru smiled through gritted teeth. "How super!"

Dorothy stepped aside and ushered Pru in. "So, apart from the speeding ticket, how are you? Why are you limping?"

"I'm fine, Mummy. So happy to be here again — oof!" Pru suddenly came to a halt as if in spasm, her right side collapsed on itself, a look of pain on her face.

"My God, whatever's the matter?" Dorothy rushed to her aid.

Smiling bravely and steadying herself, Pru replied, "It's the drive. I've been sitting too long. You know Francis, he never lets us stop."

Her mother glowered at the blameless Francis, who was standing on the drive with several heavy bags at his feet. He gawped at his wife with his mouth open in astonishment.

"Francis, don't stand there like a halfwit. Bring Pru's things in while I get her comfortable."

"I'm fine, Mummy. Really I am. Ow! Don't take my arm, it radiates the pain into my leg."

The pair walked into the cool shade of the beautiful old hallway, leaving Connie to help Francis with the bags.

"How was the drive?" she asked him knowingly.

He smiled at the sister-in-law he was so fond of. "The usual."

"How was she with the police?"

He sighed. "Forceful is the best word for it."

"Ah."

"Quite."

They looked at one another and laughed.

"Let's get these bags in and I'll fix you a brew — unless you fancy something stronger?"

"Oh, Con, you are a dear. I think a nice cup of camomile tea will do me nicely."

Pru, meanwhile, had followed her mother to the large cream drawing room overlooking the sea.

Dorothy plumped the cushions on the long and inviting sofa.

"Here, darling, put your feet up. I'll have Connie bring you tea and a hot-water bottle."

Connie, hearing this as she entered the room, looked at Pru suspiciously.

"Hi, sis. What's the matter?"

"Nothing really. The osteopath thinks it's a slipped disc, but I'm fine. Aargh!" She screwed her eyes up at the alleged sudden pain. "It's only when I move. Mummy, would you find my bag? Francis will know where it is. I have some painkillers in it."

"Of course, darling."

As soon as their mother had left the room, Connie rounded on her sister.

"There is nothing wrong with you. And, no, you are not having the big bedroom."

"Connie, I am in severe pain here. I don't want to spoil anyone's holiday, but I simply can't sleep on that bed in the blue room. It just isn't firm enough."

Connie stood with her hands on her hips. "If you think I'm going to relinquish the big room because you're pretending to have a bad back . . ."

Dorothy returned. "Here's your bag, darling. Connie, Pru must have the big room. You'll be fine in the blue room. Golly, how selfish you are! I'll tell Francis to swap the luggage round." She swept out of the room calling, "Francis, Francis."

Pru, with a gleeful look of triumph, preened. "Well. That's sorted then. Get me a cup of tea, would you?"

CHAPTER
FOUR

"I can't believe Mummy fell for that. Bad back, my arse." Connie was in the blue bedroom, unpacking the first of their four bags while Greg lay on the bed fiddling with his laptop.

He was exchanging very personal emails with Janie. Her descriptions of what she was wearing and what she was doing to herself at that moment were turning him on. He rolled on to his stomach to conceal his excitement.

Connie was moving about the room with hangers and holiday clothes. "Do you want me to unpack your case for you, Greg? Might as well, while I'm doing mine."

He was typing something and had a little smile on his lips. He didn't answer his wife.

"Greg?"

"Hmm?"

She walked to the bed and bent over him to see the screen, which instantly went dark as he pressed the sleep button.

"What are you up to that's making you smile?"

"Oh, one of the guys at the gym. Just been to Berlin on a stag weekend. You wouldn't want to know what he's been up to."

"Were you invited?" she asked airily, picking up a couple of T-shirts and placing them in an open drawer.

He closed the lid of the laptop and turned to face her. "Yep. But why would I go out for hamburger when I have steak at home?" Eyeing up his wife's shapely, hourglass figure, he made a grab for her as she passed the bed on the way to putting an emptied case away.

"You have a much nicer arse than your sister . . . or your mother, for that matter."

"Do I?" Connie giggled and wriggled out of his grasp to check herself in the cheval mirror.

"Yes, you do." He grabbed his wife's waist again as she walked past the bed.

"Greg, I'm not sure there's time for that!"

He pulled her down beside him, and lifting her hair from her neck began nibbling the way she liked best.

"Greg, I have to make supper for the kids. Pru won't, and I don't want any of that wholefood budgie stuff Francis dishes up."

Her husband persisted with the nibbling and then allowed his hand to drift to her breast. He felt her nipple stiffen under her T-shirt.

"Come on, darling. Just a quickie. It'll release all the tension in you."

Ten minutes later she did feel a lot better. She looked at Greg's handsome face as he slept and marvelled at how lucky she was to have a husband like him. He wasn't a tall man, but his dark grey eyes and tanned face made her heart flip still. He was a great dad to Abi, who adored him, and he had never strayed in the twenty years they'd been married. Of course, it wasn't all sweetness and light, she reflected. There were weeks on end when she didn't see Greg. He worked too hard and was always away on business, selling Carew games to the rest of the world. She knew she should be grateful; Abi went to a brilliant school and they had never wanted for anything, but there were times when she resented having to hold the fort. All those nights out without her husband, feeling like a spare part. Parents' evenings alone, school plays alone . . .

She pushed these thoughts from her mind. Connie pitied the wives of the men who'd been on the Berlin weekend. Life was good — wasn't it?

Next door in the master bedroom, a fully dressed Francis was astride a shirtless Pru.

"Gently, Francis. Careful." Pru's voice was muffled in her pillow as Francis massaged her back.

"Sorry, Pru. I had no idea your back was so bad. Why didn't you tell me? I shouldn't have let you drive."

"We'd never have got here."

"I know, but I like to look after you and Jeremy, you know that. That was the deal we made when your career took off and we decided that I should stay at home."

"Yes, darling. And very good you are too. So good, I think my back feels a lot better."

Francis got the message and climbed off her.

Pru stood up and did a few stretches. "Yes, I think you've worked a miracle. Get me a nice G and T, and then you can make a start on supper. We don't want Connie's fish finger feast on the first night."

★   ★   ★

"I hope your mum makes supper tonight." Jeremy was lying across Abi's bed. "I'm really hungry. I only had, like, freakin' sushi in the car."

Abi laughed and threw a pillow at her cousin's head. "We had Marks and Sparks sandwiches and crisps." She stood sideways to the dressing-table mirror and sucked her tummy in. "Jem, d'you think I'm getting fat?"

"No."

"You didn't even look."

"I don't need to. You look the same as usual."

"Maybe I should go on a diet."

"I don't like skinny women."

"So I'm not skinny?"

Jeremy picked up the pillow and threw it back at Abi. "Shut your face. Don't get so paranoid."

"Gran said I had puppy fat."

"She doesn't know what she's talking about, man. At Christmas my mate Sean thought you were hot."

"The one with the teeth?"

"There's nothin' wrong with his teeth. Anyway, his mum's got him braces now."

Abi mimed putting two fingers down her throat and made a retching noise. "Lovely."

"That's harsh." Jem laughed. "He's a good mate."

Francis's voice trilled up the stairs: "Dinner, all. Come and get it."

"Shit," said Jeremy. "Dad's got to the kitchen first. Bloody buckwheat and quorn again."

Dorothy and Henry had come over from their bungalow next door to join the two families for supper.

58

Dorothy was rummaging in the fridge, looking for the magnum of champagne that she'd won in the Lifeboat raffle.

"Henry!" She turned, brandishing the bottle.

"Yes, my darling?"

"Make yourself useful and open this. I'll get the glasses."

"They're on the table already, Dorothy." Francis indicated with his chin as he poured boiling water on to a bowl of couscous.

Dorothy was waspish. "Dear Francis, you're a wonder! How lucky Pru is to have you. Tell me, what have you knocked up for our gastronomic delight tonight?" Privately, she thought he was too much of a softie. She preferred men to be men and wasn't in favour of all this "new man" business.

Francis smiled, Dorothy's sarcasm sailing over his head. There was nothing he liked better than cooking a meal for the family.

"Oh, you know me. Something wholesome, nutritious and delicious, I promise."

Dorothy turned away from Francis and looked wryly at Henry, who stifled a snigger, disguising it as a cough, before saying, "Right, old girl. Glasses ready? She's about to blow." And with that the champagne cork came away smoothly in his gnarled but experienced hands.

"Hey, Poppa." Abi entered the kitchen and gave her beloved grandfather an affectionate hug. "Got a glass for me?"

"Ah! Ha-ha! There you are, my favourite grand-daughter." He poured her a fizzing glassful.

"I'm your only granddaughter, Poppa!"

"Well, let me look at you." Abi did a little twirl. "My goodness, you are a beauty. So tall and so slim. You remind me of Granny when I first met her."

Dorothy, who had impatiently wrestled the bottle from Henry's hands and was now pouring herself a glass, looked up. "Yes, but I had an eighteen-inch waist."

"So you did. So you did," Henry replied. Then, winking at Abi, he added, "Mind you, in those days they knew how to make a good corset."

Jeremy had joined them and gladly took the glass his grandmother offered him.

"See, Abi! You don't need to go on a diet."

Connie caught this last comment as she arrived with a satisfied-looking Greg. "Abi! You are perfect as you are! You certainly do not need to lose weight."

Abi looked sheepish. "Granny said I did."

Connie turned to her mother. "Mummy, I don't ever want to hear you say anything like that again. You always went on about my weight when I was Abi's age, and it's so hurtful."

"Not my weight," said Pru, gliding into the room with no sign of a limp. "I've always had trouble putting weight on."

Connie retaliated swiftly, "Yes. Just a pity your ego couldn't be put on a diet too."

Henry looked at his daughters sternly. "Stop that this minute. And Dorothy, keep your opinions to yourself."

60

Dorothy, looking pious, said, "I won't say another word."

"Good."

There followed a strained tension that only very close families recognise.

"Well . . ." Francis put down his champagne flute. "Who's ready for aubergine and haloumi bake, tagine of chickpeas and herb-laced couscous?"

There was a surprising amount of food left over.

"That was delicious, Uncle Francis. I feel fully vegetable and pulsed up," said Abi, taking her half-eaten plate to the bin.

Jem jumped up and did the same. "That was top, Dad. Thanks. Do any of you mind if Abi and I leave the table and watch telly in the rumpus room?"

"That's fine," said Henry. "I want to talk business with Greg anyway."

"Great," said Greg, topping up his and Henry's glasses with the remains of the bottle.

"Let's go to The Bungalow." Henry took Greg's arm, adding in a lower voice: "We might catch a bit of the cricket while we're at it."

"Anyone want a coffee or tea?" Connie asked her mother and sister. They nodded. "I'll go and make some."

"No, absolutely not — I'll go and do it," said Francis, leaping up. "You girls have got plenty to catch up on."

"That is so sweet of you, Francis. Much appreciated." Connie gave him a warm hug and then hurried after Dorothy and Pru.

As the women walked away, Francis collected the remaining plates and scraped them into the bin.

"Here you are, ladies," he said ten minutes later, carrying a tea tray laden with mugs and organic muesli biscuits. "Where shall I put it?"

"Coffee table, Francis," said Pru, barely looking at him.

"Well, the kitchen's all clear for the morning. I'll just pop over to The Bungalow to say good night to Henry and Greg."

"OK. See you in the morning. And thank you for supper, Francis." Connie smiled at him as he left.

Pru turned to their mother. "How are you settling into the new bungalow, Mummy?"

"It's perfect, darling. Easy to clean, lovely and warm. Everything brand new. What else would we do with all that garden. It was the ideal plot and it's the best thing your father ever persuaded me to do."

Connie looked unconvinced. "How could you bear to leave Atlantic House and live in a modern box?"

"Easily. When your father and I bought Atlantic House we were considerably younger than we are now. Your father can't get up on the roof to paint gutters any more. It takes him two days just to mow the lawn. And I am fed up with all the housework. The Bungalow takes twenty minutes, tops. Also, now we have our separate rooms and bathrooms, we get along so much better."

Connie raised her eyebrows. "Don't you miss cuddling up to him at night? I think he misses you."

62

"Sex is very overrated, darling. I'm glad all that side of things is finished. Much nicer to do the crossword together."

"Too much information, Mummy!" Connie preferred not to hear her mother talk about her sex life.

"Well, I'd love separate rooms," sighed Pru. "Francis and I have never bothered too much with that sort of thing."

Connie looked astonished. "Don't you have sex either?"

"No. Still, it's not as if I'm a panting twenty-something, is it?"

Connie thought for a moment. "When did you last make love?"

"I can't remember. Couple of years, at least."

"Two years!" Connie was shocked. Greg had told her that if they didn't make love at least three times a week his testicles would be damaged. "Poor Francis! He must be feeling so neglected!" Connie was indignant on her brother-in-law's behalf. "I make sure Greg is very happy. I always have."

"And you?" her mother asked. "How about you? Does he make sure you're happy?"

"Yes. Well, it's not as if the earth moves every time. But it's the glue that holds a man and woman together in a marriage."

Pru tipped her head back and laughed. "Dear little Connie. It's as if the feminist movement never happened."

"No. It's not to do with that. It's . . ." Connie felt flustered and hated her elder sister for trying to belittle her.

Dorothy stepped in. "Darling, one day you will pray for separate bedrooms. Believe me." She stood up and said pointedly, "Now, I am off to my peaceful bed in my horrid little bungalow." The comment was aimed at Pru, who didn't react. Dorothy continued: "I suggest the pair of you head off for an early night too."

Both girls tutted in annoyance behind their mother's retreating back.

Dorothy heard and, without bothering to turn round, added: "With luck you'll be asleep before either of your husbands return."

While the women had been chatting, Henry had been catching up with Greg. He poured them each a large glass of Scotch and motioned for Greg to sit in one of the two armchairs.

"So, my boy. The business is looking in excellent shape."

Greg stretched his legs out in front of him. "Yes, we've had a good first half of the year and the Japanese are meeting the delivery dates on the new apps, which I believe will increase our turnover significantly over the next twenty-four months."

They discussed markets, initiatives and overheads for a while, and then Henry said, "You know, my old father wouldn't recognise the company now. He would have hated all these virtual games. His mantra was always 'Nothing can beat the fun —'"

Greg finished it off for him: "'— of a family sitting round the table playing Ludo.'"

Henry looked at him in surprise. "Have I mentioned that before?"

"Once or twice."

"Well, you've been with the company . . . ooh, how many years is it?"

"Coming up for twenty-two."

"Twenty-two years. My goodness! And look at you now: managing director."

Every year Greg and Henry had this discussion. Greg had joined the company as a graduate trainee. His excellent degree in business and marketing meant he'd been marked out as management potential, but he'd had the nous to ingratiate himself with his colleagues and bosses, getting noticed as the lad who wasn't afraid to get his hands dirty sweeping the shop floor or making a good impression on visiting VIPs. Within a few months, Henry had begun grooming him for bigger things.

Henry liked to have Greg as his eyes and ears among the workers. Greg never pulled any punches. He told Henry who was good, who needed help and who was just plain useless. He also persuaded Henry to make improvements to staff working conditions by loosening up the rosters, smartening up the canteen and improving holiday leave. None of this did him any harm with his workmates or with Henry. One summer he'd received an invitation to a private barbecue at Henry and Dorothy's house. He could still remember how hard he'd tried not to flirt with Connie. She was almost eighteen and reminded him, in certain lights, of a young Brigitte Bardot.

"I'll tell you honestly, Greg," Henry said now, "I didn't think you were good enough for Connie when you asked me if you could marry her. But you've been a marvellous addition to the family and the company. Cheers!" They raised their glasses to each other.

Greg had heard this speech many times before.

"I am lucky to have her and Abi and a job with a company I'm so proud of." This answer always achieved a satisfactory end to the conversation. Henry grinned over his empty glass. "Get me another of these and let's see how we're doing against the West Indies, shall we?"

Henry enjoyed male company. He was fond of his sons-in-law. Both so different, but decent husbands to his girls. He heard the front door open and Francis's voice called out, "Helloo."

"Come in, my boy, come in," Henry roared. Francis appeared in the sitting room.

"Hi. Am I disturbing you?"

"Not at all, old boy. Get yourself a glass of Scotch and sit down."

Greg shifted his legs so that Francis could get past him to the drinks tray.

"How are the women?" Greg asked sardonically.

"Fine. All having their cup of tea and chatting nicely."

"How do you put up with them?" asked Greg.

Francis looked bemused. "I like them. I like women. Between us three, we've done pretty well."

Greg was about to say something horribly misogynistic when it struck him that it might upset his father-in-law. Coughing, he replied, "Quite so. Very lucky indeed.

66

Women. God bless them." And he raised his glass in salute.

On the television the England team were fielding like demons and the West Indies were falling apart. None of the men found it necessary to talk. This was the pleasure of being a man.

Henry must have dozed off for a moment, because the sound of his wife's voice woke him with a start.

"That's it, boys." Dorothy stepped over their sprawled legs and reached for the remote control. "I'm turning this off."

"We were enjoying that!" protested Henry.

She sniffed the air. "You've been enjoying too much whisky — I can smell it. Come on, chop chop. You've all got beds to go to."

The men slowly stood and stretched. Henry shook hands with Greg and Francis and slapped them both on the shoulders. "Good to see you, fellas. Sleep well. Sorry about She Who Must Be Obeyed."

"I heard that!" came his wife's voice from the hallway.

After closing the door on "the boys", Henry went to the kitchen where his wife was making two cups of Ovaltine. "Nice lads," he said. "The girls are happy enough, aren't they?"

"I think so."

"Lucky fellas to have such good wives." He patted her bottom. "And I'm lucky to have you."

She handed him his mug of Ovaltine. "Down, boy!"

CHAPTER
FIVE

It was the first morning of the holiday proper. Francis loved this time. He had got up early and gone for a walk on the cliff path. The sun was promising a warm day and as he felt its heat on his muscles, he broke into a gentle jog which felt really good. He was of medium height, slim build and thinning hair. An average-looking man, but with a kind face and expressive eyes. His mouth was regular and he had exceptional teeth. White and even. Flossed every morning. He stopped on a stretch of springy grass and lay on the turf, closed his eyes and felt the sun on his face. The phone in his pocket vibrated, signalling a text message.

Call me! x

It was from Belinda.

Francis looked around, guiltily, and deleted the message. Stuffing his phone back into his pocket he headed for home.

He let himself quietly back into the house and tried to focus on his chores. He emptied the dishwasher, set up a recycling station, emptied the kitchen bin and put the coffee on. Then he sat down with the previous day's crossword and attempted to put Belinda out of his mind. He almost leapt out of his skin when Jeremy and Abigail appeared with a cheery "Morning."

"Oh." His hands shook as he straightened his reading specs. "You made me jump."

Abigail gave him a squeeze on her way to the fridge, "Soz, Unc. Didn't mean to!"

Jeremy looked at his father. "You all right, Dad — feeling OK? You look a bit pale."

"Erm, yes." Francis laughed self-consciously. "Do I? Gosh, no, nothing wrong. Just a tad preoccupied, that's all."

"With what — not worrying about tonight's dinner, are you? Lentils and broccoli stir-fry or quinoa and broad bean stew? God, please let Aunt Con cook tonight, Dad — we're wasting away!"

"Don't be cheeky," Francis said, aiming a swipe at his son with a tea towel.

Abi swung a large bottle of orange juice towards Jem. "Want some?"

"Yuh. Thanks." Jeremy sat at the breakfast table, expecting his cousin to sort it out for him.

"Can I cook you some scrambled eggs?" his father asked.

"Nah. Abi, get me some crunchy nut cornflakes, would you?"

"What did your last servant die of?" Abi replied, bashing him on the head with a teaspoon as she passed.

"So, kids, what are you up to today?" Francis asked, reaching for the box of cereal.

* * *

The cousins found themselves a warm spot in the dunes. The tide was on its way in and the sea was calm and glistening.

Abigail stretched her arms above her head and took a deep breath. "I love the first day of the holidays, don't you?"

Jeremy, who had been watching a gorgeous redhead wriggle into her bikini while attempting to keep her towel round her, gave a distracted, "Mmm."

Abigail followed his eyeline. "You're punching way above your weight there, boy."

Jeremy pretended to be confused. "What? Hmm? Oh, the ginger? Hadn't noticed her. But now you mention it she's all right, I suppose."

The pair of them lay watching the girl as she carefully applied sun cream to her generous bosom and milky thighs.

Jeremy sighed lustily. "Do you suppose she'd like some help with that?"

Abigail giggled. "Men! Don't you think of anything else?"

"No."

The pair laughed, enjoying the friendship they had always shared. More like brother and sister than cousins.

Abi settled down to read her gossip magazine and Jeremy's attention was now drawn from the redhead to the rest of the beach. There were a lot of gorgeous girls about this summer, he thought longingly. But how was he going to meet one? He would be seventeen next year and girls occupied his every waking moment and his dreams too. He turned on his side towards Abi and, shielding his eyes from the sun, asked, "Any of your mates coming down this year?"

"No. They're all busy. I wanted Clemmie to come, but her mum's getting married again or something, so she can't."

Jem was sorry to hear this. Clemmie was hot. He said, with some wisdom, "Parents enjoy ruining kids' plans."

"Yeah." Abi turned on her side to face Jeremy. "How were your GCSEs?"

"All right, I think. Mum tried her best to bribe me into getting straight As." Here he imitated his mother's voice:

" 'One hundred pounds for every A you get, young man.' "

"Sounds good to me."

"Well, we'll see." He shifted his weight to get more comfortable. "By the way, what are you going to do for your birthday this summer?"

Abi's birthday, falling in August, was always spent in Cornwall. Usually her parents organised a barbecue in the garden with local kids and any holidaying children Abi and Jem had befriended on the beach. But this year would be her seventeenth and she was hoping for something better.

"I want to have an all-night party, on the beach. Dancing till dawn, no parents, sexy boys and plenty of booze."

Jem sniggered. "Yeah, right. And Auntie Connie's agreed to that, has she?"

71

"She doesn't know yet. She might never know. Maybe you and I could organise it without her or Dad ever finding out . . ."

It was almost midday and Francis was at the kitchen table writing a shopping list when Connie came in.

"Morning, Francis." She kissed the top of his head.

"Morning, Connie. Good lie-in?"

"Marvellous. I've been reading. It's bliss not to have to get up for anything. Greg's still asleep. I've left him to it."

"There's coffee in the pot. Would you like me to make some toast?" he asked.

"You're a darling, Francis. Yes please." She slumped into a chair. "How's my hypochondriacal sister's back this morning?"

The two of them shared a smile at their mutual understanding of Pru's ruse. Connie knew that Francis had his wife's number, but he was far too loyal (and too smart) to ever criticise his wife. Pru was lucky to have him, but Connie doubted that her sister appreciated the things Francis did for her, the sacrifices he'd made.

"A lot better, I think. I've run her a hot bath to loosen it."

"Yes. I noticed there was no hot water." Connie sighed and stretched her arms above her, watching her brother-in-law as he popped two slices of bread in the toaster. "Francis?"

"Ye-es?" He was chewing the end of his biro now and looking at his very long shopping list.

72

"You must be glad of this summer break. How have things been?"

"Oh, you know. Busy running around ferrying Jem to and from his various social activities — I was pretty strict about making sure that he found time to study — but lately it's been all work and no play, what with his GCSEs."

Connie nodded. "I know what you mean. I seem to spend all my time chauffeuring Abi. I worry about her. She's so beautiful, I can't help being afraid that she'll be lured away from the straight and narrow." She brushed at a couple of Jeremy's cornflake crumbs left on the table. "She'll be seventeen soon. My little girl is almost grown up."

"You can't hold them back, Con. Do you remember how you were at that age?"

"Christ — I don't want to remember!" She laughed and swept the cornflakes into her hand before getting up and putting them in the bin. "How are things with the PTA? Last time we talked, you were really getting stuck into all that stuff."

Francis gave a nervous laugh. "Oh, pretty much what you'd expect: so far so boring!" He hurried to change the subject: "But Pru's the one with the stress, not me."

"You work hard too, though, looking after the house and Jeremy."

The toaster popped and Francis grabbed a plate, a knife and the butter dish, then put it all down in front of Connie.

She thanked him. "Greg's always putting in long hours at work, so I'm in the same boat as you. Being the one who stays home, keeping things running smoothly — that's important work too. I like to think I'm providing a sanctuary for him to escape to, leave the stress behind."

Connie ploughed on: "He and Pru are lucky to have us. It's the little things, isn't it? Making sure the fridge is stocked with their favourite food. A well-ordered house with clean towels and a comfy bed."

Francis was still distracted. "Well, yes . . ."

Connie went for the big one: "A nice cuddle in the marital bed at the end of a long day." She stopped to observe his reaction to the last comment. Apart from a slight pause in writing his list, Francis made no response.

"Greg and I have been married for twenty years, and the physical side of our relationship is terribly important. Good sex keeps a couple together, don't you think?"

Francis stopped writing and blinked at her, not sure he'd heard her correctly. "Sorry, Connie. What did you say?"

"How long have you been married to Pru now?"

He put his pen down and tore the list from the pad.

"Eighteen years this November." Connie and he were close and enjoyed each other's company, but he was feeling distinctly uncomfortable at the turn this conversation was taking. "Anything you need from the village? I must get this shopping done." He was standing now and looking around for his mobile phone and car keys.

74

Connie knew when to pull back. She'd have to continue this conversation slowly over the coming weeks.

"No, I don't think so. I'll probably have a little expedition down there myself this afternoon to pick up supplies — Greg loves the chilli jam they do at the deli. But thanks anyway."

"OK, see you later." He found the keys and his phone on the side. As he picked them up, his phone buzzed with another text. He glanced at the name of the sender. Belinda again. He put the phone in his pocket without opening the message.

Curious, Connie decided to tease him further: "Aren't you going to see who that is? Or is it your secret lover?"

Francis was fumbling with his linen jacket. "School PTA round robin, I expect. Bound to be something that can wait. I don't want to miss the fresh granary loaves at the baker's. Tell Pru I'll be back in an hour or so."

He could feel the phone burning in his pocket. His heart was thumping in his chest and his breathing got faster. He hopped in the car and set off down the drive and out on to the sandy beach lane, relieved to have escaped before Connie asked any more awkward questions. Why did he feel so furtive and guilty? It wasn't as if there was anything between them . . . Or was there? No, he'd done nothing to encourage her.

A small child in jelly shoes, bucket and spade in hand, suddenly stepped out in front of him. Francis executed a perfect emergency stop and smiled at the child's harassed mother, who shouted an obscenity at him and yanked her daughter back on to the verge.

He had to put all thoughts of Belinda aside and concentrate. Belinda . . . Attractive, full-hipped and full of life. He had met her when her fourteen-year-old daughter, Emily, had joined Jeremy's school last September. Belinda was a merry and willing new recruit to the PTA. A divorcée in her early forties, she'd made a beeline for him from the start. It wasn't Francis's style to strike up relationships with people; he was happiest with his family around him and the few friends Pru liked to socialise with, but there was something about Belinda that was hard to resist. She was constantly inviting him over to her place for lunch. He hadn't taken up the invitation . . . yet.

He carefully reversed into a tight space in the Higher Barton village car park and turned the engine off. Unable to resist any longer, he reached for his phone and looked at the screen. Belinda's name was top of the list of incoming messages:

Hi Frankie. Amazing coincidence — am coming to Cornwall Wednesday. Staying in Treviscum Bay. Anywhere near you? Emily and I would love to see you. xxxxx

"Oh, shit shit shit!" Francis said out loud. It was Sunday today. She'd be here in three days. What was he going to do? How did she know where he was? Had he told her he was coming to Treviscum Bay? Was she stalking him? How would he explain this to Pru? "Shit shit shit," he said again.

Normally, Francis liked nothing better than a trip to the shops in Higher Barton. He enjoyed renewing old acquaintances with the shopkeepers and chatting to the baker about his latest lines. Today, however, he had found it impossible to concentrate on the lengthy explanation the baker had given him about his new range of gluten-free products.

"Would you like to try a loaf? It's hard to tell the difference."

Francis had ended up buying four more loaves than he'd intended. He'd wondered, with more anxiety than was necessary, whether there was any room in the freezer, admonishing himself for not checking before he'd come out. He'd fretted all the way home, trying to focus on the loaves instead of contemplating what would happen when Belinda arrived.

"Francis, there you are." Pru was lying on a comfortable lounger outside the sliding kitchen doors, on the sunny terrace.

"Hello, Pru," Francis called over-brightly, setting down the six or seven plastic carrier bags that were cutting into his fingers. "Let me empty the car and I'll make us a cup of coffee."

"Did you get my paper?"

"Yes, dear!" He gave her a beaming smile, hoping that it would cover any remnants of guilty thoughts about Belinda.

Pru gazed at him steadily. Frowning slightly. Oh God, did she suspect? He looked back at her, unable to move.

She spoke. "Well, go on then. I'm waiting."

"What for?" He felt a squirt of fear in his stomach.

"Get. My. Paper."

Weak with relief, he rummaged in the carrier bags: "Yes. Yes. Of course, darling."

"What's for lunch, Dad?" Jeremy and Abi walked in through the sliding doors bringing sandy feet with them. Francis visibly jumped again.

"Don't creep up on me! How many times have I told you! You'll give me a heart attack!"

"OK. Chill, Dad. What's making you so nervy today?"

"Nervy?" Francis snapped. "I am never nervy!" He looked at the two pairs of sandy feet. "Get outside and clean those bloody feet. Both of you. This is my holiday, too, you know."

"Blimey, Dad, no need to shout."

"I am not shouting," shouted Francis.

"Sorry, Uncle Francis. Come on, Jem." Abi steered her cousin outside and threw over her shoulder, "I'll be back to help you lay the table in a minute, Uncle Francis."

Francis slowly resumed unpacking and storing the groceries, then made a start on washing the lettuce for his organic poached salmon salad. His thoughts were a mess. Should he tell Pru about Belinda? How would he introduce Belinda? How long was she planning to visit? Oh God, oh God.

"Francis?" Pru's querulous voice made him jump yet again. He clutched his chest with a damp lettuce hand. He turned to face her. "Yes, darling?"

She studied him intently, until he felt as if his mind was being read. Eventually she said, "Are you all right? You look very pink and glazed."

"I'm fine. Just, erm, thinking about some jobs I need to do."

"Oh, good. Would you put the dripping tap in our en-suite basin on the list? Get Greg to help. He does bugger-all when he's here. When's lunch?"

"About ten minutes."

"Bring it up to me, would you? I'm expecting a conference call any minute."

"Yes, Pru." But she'd already left the room.

Abi and Jem reappeared with clean feet and found Francis looking worse than ever.

"Dad, you don't look at all well. Sit down and I'll make you a drink."

Francis did as he was told.

Abi started to lay the table. "I'll fix lunch, Uncle Francis, and Jem and I will wash up. You need a rest."

CHAPTER
SIX

Francis looked so poorly that even Pru noticed. Mildly concerned, she graciously vacated the big bedroom saying that she would take her conference call in the rumpus room, while Jeremy drew the curtains and settled his father down for a nap.

"I'm absolutely fine, Jem."

"You're not, Dad. You don't look yourself. What time did you get up this morning?"

"Not too early. Five-ish."

Jeremy raised his eyebrows as his father lay down on the bed. "Did you run?"

"Only a little jog."

"Well, there you are. You're just a bit knackered. Get some kip and we'll see you later." Jeremy pulled a soft rug over his father's legs and left him to it.

Lying alone in the semi-darkness, Francis could hear the quiet roar of the ocean through an open window. His mind was in shreds. What should he do? Belinda was coming. Belinda was coming. Belinda was coming. *Come on, man — pull yourself together — have a sleep and the answer will come to you. Belinda is coming, Belinda is coming.* The rhythm of these words took him into a restless slumber.

Downstairs, the rest of the family sat down to the tasty salmon salad Francis had prepared. There was an odd silence as they ate, missing Francis's attentions. Everyone finished quickly. Thanks to a bit of teamwork, they tidied up the kitchen in no time and cleared off to do their own thing.

"Come along, Henry." Dorothy was standing impatiently by the back door. "It's at least forty minutes to Lostwithiel."

"Lostwithiel? Why are you going there?" asked Connie.

"There are some staddle stones for sale. Supposed to have come from Daphne du Maurier's house in Ready Money Cove. They'd look rather good on our drive."

"What are staddle stones, Granny?" asked Abi.

Henry answered, "Those stone mushroom things. I'm not prepared to pay over the odds for them, Dorothy."

Dorothy waved a hand airily. "Your Poppa has short arms and long pockets. Now come along, Henry."

Abi looked at Jem. "Fancy a bike ride?"

"Sure," he said, draining his glass of squash.

Abi dropped a kiss on her father's head. "Bye, Dad. See you later."

Greg was desperate to find a quiet place where he could talk to Janie on his mobile. Connie and Pru were still in the house. He walked to the stairs and called up: "Connie? I'm going to the garage — fill up with fuel while I can. See you in a bit."

Connie appeared at the top of the stairs in shorts and T-shirt with a towel and a book under her arm. "OK, darling. I'm going down to the beach for a snooze and a read."

Greg felt a sense of liberation flood through him. He had the whole afternoon undisturbed with his phone and Janie.

Connie, too, was feeling liberated as she sauntered along the path to the beach. An afternoon with no responsibilities. Bliss! No need to talk, listen or do anything but lie down and read or sleep.

"Connie, wait for me." A familiar voice broke into her bubble. Connie kept walking.

"Connie!" Irritation in the call now. "I said wait!"

Connie breathed deeply, stopped and turned. Pru was at the top of the path, closing the garden gate. She looked cross and hot as she drew level with Connie.

"Why didn't you tell me you were off to the beach? You knew I'd have said I'd come."

"Yes, I did know, but actually I was hoping for a bit of peace and quiet."

"Oh, me too. Don't you find Mummy's endless chatter and sparring with Daddy awfully wearing?"

"Yes."

"And the kids! They're good kids, I know, but the noise, the mess — it's exhausting."

"Yes."

"And now Francis has decided to take to his bed. I just had to get out of the house."

"Yes."

They found themselves a sheltered spot of dry sand in the sunshine and rolled out their towels, smoothing them to remove any wrinkles and sitting down gently so as not to get any sand on them.

Connie slipped out of her shorts and top to reveal a well-cut bikini and curvy thighs. She picked up her book and began to read.

"What are you reading?"

"Something from my book club."

"You're lucky to have the time."

"To read or join a book club?"

"Both."

Pru unpopped the fastenings on her stripy beach robe and rolled it up carefully to use as a pillow. She was wearing a one piece in navy and white.

"I don't like bikinis," she said pointedly. "Not at our age."

"I am not your age."

"You know what I mean."

Pru reached into her bag for sun cream, factor 50, and made a huge amount of slapping noise as she put it on.

"Would you put some on my back?"

"OK." Wearily, Connie put her book down, sat up and creamed her sister's white and bony back.

"Thank you," Pru said. "Would you like me to do you?"

"No thanks," said Connie, settling down again. "I want to go brown."

"The sun is so ageing to one's skin. You should look after yours."

"I'm wearing factor 15."

"Not high enough."

"It's Cornwall, not Africa."

"I'm only saying."

"Sorry. Look, I want to read my book, OK?"

"I'm not stopping you." Pru plonked a ridiculous orange floral floppy hat on her head and lay down.

Connie waited in case her sister had anything else to say, but she stayed silent. Breathing a sigh of relief, Connie started reading again. Pru began to snore. Heaving a sigh, Connie dropped her book and closed her eyes. Within minutes she was snoring too.

When they woke up, the sun was a little lower and the tide was on its way in. They moved their towels further up the beach. As they settled, a light breeze picked up and Pru shivered. She put her robe back on.

"Are you worried about Francis?" Connie asked Pru. "He certainly isn't looking very well."

Pru looked at her as if she were mad.

"No. Why should I be? He's fine."

"He seemed a bit tired and distracted."

"What has he got to distract him?"

"You tell me."

"I am telling you: nothing. He's fine. Probably wants a bit of attention."

"Maybe he wants *your* attention."

"Poor Francis, not getting any sex? Is that what you're trying to say?"

"Yes. No. Well, yes."

"Francis is as little inclined as I am. It's something that we used to do and don't need to do any more. We've grown up."

"So, grown-ups aren't allowed to have sex?"

"Exactly."

"But Greg and I have sex."

"Yes. And look at Greg. He's not exactly a grown-up, is he?"

Connie propped herself up on her elbows and looked at her sister. "What is that supposed to mean?"

Pru squinted, shading her eyes. "Well, he's still a little boy. The way he dresses, his gadgets, the car he drives, the swagger as he walks."

"I'd rather have a man who knows how to have fun — and, yes, sex — than a downtrodden servant."

Pru sat very still for a moment. Then, in a dangerously neutral voice, she replied, "You think Francis is a down-trodden servant?" She started to wag her forefinger in front of Connie's face. "That downtrodden servant lives in a beautiful house, with a joint account he can access at any time, and a son who is happy and doing well at school, and a wife who works her backside off and brings home a considerable side of bacon. Does that sound like a downtrodden servant to you?" She paused spitefully and added, "Or does it take one to know one?"

Pru settled her sunglasses over her eyes and lay back on her towel to emphasise that the conversation was closed.

Connie, smarting, settled back down too. Her sister could be such a bitch, She couldn't help feeling worried about her brother-in-law. He was a nice man and she couldn't bear to think of him being lonely and forced into celibacy. He wasn't the type to have an affair, but he was attractive in his own way. Not compared to

Greg, of course. Loads of her friends fancied Greg, but he had never given her cause for concern. Good job too, or she'd roast his nuts for Christmas.

"Hi, Mum! Hi, Auntie Pru." The shadows of Abi and Jem fell across them. "Presents for you!"

The youngsters handed over two cones of whippy ice cream with chocolate flakes stuck in the top.

Connie and Pru made space for their offspring on their towels.

"Hi, kids. What have you been up to?"

Abi started. "We cycled to Pendruggan — you know, the village where they're filming that telly detective thing you like, Mum."

"Oh yes. Were they all there?"

"Yeah. We had to be quiet because they were filming some dead body being found on the village green or something. We watched for about half an hour, but it was so slow and boring we decided to cycle into Trevay and have a coffee on the harbour." Abi, finishing her sentence with an upward lilt as if asking a question, took a lick of ice cream.

Jeremy continued, "Yeah, and we bumped into Big Ben. He said that a woman who says she knows our family is coming to stay in one of the holiday lets at the back of Atlantic House."

Big Ben was a tiny man who had bought Dairy Cottage and The Byre, two of the outhouses that had originally belonged to Atlantic House. For the past few years he'd been renting them out as holiday lets.

"Really?" asked Connie. "I wonder who that is?"

"He didn't say. But whoever it is will be arriving on Wednesday."

"I hope it's someone nice and not a terrible bore."

Abi laughed, "Oh, Mum, you're sounding more like Granny every day!"

Connie gave her daughter a friendly shove.

As Abi regained her balance, she caught sight of a man watching them.

"Mum, that man's staring at us."

Connie looked over the top of her sunglasses. "Where?"

"See the pink beach tent? Just to the right of that. He's quite hench, for an old bloke. Bare chest and blue shorts. Curly hair — too long for his age. Talking to a couple of the lifeguards?"

Connie followed Abi's directions and spotted him. She pushed her sunglasses back up her nose and nudged her sister. "Pru, look. See him?"

Pru was alert and as still as a pointer dog. Breathing out very slowly she replied, "Yes. I see him."

They spoke together: "Merlin Pengelly."

Abigail giggled. "Who is he?"

"An old friend of mine," said Pru.

"And mine," said Connie.

The women eyed each other for a moment. Pru broke the silence first.

"Come on, Connie." She stood up and started to roll her towel. "Time we were going back."

Connie was already up and shooshing Abi off her towel.

The man continued to watch them with a slow smile spreading across his handsome face. He waved at them.

"Oh my God, he's waving," Connie flustered.

"He's coming this way."

Merlin's brown athletic legs were carrying him towards them. Fifty metres, thirty and finally with only a couple more steps to go he stopped and raised a sunkissed eyebrow, allowing his sea-green eyes to gleam flirtatiously.

"Connie? Pru? Is it really you?" The two women looked uncomfortable. "You do remember me, don't you?"

Pru acknowledged him and answered coolly: "How could we forget, Merlin."

He leaned forward as if to kiss her cheek, but she offered her hand to shake instead. He ignored it. She felt his warm skin brush her face.

He stepped back. "I'd know you anywhere, Prudence Carew."

"Meake."

"Sorry?"

"I'm Prudence Meake now."

"Oh, you're married. Congratulations."

Pru introduced Jeremy, "And this is my son, Jem."

Merlin reached out to shake his hand. "Good to meet you, Jem." He turned to Connie. "Don't tell me you're married too, Connie?"

"Of course I am."

"Oh yes. I remember reading about it. After our summer you married one of your dad's employees."

Connie looked crossly at him. "I married a man who loves me. He's managing director of the company now."

"Is that so?" He nodded his head slowly, his piercing eyes smiling sardonically. "Well, you did all right for yourself, didn't you, eh?"

Abigail couldn't bear to be left out a moment longer. "Hi, I'm Abi. Connie's daughter."

He turned his glittering gaze to her. "Well, well. You're a beauty, aren't you."

Connie snapped, "She's not seventeen yet, Merlin."

Merlin laughed. "And so were you once, Con. So were you."

Jem, conscious that there was something rather uncomfortable about this encounter, felt a primeval urge to protect the women, though he wasn't sure why.

"My father and Uncle Greg are up at Atlantic House," he said loyally.

Merlin shifted his gaze from Pru to this young boy with the beginnings of soft whiskers on his chin and hair gelled in the way the "up country" kids seemed to favour.

"Is that so?" he drawled. "I'll make sure I look out for them." He turned his attention back to the two sisters. "You've still got Atlantic House then?"

Connie answered, "Yes."

"There are a few memories there, aren't there?" he said.

"Come along, Connie, we must get back to the house." Pru was stuffing her towel into her beach bag.

Merlin ignored her and sat himself down on the sand. Fishing in his shorts pocket, he brought out a bag of tobacco. "Stay a while longer. We've got catching up to do." He calmly set about rolling a cigarette. "Want one?" He pushed the leather pouch towards Jeremy.

"No thanks. I don't smoke."

Merlin looked up at him and winked. "Not tobacco, anyway, boy. Eh?"

"Jeremy's only sixteen, Merlin. Don't tease him," Pru scowled.

"Oh, right." Merlin screwed up an eye as the wind blew smoke into it. "How about you?" He was looking at Abi. "Or are you a good girl?"

"How do you know my mum and my auntie Pru?" asked Abi.

Merlin took a deep drag on his cigarette and smiled. "Shall I tell her, girls?"

"Merlin is an old friend of your mother's and mine. We knew him when we were about your age, Abi. That's all," said Pru with feigned disinterest.

Merlin again raised an eyebrow. "That's all?" he smirked. "That wasn't the way it seemed to me." He turned to Abi. "These two broke my heart. The prettiest girls on the beach — and they knew it."

"Tell me more," said Abi.

"Hmmm." He looked at Connie and Pru and gave a sad smile. "I would, darlin', but I think your mum and Auntie Pru might not want me to. Another time, eh?"

"Yes, another time," said Connie.

"Good idea," said Pru.

Abi's eye was caught by the sight of her father walking down the beach towards them. "Hey, Daddy!" She waved. "Over here!"

Merlin stood up. "Time I was off. Good to see you, girls. Catch you later." And he was gone.

Greg arrived hot and perspiring. He had on a white singlet vest and board shorts pulled low to reveal the back of his designer underpants.

"Hey, kids. Hey, Con." He reached his wife and pulled her into a hug. "Jem, Abi — want to surf with me?"

"Yeah. Love to. Great."

"Good," he replied. "Who was that guy you were talking to?" He nodded towards the retreating back of Merlin.

"Merlin Pengelly. One of Auntie Pru and Mum's old boyfriends," said Abi.

"Yeah? Which one, Con?"

Connie and Pru studiously avoided looking at each other until Connie said, "He was one of a group of us who used to knock around together."

"Really?" Greg smiled and held Connie closer. "Should I be jealous that he's resurfaced?"

He took another glance at the sauntering Merlin, who had reached the top of the beach. As if he knew he was being watched, Merlin turned and gave the family group a flamboyant salute before disappearing from view.

"Golly, no!" Connie hastily replied.

"Good. He looks like a right prick."

Back at the house, the freshly showered sisters started preparing supper.

Connie was squirting a generous amount of tomato ketchup into Pru's gently simmering bolognese sauce.

"Do you know how much sugar there is in that poison?" Pru tutted.

"Sugar brings out the flavour of the meat and ketchup is good for you. I read it in the *Daily Mail*."

"And you believe everything you read in that rag, do you?"

"The same way you believe everything in the *Guardian*, yes."

They carried on with their jobs, each silently distracted by their meeting with Merlin earlier.

Pru broke the silence first: "I used to think that you and I had no secrets."

Connie paused momentarily as she was folding paper napkins. "We don't, do we?"

"You tell me."

Connie turned to face her sister, who was taking wine glasses down from a cupboard "Tell you what?"

"Why didn't you tell me about Merlin?"

Connie swallowed hard and went on the attack. "Yawn yawn — ancient history."

"I agree, but I still can't believe you could be so spiteful." Pru settled the glasses on the table and stood with her hands on her hips and an angry glint in her eye.

"Spiteful?" Connie retaliated quickly. "That's something you'd know all about. Take the plank out of your own eye before you look at the splinter in mine."

"Not the old grudge about the blue bedroom again? Grow up!"

Connie advanced on her sister, the kitchen table between them, "Don't you *ever* speak to me like that again. You've got your own way in life at every turn."

92

"And you haven't? I've worked hard for everything Francis and I have."

"Meaning what? That I'm an intellectual pygmy who's never had a job?"

"If the cap fits."

Connie moved fast around the table and stuck her face into Pru's. "Say that again."

"Prudence. Connie. What is this racket?" Dorothy had come through from the terrace.

The girls backed away from each other and continued with their jobs.

"Were you rowing?"

There was no answer, but Dorothy knew her girls well enough not to need one.

"I'll take that as a yes." Neither of them would meet her eye. "Right, I'm here now. Give me a job to do and let's all calm down."

The three women busied themselves for the next half hour and the atmosphere gradually thawed.

Eventually Pru spoke: "OK, I think that's everything. Table laid, bolognese done. Trifle made. Just the salad to do when the kids and Greg come back. Fancy a drink, Mum? Connie?"

"Not for me, darling. I'm going home to spruce myself up." Dorothy set off for The Bungalow with a parting wave.

"Yes, please." Connie offered an apologetic smile to Pru. "I reckon we deserve a glass of something cold and white. Shall we take it outside?"

Pru laid a tray with an ice bucket and bottle of Pinot Grigio, two glasses and a bowl each of olives and cheese straws.

Carrying it out on to the terrace, she saw that Connie had plumped the cushions on the silvered wood of the ancient set of garden chairs. The lowering sun was still warm and the sea reflected its gold.

Pru raised her glass. "Cheers."

"Cheers."

They watched the sun as it set low in the sky and looked out to the beach below to spot their surfers.

Connie could see Greg standing in the shallows, taking photos of Abi and Jem as they cruised the waves on their boards.

She took a long sip on her wine. "Merlin looked good, didn't he?"

"Yes. Very." Pru conceded.

CHAPTER
SEVEN

Greg paddled out behind the breaking waves and waited patiently. He counted the rollers coming towards him, one, two, three . . . small ones gently lifted and lowered him. It was quiet. Only two other surfers, both men, were waiting with him, out in the deep. Four, five . . . every seventh wave was the one to look out for. Six, seven . . . he saw it coming. Swelling and rising to meet him. He paddled like mad with his salt-wrinkled hands and looking behind him saw the water break as it rose above him. He caught it well. Came up on to his knee, got his balance and was standing on the board and riding the foaming water towards the beach.

"Yee-ha!" he cried, hoping someone was witnessing his brilliance. Then something threw his balance and he was dumped in a tumble of heavy water and sand. Winded and underwater, he felt the rough sand tear at his cheek and ear. Gasping his way into fresh air he found the strength to stand and, as nonchalantly as possible, retrieve his board. He stood in the shallows catching his breath.

"All right, Dad?" Abi swept up beside him, still upright on her board.

He tried to regulate his heavy breathing. "Yeah, yeah. Fine. Did you see me? I was out in the impact zone, wanting a bit of aggro, and caught a really good tube."

"Dad, quit the dude talk. It's not funny."

"Listen, babe, I've been a surfer for thirty years."

"Yeah. Which is why you're a bit too old for it now. You know what the surfers call someone like you?"

"Cool?"

"Nope. A grey belly."

"Really?"

"Yeah." Abi put her wet arm round his crestfallen shoulders.

"Looked as though you took a bit of a tumble."

"Nah, nah. All part of the fun. Go on. Get back in. I've got my camera in my bag. I'll take some action shots of you and Jem."

"Great! I'll tell him. We'll come up the beach together, OK?"

Greg waved his daughter off, envying her energy and fitness as she ran into the sea. He looked at his "grey belly" and sucked his muscles in. Or at least, he tried to. It didn't seem to make much difference. Letting them go again, he walked to their pile of belongings and found his camera.

By the time the surfers got back to the house, Connie and Prudence were opening a second bottle of wine on the terrace.

"Hi," giggled Connie, clearly rather tiddly. "My sister and I deserved a little drinky. Want one?"

"Definitely. Let me have a shower and I'll be down."

Greg's legs ached as he climbed the stairs. He got to their bathroom and turned the shower on, having a quick pee in the loo while waiting for the hot water to come through. He saw himself in the mirror. He admired what he saw. He'd had a fantastically erotic call with Janie that afternoon. She'd been home alone in her Battersea mansion flat, taking a bath. God, how he'd wanted to be there with her.

With renewed vigour he jumped under the shower and almost had a heart attack. The water was icy cold. The kids must have taken the lot.

Supper was a quiet affair. Francis came down and managed a few spoonfuls of the spag bol. The kids went off with theirs on trays to watch a movie in the rumpus room. Connie was trying to sober up and Pru had got her laptop out and was doing some work.

Greg helped load the dishwasher then took a gin and tonic into the drawing room and settled down to have a quiet read of the paper.

The door banged open, shattering his peace, and Abi entered. "Daddeee?" she wheedled, plonking herself down on the sofa next to her father.

"Hmmm?" He turned the page noisily and refused to look at her.

"You know it's my birthday in a couple of weeks?"

"Is it? I really don't remember."

Abi smacked his arm. "Yes you do! Don't be so mean."

Greg rubbed his arm. "What do you want, you ungrateful child?"

Abi brightened. "A party."

"Well, I'm sure your mother will organise the usual."

"That's the problem." She pouted. "I don't want the usual pizza and soft drinks on the lawn, everyone collected by nine thirty. I want a proper party. On the beach. No adults."

"No."

"But, Dad . . ."

"No."

"I'm seventeen."

"And?"

"I'm almost eighteen."

"That maths tutor is worth his weight in gold."

"I'll ask Mummy. She'll say yes."

"I wouldn't be too sure about that."

"When she was young, *she* had parties on the beach, with Auntie Pru. They shared a boyfriend. We met him on the beach today."

Greg looked at Abi. "What, that bloke on the beach with the long hair?"

"Yep. Merlin."

"Oh good God! There's nothing sadder than an old hippy on the pull."

"I thought he was rather hot . . . for an old man."

"Do I look like an old man?"

"Yeah."

"Thanks."

"Well, you are, like, over forty or something."

"Thank you again."

"Mummy and Auntie Pru went all mysterious about him."

"Did they? In what way?"

"They went all secretive. I mean, he did look quite hot."

"Did Mummy say that?"

"She didn't have to." Abi smirked.

Greg thought for a moment. "Don't be so silly. And by the way, you're not having a party on the beach."

"*Muuum.*"

"Yes, Abi? And don't throw yourself on my bed. I've just tidied up."

"Can I have a party for my birthday?"

"Of course. We always have a party for your birthday. I was thinking one of Dad's barbecues . . .?"

"I was thinking one on the beach, no oldies."

"Oh, darling, Granny and Poppa will *have* to come. They'd be terribly hurt if they weren't invited."

"Why don't you and Dad take them out for dinner instead?"

It dawned on Connie that she, too, was now classed as an oldie. She absorbed the blow.

"You mean, instead of me and Daddy coming to your party?"

Abi nodded.

"No way, young lady. The beach and boys and booze is absolutely out of bounds. I'm aware what goes on, you know. I'm not so old that I can't remember these things."

Abi perched on the bed. "Go on then, you dark horse. Tell me what you got up to."

"Nothing." Connie grabbed a pair of Greg's shorts and started to fold them.

"Yes, you did! You and Auntie Pru had a big old rosy glow round you both when you saw old whatsisname today."

"His name is Merlin. An old friend."

"I think you had the hots for him, and I reckon he still fancies you."

Connie couldn't stop the flush creeping up her throat. She sat at her dressing table and started to brush her hair. "Don't be so silly."

"That's what Dad said when I told him."

Connie spun on the dressing table stool. "You told your father that you think I fancy *Merlin*?"

"Sort of."

"Well, guess what: you are *sort of* not having a party on the beach. OK?"

Next door in the master bedroom, Pru had had to forgo her bedtime bath due to the slow heating of the hot-water tank, but Francis, feeling much better now, was mixing some massage oil for his wife's back.

"What's that smell, Francis?"

"I'm burning lavender oil. For relaxation."

"Oh."

Pru went to the bathroom to undress, wash and then clean her teeth. She looked at herself in the mirrored wall over the bath. Breasts small and still high. A few stretch marks on the tummy, but her hips were as narrow as ever. She shut her eyes and remembered how Merlin used to kiss her. How he'd admired her flat chest when she was so self-conscious about it. She remembered his body — how good it felt.

"Come on, Pru, darling. This is going to help you sleep," Francis called from the bedroom.

Pru opened her eyes and saw her face as Merlin must have seen it today. A few lincs, skin beginning to sag round the jaw. She stepped back into the bedroom and attempted a slow, undulating walk towards her husband. Maybe sex *would* do them both good. Francis looked at her.

"Your back must be bad — it's affecting your walk, love. Come on. Lie down and I'll sort that out for you."

As Pru lay under the kneading fingers and warm oil, she tried to keep all thoughts of Merlin out of her head.

Francis was trying, but failing, to keep all thoughts of Belinda out of his. He pictured her generous cleavage, her fleshy hips made more curvaceous by her slender waist — what would it be like to drip warm oil over her skin? How he would love to run his hands over her dainty feet and scarlet-painted toes. She'd be here in a few days. Oh God.

Pru, meanwhile, was indulging in something she hadn't done for a long time — a fantasy. In her mind she was lying naked in the dunes with Merlin running his rough, sea-hardened hands over her shoulders, rubbing in sun cream. She was nineteen again and hopelessly, passionately in love with him.

As quickly as the fantasy had grown in her memory, it was gone. A phantom. In its place stood reality. A different Pru. A different life. This was her life. Sensible, responsible, mature.

She was grateful to Francis and all he had sacrificed to care for her and Jeremy. A good man. A man she could rely on. She called his name and he heard it, muffled as it was against the pillow.

"Francis?"

"Yes, Belinda?"

He stopped his massaging instantly and watched Pru lift her head and slowly look over her shoulder at him.

"Who's Belinda?"

Greg woke up on the sofa. It was almost midnight. Connie must have forgotten about him and gone to bed. Shivering slightly, he stood up and winced as a cramp shot through his left shoulder. The surfing had really done him in. He resolved to start running again, from tomorrow. Or was that today?

He bent to turn off the one table lamp someone had thought to leave on for him and felt his way to the kitchen to pour a small brandy. His laptop was still on the kitchen table where he'd left it. He sat down, hoping to find a message from Janie. Hope was rewarded.

Hi Greggy,
The office is very quiet without you. Old octopus arms is bound to spend all week feeling me up whenever I am in the kitchen on my coffee run. He drops teaspoons so that he can bend down and look up my skirt to see if I'm wearing stockings and suspenders. Don't worry. Only wear stockings when you are here.

How is it in the bosom of your family? Poor you. I can't wait for Abigail to leave home, so you can leave too. Not long now! Then you can tell the old boot about us.

I'm getting ready to go out. My brother's old flatmate, Adrian — remember the one just back from Afghanistan? — is taking me out to dinner. Don't want to go, but he's a nice guy and I'm doing my bro a favour. One for the troops!

Phone me tomorrow and I'll tell you all about it. Think of me when you go to sleep tonight.

Love you, sexy boy,

Janie xxxxxxxxxxx

Who the hell was Adrian? She'd never mentioned him before. Some upper-class twit in charge of a tank regiment with a six-pack and an inheritance to look forward to? What would she wear for this . . . he hesitated to say the word *date*. Her lingerie collection was vast and very, very cute. Greg tapped out a brief reply.

Hope you haven't enjoyed your evening too much. Speak in the morning.

G x

He drained his brandy and went upstairs. In their bedroom he was deliberately noisy, which woke Connie up.

"What time is it?" she mumbled.

"Sorry, love. Did I wake you?" He slid into bed next to her and slipped his hand round her tummy and kissed her neck. Connie yawned.

"I can't sleep," he told her.

"It's because you've been asleep on the sofa." Connie's eyes were shut tight.

"No, it's because I fancy my wife like mad and need to make love to her."

"OK." Connie turned on to her back. "Pull my nightie down when you've finished."

CHAPTER
EIGHT

"Who's Belinda?" Pru demanded, her gimlet eye glinting under a perfectly arched eyebrow.

"Did I say Belinda?"

"Yes, you did." Pru turned to face him, both gimlet eyes fixed on him now.

"Oh. Ha ha." Francis tried to laugh it off. "She's, er, she's . . ." His imagination kicked in: "She's the ghastly woman on the PTA. Haven't I mentioned her? Only been at the school a year and already making waves. She wants to overturn some ideas the committee have sanctioned. I had a message from Chairman Bob on my phone earlier and it's been on my mind."

Pru turned back to her pillow, bored with anything to do with her son's school and her husband's dealings with it. "Oh. Poor you. Continue with the massage."

Francis closed his eyes in a prayer of silent thanks, and tried to get some control back into his shaking hands. He reached for the massage oil. It slipped from his grasp and fell on to the cream-and-beige patterned carpet, leaking a new pattern of its own.

"Oh crikey, Dorothy's carpet!" He bent to pick it up, overstretched and slid off the bed himself, knocking the bottle over again.

Pru peered at him. "What are you doing?"

Francis was panicking. "The bottle. The oil. Dorothy's carpet."

Pru was unperturbed. "Oh, for God's sake. Forget about the carpet. It's hideous anyway. Put it on the list of jobs that need doing."

He got to his knees with the oil bottle now safely in his hand. "Right." Standing, he found the lid and carefully screwed it on to the bottle. He walked to the bedroom door and opened it.

Pru watched him as if he were mad. "Where are you going?"

"I'm going to add this job to the list."

"Not now, you fool," she said, irritated. "It'll wait till tomorrow. Carry on with the massage and then we can all get some sleep."

"Oh, I see. Right. Silly me. Massage it is."

He resumed his position and carefully added more oil to his palms.

"Hmmm," murmured Pru. "You are very good to do this for me, Francis. I'm lucky to have you."

He continued in relieved silence until she started laughing, her body shaking under his hands.

"Sorry, Pru. Is that tickling?"

"No, no," she giggled. "For a moment there, I thought you might be having an affair."

And now it was morning and he felt sick with guilt about the lie he'd told his wife, the first ever, and the affair he hadn't even started yet. Would never start! What was he thinking? He got out of bed and observed

106

the sleeping form of his wife. The woman who needed him. Trusted him. Relied on him. Eighteen years ago he had left his job and a good career for her. He was a well-qualified social worker. It was his true vocation. His calling. Francis had known he could make a difference to people's lives. Then he met Pru.

He had been in a case meeting at the local council offices when she had stalked in, slammed her briefcase on the table and demanded, "Which one of you is the head of planning?"

She was tall, dark and handsome, and Francis had immediately fallen under her powerful spell.

His colleague told her, "None of us are, madam. You're in the wrong place."

"You won't get rid of me that easily. This is the planning office."

"No, this is Social Services. The planning department is in the building next door."

"I was directed up here by the idiot girl on reception."

"You need to leave this building and go next door."

It took a while, but eventually she was persuaded that she had gatecrashed the wrong meeting. Picking up her briefcase, she had pointed at Francis: "You. Show me where the right bloody room is."

On their way to the building next door, she'd asked, "What's your name?"

"Meake — Francis Meake," he stammered.

"Well, Francis, I'm indebted to you for helping me when I made a complete fool of myself. Let me take you for a drink by way of thanks. I hope you drink

Scotch?" She didn't give him time to answer. "I'll collect you from the car park at five thirty."

Within three weeks, to the astonishment of their respective friends and family, she had proposed and he had accepted. He loved the fact that, under her confident exterior, lay a woman who needed him. In return she loved him for his loyalty and gentleness. Here was a man who would never hurt her already wounded heart.

A month later, he had worked out his notice and set about finding a home for the pair of them. His final pay cheque was just enough to pay the deposit on the engagement ring Pru had chosen for herself. She paid the balance.

Her work as a commercial property surveyor was arduous and sounded very complicated. She had a good business brain, like her father and grandfather before her, but had no desire to get into the toy market: "I had enough of board games when I was growing up," she once told him. "I prefer to work in the real world."

She was a partner in her firm and very well respected. She worked long hours all over the country, but her goal was to open a New York office and grab some of the big bucks. It had taken her only five years to achieve that dream. Five years after that, she opened a Hong Kong office.

Their wedding was plain and simple. The bride wore trousers. Her parents were happy for her but concerned for Francis's welfare.

"She'll eat him alive," whispered Dorothy in the registrar's office.

Henry patted her knee and whispered, "She's got what every working woman dreams of: a wife! Besides, I think he will be good for her. Pru needs someone steady."

They married early on a Monday morning in order to be sure of catching the afternoon flight to New York. Pru had several meetings lined up and rather than rearrange them, she'd decided to combine business with pleasure. When they returned on Thursday morning, it was to their four-bedroom, faux Georgian townhouse in Greenwich. Well, Francis returned to it. Pru went straight to the office to report on the business she'd secured in America.

Francis revelled in his new role.

Every night he would cook something healthy and delicious for his wonderful, powerful wife. Sometimes she'd come home late, but always with flowers or a scented candle, and always he forgave her. Sexually, he was inexperienced, but Pru enjoyed taking the lead in bed. They were both thrilled when Jeremy was conceived.

Pregnancy didn't suit Pru. She worked till her waters broke and was back at her desk within five days of the birth. Francis adored being a father. He was a natural. Night feeds, nappies, projectile vomiting — all were constant sources of fascination for him.

He set up his own daily timetable. Up before Pru to prepare her breakfast and wave her off. The mornings were devoted to Jem and housework. The afternoons walking the pram to the shops. He loved taking Jem out in his pram. All the young mums cooed over the baby and marvelled at Francis's maternal skills.

"Your wife's so lucky. My husband has never so much as changed a nappy," was a constant refrain.

It was around this time that their sex life started to dwindle, though. Francis would be too tired after a long day with the baby and Pru felt she had done her bit in providing a healthy son. Nothing was ever discussed; with the passage of time the subject was simply forgotten.

Francis had put all of this aside and barely acknowledged any sense of frustration — until Belinda came along.

Belinda touched something in him, there was no denying it. Francis could not admit even to himself that it was his loneliness that made him susceptible to her charms. He wasn't naturally gregarious or outgoing; all he'd ever craved was a family of his own. His mother had died when he was young, and his father, a GP, had employed a series of nannies and housekeepers to look after him. Though he hadn't been neglected, he had missed out on a truly happy childhood. Much as he liked the Carew family gathering in Cornwall each year, he yearned to cram Pru and Jem into a camper van and travel all over Europe, seeing the sights. He could imagine them picnicking in the Dolomites or waking up next to Vesuvius. At the same time he envied the mums at the school gates, who spent their summer holidays in caravans near the seaside or took family day-trips to Alton Towers. He could never imagine Pru doing anything so "ordinary", though he was sure Jem would have loved it.

Francis had always got along with the mums (and some of the dads) of Jem's playmates and school friends. He had been a regular at the Baby Times Coffee Morning Club, enjoying the discussions on breast-feeding versus bottle, postnatal depression and the relationship between parent and child. And he was chatty with the mothers at the school gates and in the PTA. But none of them had ever shown the slightest interest in *him*. Until Belinda.

She had turned up the previous year, at the beginning of September. It was the first sitting of the PTA after the summer holidays. Francis could still remember the moment Chairman Bob had announced: "Before we get down to the business of the day, I'd like to welcome a newcomer. This is Belinda . . ."

The PTA members had duly craned their necks for a glimpse of the voluptuous woman at the end of the table. She was wearing a psychedelic orange-and-pink kaftan. Her curly blonde hair was piled loosely on top of her head. Dangly earrings framed her chubby cheeks and as she smiled and gave them a little wave, bracelets jangled on her wrists.

"Hello, everybody."

Several male eyes had wandered to her delightful cleavage and remained there, transfixed.

Bob had continued: "Belinda's daughter, Emily, has joined us for year nine. Is she fourteen this year, Belinda?"

"Yes. That's right. A little Piscean to my Scorpio."

111

Somewhat bemused by this, Bob had ploughed on, "Belinda is very keen to help with admin and organising our fundraisers."

"Actually, I have an idea for a Halloween quiz night," she'd volunteered.

The dreaded Mrs Dredey, PTA stalwart, had interjected, "Well, we usually do a harvest supper, and we can't do two fundraisers in one term. There wouldn't be the support."

"Nonetheless, we'll make a note of the suggestion. Fresh ideas always welcome," Bob had beamed, bending to his notepad to scribble: *Belinda Halloween*. He'd sat up again, "Now, I think it'd be a good idea if we all introduced ourselves round the table. You first, Mrs Dredey." Each of them had given their names in turn. Francis had been last: "My name's Francis Meake. Welcome."

Belinda had rewarded him with her twinkling smile. Since that night, she had made it her mission to sit next to him at meetings, pulling her chair as close to his as possible so that he could feel the heat emanating from her. She would bend low, delving in the handbag at her feet for a notepad and pen, all the while displaying her plumply rounded breasts for his benefit.

When tea and biscuits arrived, she would lean across him, tickling his cheek with her curly blonde hair and leaving wafts of her musky perfume in the air around him. While the committee embroiled themselves in some lengthy dispute over the roster for putting out the stackable chairs in the school hall and then putting them away again afterwards, she would put her lips to his ear and whisper little jokes about Chairman Bob and Mrs Dredey. Despite himself, Francis had found her intensely exciting. He loved being in her company. She had a saucy wit that made him laugh and she was interested in him — something he'd never encountered in a woman before. Soon he'd found himself telling her about all sorts of things, including Pru and the Carew family. She was easy company. Once, when he'd had an hour to kill between their PTA meeting and a trip to the dentist, Belinda had made a suggestion: "Why don't you come to lunch at mine, Frankie? We've got two hours before we have to collect the kids, and I've got half a bottle of red and some asparagus quiche that needs eating up."

"Ah, very kind of you, but no," he'd said, with more determination than he'd felt. "I'd better not risk a ticking off from the dental hygienist!"

She had looked at him sadly, pouting a little. "Shame. Some other time, perhaps? There are so many things I'd like to talk to you about." She'd stepped closer, smiling, and dropped her voice an octave: "None of them involving flossing!" Her rosy apple cheeks had moved up towards her eyes, making them twinkle.

He'd swallowed hard and a drop of saliva went down the wrong way. He had started to cough, and then couldn't stop, gasping for breath and choking.

Immediately she'd whipped behind him, one arm round his waist while the other thumped a point between his shoulder blades. He had felt her warm bosoms jostling his back. She'd thumped a couple more

113

times and eventually he had stopped spluttering and begun to take deep breaths of fresh air. She'd let him go and walked round to face him.

"Better?"

"Yes. Thank you."

She'd put her hands on his shoulders and kissed both his cheeks. "My pleasure." She'd winked at him. "Bye, Frankie. You owe *me* a lunch now!"

He had watched as she'd undulated towards her ancient, bright pink Citroën 2CV. It had a soft top and a hand-painted daisy on the driver's door. She'd got in, causing the suspension to rock, and then driven away, one hand waving through the open roof.

He'd returned her wave, unsettled by her casual intimacy. The arm round his waist. The kiss . . .

And that was when the inappropriate thoughts about her had started.

And she'd be here on Wednesday. Shit shit shit.

Down in the kitchen the early morning sun was streaming through the open French windows. Greg was sitting at the table, working on his laptop. He jumped when he heard Francis's footsteps and quickly shut the laptop lid.

"Oh, Francis. It's only you." He relaxed and opened the computer again. "Pour me a coffee while you're up?"

"Sure." Francis was used to taking orders. "What are you working on?"

"Oh, just some stuff in the office. My secretary doesn't seem to understand I'm on holiday!" Greg rolled his eyes and clicked his tongue.

114

Francis carried two steaming coffees to the table and gave one to Greg. "Glad I don't have that kind of responsibility. What's the problem?"

"Well . . ." Greg felt the need to share a little of his guilty secret, "It's not so much work. It's my secretary. She's fallen in love with a man at work. A married man."

Francis tutted.

Greg continued: "And I've turned into a bit of a shoulder for her to cry on."

Hiding his surprise at this unlikely role for Greg, Francis said, "Office romances usually end badly, in my experience."

Greg smirked. "Oh, you have experience of office romances, do you?"

"No, of course not! It's been years since I've worked in an office, and even when I did . . . But conventional wisdom suggests —"

Greg cut him off: "Didn't you meet Pru at your office?"

Francis was losing his way in this conversation. "Well, yes, but it wasn't like that." He made an effort to steer the subject back to Greg. "What does Connie say?"

Greg started, and looked over his shoulder to the doorway. "Don't tell Connie, for God's sake!"

"Why ever not? She might have some useful ideas and advice."

"No, no, old boy," spluttered Greg. "You see . . ." he lowered his voice confidentially, "the chap my secretary is seeing is a great friend of ours. Connie knows the wife. I couldn't let her carry such an unbearable secret."

Francis nodded. "I see. No, that wouldn't be fair on Connie. So what are you going to do?"

"Well, I have suggested that Janie, the girl I'm talking about, should go out with a friend of her brother's. Lovely chap. Army. Just back from Afghanistan. They went on a date last night."

"Good. How did it go?"

A haunted shadow flitted over Greg's features. "I don't know. She hasn't answered my email yet."

"Oh." Francis fell silent, then smiled. "Maybe she had such a great night with this chap that she's not in the office yet."

Greg looked glum. "Wouldn't that be marvellous for her."

"I'm sure it'll all work out." Francis's mobile started to ring. His thoughts still occupied with Greg's problem, he answered without looking at caller ID.

"Hello, Francis Meake." Suddenly, his face took on a slight flush. "Hello, Belinda . . . yes . . . yes . . . That's right. Treviscum Bay . . . We're Atlantic House . . . yes, what a coincidence . . . TODAY? . . . I thought you were coming on Wednesday . . . A last-minute cancellation . . . lunchtime . . . yes, Dairy Cottage is right next door to us . . . yes . . . quite a coincidence . . . OK . . . see you later . . . bye."

Greg watched Francis place the phone on the table as if it were a grenade with the pin missing.

"Are you all right, old man?" he asked.

Francis picked up his coffee cup but his hand was shaking so much he had to put it down.

Greg tried again, "Who's Belinda?"

Pru strode into the kitchen.

"A mother at Jeremy's school. On the PTA." She stopped when she saw Francis's ashen face. "What's the matter with you?"

Francis looked up from where he sat, into his wife's perceptive eyes. He blurted, "It's Belinda. She's rented Dairy Cottage. She's arriving with her daughter today."

Pru looked quizzical "Ah, Big Ben told the kids that someone we knew was coming down. I thought it was Wednesday."

"Big Ben had a cancellation." Francis looked as if he were in shock; which of course he was.

Pru gave him a funny look, then said, "Well, you don't have to have anything to do with her."

"I, er, no . . . at least . . . that is, she may want to talk to me about, er, school things."

"That's OK. It'll keep you busy. Is her husband coming down, too?

"She's divorced."

"Better still! We'll never see her. She'll be out looking for a holiday romance." She rubbed Francis's shoulder. "Now, how about you get me some of your granola and blueberries?"

Francis gladly did as he was told, but a feeling of impending doom settled over him like a fog over the moors.

CHAPTER
NINE

Francis had done the washing up, ironing and vacuuming and was wondering whether he should change the sheets. Physical activity, and cleaning in particular, was a good distraction. He had always liked cleaning; it helped focus his mind.

He wished he was alone in the house, but the threat of showers was keeping everyone indoors.

Pru was in their room talking loudly on her mobile. She'd waved him out when he'd attempted to spray stain remover on the oil-marked carpet.

As he walked back out on to the landing he could see the kids mowing the lawn. Or rather, Jem was driving the ride-on machine, another of Henry's gadgets, and Abi was sitting huddled in her hoodie, reading a magazine.

Downstairs, Connie was littering up the kitchen with her mother and father. Henry had bought himself an iPad while on the trip to see staddle stones in Lostwithiel. He didn't have a clue how it worked so Connie, not exactly a high-tech whizz herself, was attempting to get it up and running.

"Don't keep touching the screen, Henry, you'll put fingerprints all over it," said Dorothy.

"Mummy, you're supposed to touch the screen, that's why it's called touch screen," said Connie irritably, trying to make sense of the instructions.

Dorothy was getting bored and impatient.

"Why did you buy the thing, you silly man?"

Henry frowned at her. "Why don't you go and decide where to put your bloody staddle stones and leave me and Connie to sort this out."

Dorothy was huffy. "It's starting to rain."

"Well, make some coffee then. Francis has washed the machine out," said Connie.

Francis heard this and was dismayed. He took pride in cleaning out the coffee machine and really enjoyed making the first pot with a sparkling appliance. It was clearly not to be. Gathering up the hoover and his trug of polishes and dusters, he put his bum to the drawing-room door and pushed it open.

Greg was lolling on the sofa, squashing the newly plumped cushions. He was on his mobile. He signalled Francis to sit down and be quiet. "I'm glad you had a good time . . . of course I'm not jealous . . . So what's Adrian like? . . . Is he? . . . Does he? . . . Did he? . . . Sounds a lot of fun . . . What did you wear? . . . What time did he drop you off? . . . That's late, you must be tired this morning . . . Mmmm . . . yeah . . . It's OK here . . . Yeah, having a great time . . . Connie's really brown, nice tan marks . . . Not jealous, are you? . . . ha ha ha . . . OK, you'd better answer it . . . Speak later . . . Same to you . . . bye, bye." He hung up. "Janie," he explained.

"Ah," said Francis. "How did the date go?"

Greg put a fingertip in his mouth and started to bite the nail. "Too bloody well."

"That's good, isn't it?"

Greg stopped chewing and gave a half-hearted smile. "Yeah, sure it's good. For her. But not for my mate. I mean, he really likes her."

"But he's married."

"Sometimes, it's not enough to have one woman in your life."

Francis thought of Belinda and coloured. "Hmmm."

They sat in silence for a bit before Greg said, "If my friend left his wife for her, it would cause a hell of a stink."

"Divorces are never easy."

"No."

"Does he have children?"

"Yes. It would be horrible for Abi."

"Abi? That's a coincidence. Same name as your daughter."

A look of fear fled through Greg's eyes. Then he laughed, "Oh! I see what you mean! Never thought of that. Ha! Abi! Yep. Popular name and all that. Anyway . . ." He slapped his hands on his knees, stood up and beamed at Francis. "What can I do for you?"

"Nothing."

"Weren't you looking for me?"

"No. I want to vacuum round."

"Oh, right, right. I'll get out of your way then."

He patted Francis on the shoulder and walked out. Francis looked at the squashed cushions on the sofa and replumped them.

120

The phone rang twice and the postman knocked once. Each interruption sent Francis's heart a message to stop beating for a second. Belinda had said she was arriving at lunchtime.

One bathroom left to do. What time was lunchtime? Twelve? One? Two? Oh God, this waiting was purgatory.

By two thirty there was still no sign of Belinda. Connie's lunch, of shop-bought Scotch eggs, bagged lettuce and plastic-potted potato salad, would have played havoc with Francis's digestion at the best of times, but today it was impossible for him to even sit at the table. The synthetic smell of cheap salad cream was the last straw.

"Nothing for me, thank you, Connie. I had a big breakfast. I'm going to get some fresh air. Do excuse me."

He went to the front door and stepped out into the watery sunshine. The clouds were parting at last. He sat on the stone bench, underneath a beautiful overhanging apple tree with low-lying, thick branches. He had overheard Henry saying to Dorothy only yesterday that they should get the tree surgeon in to trim it back. Francis liked the seclusion that it afforded him. The garden really was amazing. An Albertine rose bush bloomed lusciously nearby. He drew in great breaths of salty air, full of the aroma of freshly mown grass. His nerves were giving him nausea. He closed his eyes, hoping it would pass.

"Frankie! Look at you sitting among the apples and roses. Just like Romeo waiting for Juliet!" His eyes snapped open. Belinda was coming towards him. Francis jumped up so quickly at the sound of her voice that he forgot about the branches that were dangerously close overhead. As he stood, his skull took an almighty crack from a particularly thick branch.

"Argh, Jesus!!" Francis clutched at his head and then, looking up, he saw Belinda heading towards him. The bump on his head had obviously been a nasty one; as he took his hand away from his skull he saw blood on his fingers. Nausea welled within him. Belinda, who had looked quite normal to begin with, suddenly seemed crystal sharp, almost as if he were watching Henry's HD television, then her outline grew smudged and wonky as if in a dream. Her ample bosoms were dancing like dandelion heads in a soft breeze. Her voice was coming and going in waves of sound he couldn't make out. Closer and closer she got to him, her mouth moving and her arms outstretched. So close was she now that the light of the sun was dimmed, while the ground beneath him rose up and tipped his stone seat to the left. Her lips were almost on his own. Then darkness came.

Later he was aware of a softness beneath his horizontal body. He heard voices talking quietly nearby.

Belinda first: "I saw him sitting there, probably waiting for me, bless him. Then he hit his head on one of those branches and was out cold."

Greg's voice: "My dear, what a terrible shock for you. Let me get you a brandy."

Belinda again: "Don't mind if I do. I feel a bit shaky."

Greg: "And I'll join you, naturally. I'd never let a lady drink on her own."

He heard footsteps on the front porch, then Pru's voice: "Francis! For God's sake, get up. You'll get damp through lying on the grass like that."

Belinda: "He's had a nasty knock. This gentleman helped me get him flat. Frankie's bumped his head on the stone, look."

Pru's voice now; loud and close in his ear: "Francis! Get up."

Belinda: "He's hurt. We've called an ambulance."

Pru's voice, cold: "Who are you?"

Pru was scanning the woman in front of her. She was on the pretty side — if overweight could be pretty — and overtly girly and feminine. Pru felt rather sorry for her.

"My name's Belinda. I work with Frankie."

"Ah! Belinda. My name is Pru and I am married to Frankie." She corrected herself: "Francis."

Belinda: "How do you do."

Greg again: "Here, get this brandy down."

Pru: "Francis doesn't like brandy."

Greg: "Oh, he does. But only when you're not around. Besides, this is for Belinda and me."

Somewhere above the sound of talk and seagulls Francis could hear a siren. The ambulance, he supposed, as he drifted off back into darkness.

The hospital discharged him a few hours later, when they were quite sure the bump on his head was nothing serious. They gave him a leaflet to read on watching out for signs of concussion, a box of paracetamol and advised bed rest.

123

"Bed rest! He seems perfectly fine," interjected Pru as the doctor tended to her husband.

"Your blood pressure is a little high, Mr Meake. Are you under a lot of stress?"

"My husband is *not* stressed *or* anxious. If anyone is, it's me. My masseur says she's never felt such tense and knotted shoulders as mine."

The doctor ignored her and spoke to Francis.

"What about your diet? You're a bit underweight."

"His diet would make Gwyneth Paltrow look as if she's been on the Hobnobs!" answered Pru, as though Francis were a small child unable to answer for himself.

The doctor admonished her: "Please, Mrs Meake, let your husband answer."

"I'm fine," said Francis.

"Well, you have a nasty bump on the head and it appears from the blood tests that you are also a little anaemic. I want you to eat lots of leafy green vegetables, dried fruits, nuts. Try a steak every now and then, if you can. And try not to worry about things. Take it easy for the next day or two. OK?"

Pru, who had followed the ambulance to hospital in her own car, was driving him back to Atlantic House now.

"I'm sorry about all the fuss and bother," Francis said.

"I think it's your friend, Belinda, you should apologise to. You gave her quite a shock."

"I was surprised to see her." He looked down at his grazed knuckles.

124

"She claimed she *works* with you," Pru snorted, and gave him a short glance.

"That's something of an exaggeration. I told you, she's on the PTA and is a bit of a busybody."

"She called you Frankie."

Francis started to feel sick — his head throbbed. "Yes. It's very annoying."

They settled into a familiar silence. Francis leaned his head on the half-open window, taking deep breaths.

The car rolled into Higher Barton and finally down the narrow, sweet-smelling lane leading to Treviscum Bay and Atlantic House. Pru helped Francis out and up to their room. As he cleaned his teeth he saw the graze on his cheekbone and the swelling above his eye.

"That'll be a shiner tomorrow," said Pru, behind him. "Come on, *Frankie*, let's get you into bed." She passed him a glass of water and his tablet.

"Thank you, Pru."

"Whatever for?"

"For looking after me."

"Hmm. Don't get used to it. Get some sleep and I'll try not to wake you when I come up." She bent down and kissed him on the forehead. "Sleep well."

He woke the next morning to a gentle shake of his shoulder and a cup of tea from Jeremy.

"Here you are, Dad."

"Thanks, Jem." Francis sat up feeling very groggy while his son set the mug down on the bedside table and perched on the bed.

"How do you feel?"

"OK."

"We're all worried about you. Maybe we should look after you for a bit, instead of the other way round, eh?"

Francis smiled at his beloved son. "I'm fine. You know me, I enjoy looking after you and Mum."

"Yeah, well, stay in bed a bit. Mum says she can get her own breakfast today."

Father and son smiled at each other, sharing the joke.

Jeremy stood up and walked to the door. "Shout if there's anything I can get you. Oh, nearly forgot, your friend Belinda says she'll be over to see you in a minute."

Francis didn't have time to take evasive action. No sooner had Jem left the room than he heard Belinda's trilled "Morning" through the always unlocked front door.

He sat rigid in bed, his ears straining for any sound, above that of the noisy thumping of his heart, that might suggest she would stay downstairs. No. He could hear her armfuls of jingly bracelets jangling on the banisters, the squeak of the top landing floorboard, the turn of the bedroom doorknob.

"Frankie!" She filled the room with her hips and bosoms and burnished curls caught up in an adolescent posy of silk poppies.

"You poor thing." Now she was on the bed, opening carrier bags full of Lucozade, magazines and sweets.

"I've been so worried about you." She leaned forward and kissed his cheek.

"Oh, I do beg your pardon. Am I interrupting something?"

Greg was standing at the open door, giving Francis a sly wink.

"I have been sent by Pru —" he smiled archly at Belinda — "that's Francis's *wife*, to see if you would like a tea or coffee?"

Belinda looked innocently at Greg. "How very kind of her. A coffee would be nice."

"Excellent. I'll be back in a moment." He shot Francis a knowing look under raised eyebrows before departing.

Belinda continued where she had left off. "I am so glad I was there when you had your accident. Thank goodness Greg heard me call. He's your brother-in-law, is he?"

"Yes," Francis replied limply.

"Well, he was wonderful. Gave me a brandy and really calmed me down."

"Good."

"Now then, when you are up and about, I'm going to have a barbecue in the cottage garden, for all of you."

"That's very kind, but no need. There are a lot of us . . ."

"Yes! I've met them all downstairs. Aren't Jem and Abi sweet? They've taken my Emily under their wings. They're going to go down to the beach and look at the rock pools together."

"That's nice."

Belinda patted his hand. "Emily and I were so lucky to get into Dairy Cottage early. It's lovely."

"How did you know this was where I was staying?"

"Ooh. That bump on the head must be worse than we thought! You told me."

"Did I?"

"Yes."

"What are you doing here?" His headache was worsening and he looked around for the painkillers the hospital had given him.

She got to them first and popped two out of the blister pack, then handed him a glass of water.

"Emily and I needed a holiday and it was sheer coincidence that I found Dairy Cottage on the Internet." He swallowed down the tablets and passed the glass back to her. She took it and frowned. "I'm not stalking you, if that's what you think."

He tried to laugh and shake his head but it hurt.

She looked with great concern into Francis's face.

"Frankie, you do look pale."

"My head aches a bit."

"Well, I'll cancel my coffee and let you rest." She picked up her large sequin-spangled handbag. "I'm going into Trevay to do my big shop and then get really settled into Dairy Cottage. Emily and I won't intrude, I promise."

Francis attempted some gallantry through his swimming consciousness. "You're both welcome. More the merrier."

"What a lovely couple of weeks we'll all have." She leaned over and kissed his bruised forehead. "I'll have you right as rain in no time."

Whether it was this threat, the shock or the pills, he'd never know, but his body shut down and he slid gratefully back to sleep.

CHAPTER
TEN

Francis knew Belinda was somewhere in the house. He called her name but she couldn't hear him over the sound of running water. He found her in the shower. Her curvaceous outline was blurred by the rippled glass of the shower door, but he watched as she tipped her head back under the shower. Shampoo suds caressed her ears, shoulders and breasts before they splashed into the shower tray and slid down the drain. He called her name again, "Belinda?"

"Frankie? Is that you?"

"Yes."

"I've been waiting for you."

"Have you?"

"Of course. Take your clothes off and join me."

Naked, he opened the shower door and stepped into the humid warmth. He found her lips and kissed them. She put her arms round him and he quivered as his chest met the warm softness of her breasts. She called his name again and again: "Francis. Francis, do you want some lunch?"

What a strange thing to ask at a time like this. Nevertheless he answered, "Yes. What would you like?"

"Francis! I am asking you!" She shook his shoulder with more strength than was necessary. He opened his eyes and saw Pru's concerned face leaning over him.

"Francis! You've been out for the count!" He sat up with a jolt and looked at the bedside clock. Two p.m.

Greg put his head round the door. "Hello, Rip Van Winkle. Had a good snooze?"

The dream of Belinda was rapidly receding. "Hello, Pru, Greg. Sorry. I should get up. Things to do."

"There's nothing to do, darling. I'm going for a walk and later on we're ordering in a Chinese takeaway. Just came to check on you. Hungry?" Pru was being very kind.

"I'm fine. You go and have a walk and I'll sort myself out."

"Sure?" She was touching his hand. "I'm a bit worried about you. That bang on the head. Do you feel sick? Are you seeing double? Got a headache?"

"No, no. Sleeping it off, that's all. I'm fine. Really."

"OK. Well, I'll see you later."

Pru left with a sympathetic smile, Greg with a wolfish wink.

Francis gingerly got out of bed and crept on to the landing. From the stairs window he saw Belinda's car bouncing down the lane and then watched as she drove into her driveway, scraping only a small section of the drystone wall as she did so. He slunk behind the curtains, peeking surreptitiously as she climbed out of the car and ferried backwards and forwards between car and house, laden with shopping bags. Finally she locked the car, went into Dairy Cottage and closed the front door. He allowed himself to breathe out, then padded downstairs. His heart was pounding and his stomach felt jittery; Belinda's sudden arrival in the midst of his family life had unsettled something inside him.

The house was quiet as he entered the kitchen. A voice made him jump.

"You sly old dog. Didn't think you had it in you. Hats off!"

Greg had followed him in.

"What do you mean?" Francis tried to keep his voice light.

"Belinda! She's one sexy lady. Why on earth would her husband let her slip through his fingers?"

Francis put a wholemeal bagel into the toaster and ignored the question.

Greg continued: "You're playing it dangerously, aren't you? Having a woman like that, fancying you the way she does, on your own doorstep. Takes guts."

"We work on the PTA together, that's all."

"So why invite her down to spend the summer here?"

"I didn't," Francis said angrily. "She won't leave me alone. It's making me ill."

Greg looked disbelievingly at his brother-in-law. "Then why was she kissing you in your bed?"

Francis sat down and put his head in his hands. "I don't know. She's just being kind and caring. It's her way."

132

"Rubbish, old chap. I'm a man of the world." I understand how these things work. Some women are attracted to married men, and it's our duty to help them." He gave Francis another wink. "What the eye doesn't see the heart doesn't grieve over, eh?"

Francis bristled. "What kind of man do you think I am? I love Pru and I take my marriage vows seriously. I would never ever be unfaithful to her."

Greg sighed and crossed his legs, weighing something up.

"Look, Francis, I can help you. We can help each other. A problem halved and all that. You see, the thing is . . . I'm in a bit of a pickle myself."

"Pickle?"

"Yes . . . With Janie, my secretary."

"Oh yes. Has she had any more dates with the soldier?"

"She has. Apparently things have been going very well. Too well." He looked meaningfully at Francis, nodding his head.

"Great! So your friend can end the affair?"

"Ah, no. He's really rather, ha ha . . . put out. Jealous, maybe."

"Well, he has no right to be!" exclaimed Francis, "I think it's best all round if Janie finds a man her own age."

Greg looked momentarily wounded. "There's not much of an age difference, actually." He lowered his voice: "Look, I won't say a word to Pru about you and Belinda, if you don't mention a word about Janie to

Connie." He gave Francis a sly grin. "There's honour among brothers-in-law, eh?"

Francis was horrified. "Hang on a minute, what are you saying? I have nothing to hide, and neither should you. It's not your fault your secretary is seeing someone in your office. If you want my advice, don't get involved with their problem."

"Ah, well, there's the rub: I already am involved. You see, the reason why Connie mustn't know is because, well, it's me Janie's having the fling with."

Francis looked aghast. "You mean you're having an affair with your secretary?"

Greg glanced over his shoulder and then back. "Shh. Do you want everyone to know? We're in the same boat, you and I — we both have our little secrets."

Francis spluttered indignantly, "I don't have any secrets."

"Ah yes, but ..." Greg watched Francis slyly, ". . . you wouldn't want me telling Pru that I saw you and Belinda canoodling in the marital bed, would you?"

Francis shook his head, feeling like a man facing a firing squad. "That wasn't canoodling. That was her seeing if I had a temperature . . . or something. Belinda and I are just friends."

"Stop kidding yourself! Anyone with half a brain can see what's going on. I'll keep schtum, and in return you can help me with the Janie situation. If I ever need a little alibi, you'll be there, won't you, old bro-in-law?"

Francis's heart sank — he was snookered.

★   ★   ★

134

Pru was taking a walk on the cliffs. It wasn't like Francis to be ill. It had shaken her. To be truthful, seeing Merlin on the beach had shaken her more, and she needed to get out of the house and do some thinking. She walked across the lush lawn surrounded by lavender, box and poppies, then out of the gate and on to the cliff path. She wondered whether to walk straight on and down to the beach or turn left towards the headland. She chose the headland. The beautiful old path lined by perfumed gorse was so familiar to her. To her left were lush fields full of grain crops. Further on, a field of tall grasses was being cut for hay. Skylarks were nesting somewhere. She could hear one singing very close by, but she couldn't spot the shy little bird.

A breeze blew in from the ocean on her right, ruffling her hair. After yesterday's rain, when it had been rough and coloured with sand and seaweed, the sea now twinkled deepest blue and reflected the small clouds in its ripples. She reached a wide gateway and carefully opened and closed the heavy latch. She felt the silky wood of the gate, made oily with the years of hands rubbing over it. She smiled at the touch. This gate, leading down to Figgoty's Beach had been her meeting place with Merlin a lifetime ago.

Merlin had been her first true love. The love you get over but never forget. Above her a seagull laughed. She thought back to that long-ago summer.

She had not long turned nineteen. Connie was sixteen and very popular. She had always been the girlier of the two sisters. Her blonde hair, full bosom and friendly nature captured the affection of both sexes. Her girlfriends adored her and all the boys enjoyed flirting with her. Pru, on the other hand, was more serious. She was at university and enjoying the academic life. She had a couple of admirers. Both a bit worthy and dull, but good for the odd night out. Where Connie was pneumatic, Pru was a washboard. No bust, no hips, but with a stunning six-pack.

Connie's friends happily absorbed Pru into their group, enjoying having someone a bit older around them. Mainly because she could drive.

"Pru . . . Pru?" wheedled Connie one afternoon.

"What do you want?"

"Would you like to come to a party tomorrow night?"

"Where?"

"Newquay."

"And you want me to drive you?"

"Me and Trace and Maz."

"Only if you pay me for the petrol."

"But it's Mum's car."

"Yes, and she'll ask me to replace the petrol."

"Oh, all right, we'll split it."

The party was on the beach. A hot August night. A huge moon hung fully in the heavens surrounded by a carpet of bright stars.

As soon as Pru got to the beach road, her three passengers leapt out and disappeared while she was left to park.

When she got down on to the sand, there was no sign of her sister or her mates. She collected a tin of cider from a trestle table and mooched around the outer

136

circle of the party. Pru knew a few people, who nodded to her, but no one came forward to chat. She found a cool piece of clean sand and lay down to watch the stars. Back then she used to love searching for satellites as they tracked their way across the heavens.

A soft Cornish voice broke into her solitude.

"Can I join you?"

She turned her head, feeling the sand shift beneath her. He was wearing sawn-off jeans and a Debbie Harry T-shirt. His face was in shadow, but she could see the outline of curly hair.

She sat up. "Be my guest."

"I've been watching you."

She felt a little scared and turned towards the party to see if she could glimpse Connie.

"It's all right. I'm not a nutter. Mind you, if I was that's exactly what I'd say, isn't it?"

Pru laughed nervously.

"I thought you looked like someone I'd enjoy talking to, that's all." He smiled and in the moonlight she made out kind sea-green eyes, nice lips and slightly wonky but very white teeth.

"Oh."

He sat down next to her and rolled a cigarette. "Want one?"

"No, thank you."

"Good girl."

There was silence for a while as he sat gazing at the moonlit waves gently breaking on the sand. Pru thought she had never seen anyone so gorgeous.

After blowing a series of smoke rings, he turned to her, holding out his hand: "Merlin Pengelly."

She held it. Rough and coarse but clean and strong. "Prudence Carew. How do you do."

He laughed. "Oh, a posh girl! I've never met a Prudence before."

"Well, my family and friends call me Pru."

He looked at her steadily and took another draw of his cigarette. "Got a boyfriend, Pru?"

She wasn't sure how to answer this. The true answer was no, but under the circumstances she didn't want to look an idiot. "Oh, you know." She shrugged. He shrugged too.

"And what do you do, Pru Carew?" He smiled.

"I'm at university."

"Posh *and* clever."

"Don't make fun of me."

"I'd never make fun of a girl like you," he said softly. He stood up and held a hand out to her. "Want to go for a walk?"

She smiled up at him. "OK."

They moved away from the main party and walked and chatted and laughed together until the first streaks of dawn were visible on the horizon. He told her he was a lifeguard for the summer and in the winter he'd do some labouring. He was Cornish born and bred. In return she told him about the courses she was taking for her business degree, the family firm and Atlantic House. Hoping that he might come and find her. "I'm here all hols," she said.

She didn't know what it was that made her feel so comfortable with him, but when she finally got home to Atlantic House and her bed, it was his sea-green eyes fringed with sunkissed blond lashes that burned in her memory. His freckled nose bending towards her, slowly blurring as he gently kissed her goodbye. The feel of his warm hand holding hers as she left to go and find Connie, Tracey and Marion. He had stood and watched from the sea wall as she drove away. She prayed he would come and find her.

More than two decades on, an older, wiser Pru smiled ruefully at the memories. Merlin had taught her a lot about life. But that was a lifetime ago. She had moved on — there was no changing the past.

When she reached the top of the cliff above Figgoty's, the beach below was deserted. Pru scrambled down the steep and awkward path. Some of the rocks were slippery, but she remembered the hidden footholds and managed to jump the final six feet on to the smooth sand below. Only the locals knew about Figgoty's; no visiting families encumbered with pushchairs and windbreaks would dare make the tricky descent. The beach was sheltered by the huge natural curve of the cliffs. The sea here had a deep swell and the undercurrents could catch out the most seasoned of swimmers. It was here that she and Merlin used to escape on his days off. They would take their clothes off and lie naked on the sand before racing each other into the water and enjoying the pleasure of the cool waves running off their warm skin. She hugged herself.

Why not? she thought. *No one can see from the cliff.* She pulled her sensible Marks and Spencer hoodie over her head and stepped out of her Rohan shorts. After another quick look to make sure there was no one watching, she slipped off her bra. Placing everything neatly on a dry rock, she ran across the sand and into the icy sea. What would Francis say if he saw her now? Maybe she'd bring him down here when he felt better.

Pru didn't stop running until she was up to her shoulders, then she took a deep breath and ducked under a breaking wave. When she surfaced, she floated on her back and looked up at the periwinkle sky. It felt so good to be this liberated and unencumbered, she couldn't help laughing out loud. Turning back on her tummy, she swam through the breakers and out to where the sea was smooth. Again she lay on her back and felt the sun warming her front. Presently she heard another kind of splash over the sounds of the sea. An oar. She flipped over and saw a man in a sea canoe coming ever closer to her. He hadn't seen her . . . yet. What should she do? She bobbed quietly, her nose just above the water. He was less than six feet away now and when he saw her he almost dropped his oar.

It was Merlin.

CHAPTER
ELEVEN

Connie wondered if she could find the entrance to the cave in the wooded valley after all these years. She'd asked Greg to join her on her walk, but he was busy with emails. Though she made a show of disappointment, secretly she'd been relieved to take the walk on her own. She desperately needed to get out of the house and think about her unsettling row with Pru the other night. The appearance of Merlin had had a very strange effect on them both. She was shaken by how much emotion the memories of that summer had stirred up.

Her sandals allowed the long grasses to tickle her instep as she pushed her way along the overgrown path. She saw the remembered stile ahead of her and, after climbing it, turned right to follow the rushing stream leading through the valley and on to the sea. The first time she'd come here was with Merlin and Pru. The three of them had played Pooh sticks and Merlin had given them their first experience of smoking a joint. It had been a warm afternoon with the drone of flies in the air.

"Either of you girls know what a fuggee hole is?" asked Merlin, his blissed-out eyes turning Connie to jelly.

Pru giggled, "I wouldn't like to say."

Merlin grinned his suntanned grin and clamped the joint between his crooked teeth. "Shame on you, Pru Carew. Dirty mind!"

He took her hand and pulled her up the sloping side of the valley.

Connie watched the giggling couple for a moment then hurried to catch them up, not wanting to be left behind. The climb got steeper until they reached a small plateau. Merlin was now leading the way and the girls were scrambling after him. Giggling and stoned.

After about fifty metres, Merlin stopped and bent down on his haunches, pulling aside some tall ferns.

"'Ere it is."

The girls crouched next to him and saw an opening in the side of the valley. Carved out of the rock, it was just big enough to take a barrel of brandy or a small crouched person.

Merlin flicked his lighter and, using it as a torch, disappeared into the hillside.

The girls looked at each other nervously.

"Come on, girls. The lights are on," he called.

Pru went first, letting out a gasp as she entered the carved cavern, lit now by six flickering church candles.

"Oh my God!" she called to her sister. "Connie, you must see this."

"What is this place?" breathed Connie in wonder as she stood in the tall space.

Merlin shrugged. "No one knows for sure, but there are several of them in these parts. Prehistoric, I think. The smugglers used them to hide their stash."

At the back of the dry cave there lay a pile of blankets and an old-fashioned feather quilt. Merlin shook them out and spread them on the floor.

"Come and lie down next to me," he told them. As they did so, he began to sing the Beatles' "Come Together". His voice ricocheted richly from the walls.

Connie put her arm across his muscly chest and met Pru's doing the same thing from the other side. Merlin finished the song and put each of his arms under their heads.

"Oh, my lovely girls. Summer doesn't get much better than this!"

Connie was starting to sweat a bit as she climbed the steep slope and found the plateau. Her heart beat with a sense of stepping back in time. It didn't take her long to find the entrance, hidden now by a thicket of ferns and gorse. The plants scraped her legs and stung her feet, but she kept going until the small hole was revealed.

As she ducked her head inside, Connie cursed herself for not bringing a torch. Then she remembered that the three of them had scratched their initials just inside the entrance. She closed her eyes tightly and counted to sixty, hoping that this would trick her eyes into seeing in the dark better. When she opened them, her sight slowly adjusted. Turning her head to the right she saw the letters *CC, PC* and *MP*.

CHAPTER
TWELVE

As soon as he saw Pru in the water, Merlin stopped paddling and put his head to one side, staring at her from under his still-golden eyelashes. He dropped his gaze to her bare shoulders and then down to the water, where he could clearly see she wasn't wearing any clothes. He lifted the boat's paddle out of the water and balanced it across the front of the canoe.

"So. My little Pru has returned."

"I think it's you who have returned."

He laughed. "True, that. I haven't been to Figgoty's since you left me."

Pru snorted in derision. "Stop sounding like a schoolboy and leave me alone. I need to get out and get dressed."

"Nothing I haven't seen before, eh, Pru?"

She was shivering in the water now. "Bugger off, Merlin." She started to swim back to the beach.

He leaned on the paddle and looked thoughtfully up at the sky.

"You're not holding a grudge are you, Pru?"

Angrily she stopped swimming and turned to him. "Hold a grudge? Whatever for? You are a footnote to my youth, someone Connie and I laugh about."

He smiled, showing his attractively wonky teeth. "If I thought that was true, you'd be breaking my heart." He picked up his paddle and put it in the water. "You and I are unfinished business. Catch you later."

She watched as he disappeared around the next headland and then she swam back to shore and into her warm, dry clothes.

The climb from the beach and up the cliffs was hard. Her legs were shaky and her fingers felt weak as she fumbled for handholds in the slate. Seeing Merlin had upset some delicate balance within her. She grasped a good wedge of rock, but as she hauled her weight on to it, it came away in her hand and she slid a little, grazing her shins. Her breath was uneven and painful in her throat. She felt something rising within her — something buried but not dead.

"Come on, Prudence. It was all a long time ago. Don't let that idiot under your skin."

After a while she scrambled from her hands and knees to a bent walk and then, finally, she was standing upright on the grass-tufted path of the clifftop. Pru rubbed her eyes with her T-shirt and looked down to the beach. She saw her own footprints in the bare sand, but of Merlin there was no sight.

There was a weather-beaten bench ahead of her, facing the ocean, and she gratefully walked towards it and sat. She put the palms of her hands over her blue eyes and instantly saw an image of Merlin making love to her for the first time in the little cave up in the valley. The fuggee hole. She remembered the excitement of having given Connie the slip. She remembered how he'd held her hand and guided her through the gap in the earth bank and into the warm pitch-blackness. She could hear the rasp of his lighter and see the candle stubs sitting in solid pools of wax on the floor. She'd watched as he bent and lit their wicks. Now, she could see the tall graceful arch of the rock; white and smooth. It wasn't dank and slimy like the cave under Atlantic House. Merlin had moved to the back of the cave and collected the bundle of blankets and the faded paisley eiderdown quilt. He'd laid them on the floor, the same as he had that day when Connie had been with them.

"Do you want to lie down?"

She kicked off her plimsolls and sat on the makeshift bed.

"I've never seen a girl like you before." He was kneeling in front of her. Slowly he slid his arms round her waist, all the while gently kissing her neck and shoulders.

"Is that nice?" he breathed.

"Mm," she said, her eyes wide open.

She had been kissed by boys before, but had never understood what all the fuss was about. Now, with the warmth of his arms around her and his soft lips on her face, she felt different.

He sat back a moment to look at her. Satisfied that she appeared not to mind, he moved in to kiss her mouth. Unsure how to respond, Pru had parted her lips a little and allowed his tongue inside her mouth. She didn't know what to do with her hands, so she let them hang loosely by her side. He pulled away and looked at her.

"Not shy, are you?" he asked.

"No."

He'd taken her hands and placed them on the belt of his jeans. "Undo me," he whispered.

She squeezed the palms of her hands tighter over her eyes, remembering the way he'd made love to her and how she had felt. Special. Adult. Wanted. Until . . .

"Merlin!" the sound of that name broke through her reverie. Rubbing her eyes roughly, she uncovered them and sat blinking in the daylight.

A little round dog followed by a little round man barrelled towards her.

"Here, Merlin!" the man called in a Midlands accent. "Quiet, you've disturbed this lady. Mind if I share the seat with you?" He sat down before she could answer. "Beautiful up here, isn't it? I'm going to be scattered up here when I die."

Without saying a word, Pru stood up and walked away as fast as she could. Behind her, she heard the man say, "Well. Some people, eh, Merlin?" Her walk turned into a trot which turned into a run. She had to get back to the real world. To Francis and security.

"Mum . . . Muuuuum?" Abigail was shouting from upstairs.

Connie, who had only just sat down after clearing up the supper things, was in the drawing room with Greg. Her mind had drifted back to the initials carved in the rock wall. She took a deep breath and blew it loudly through her lips. "What?" she yelled.

147

"There's no hot water. And I've got shampoo in my hair."

"Well, use the cold tap."

"It's cold."

"Exactly."

A short silence ensued. Connie picked up her glass of wine and waited.

"Daaaad?"

Connie looked over at Greg, who was trying to watch the news.

"Whaat?" he bellowed.

"There's no hot water and . . ."

". . . You've got shampoo in your hair?" he chorused with her.

"Yes. Help."

He flicked the TV off and stood up, quietly swearing.

Connie heard him go upstairs, followed by Abi's protestations that he couldn't come in the bathroom because "I haven't any clothes on."

"I've seen you without clothes on since you were born. Now open this door."

After another five minutes or so Greg came downstairs and into the drawing room.

"There's no hot water," he announced.

Pru and Francis stuck their heads round the door. "There doesn't seem to be any hot water, Connie."

Connie looked at them as if they were all mad. "Really? You don't say? What do you expect me to do about it?"

"Oh, don't get all huffy. We're only saying," said Pru.

148

"And I'm only saying why are you all asking me? I don't know what to do."

The four of them stood, pathetically, trying to come up with a solution.

"We'll have to talk to Dad in the morning. He'll know a plumber. In fact, Mum and Dad need to do a bit of maintenance on the old place."

"That's true." Pru looked at Francis. "The tap in our en-suite basin is still dripping."

The following morning, a delegation of Connie and Pru knocked on the door of The Bungalow.

Dorothy opened it in her dressing gown.

"It's terribly early. What do you want?"

Connie poked Pru in the back, which Pru took as a signal, correctly, for her to open the conversation.

"It's almost ten. Can we come in?"

"Oh yes." Dorothy opened the door wider. "I hope you don't want breakfast."

"We've had breakfast. We just want to have a chat with you and Daddy."

"Oh God. Sounds ominous. *Henry!*" she called. "The children want to speak to you."

A muffled, "One moment," came from his bedroom. They heard movement, then he opened his door and walked out to greet them, tying the belt of his silk dressing gown.

"Good morning, all. To what do we owe this pleasure? Come into the lounge and sit down. Dorothy?"

"Yes."

"Put some coffee on, would you?"

Dorothy went to the kitchen, grumbling.

Henry sat in his armchair and smoothed his hair with his hands.

"What's the matter?"

Connie turned to Pru, who started: "Daddy, when did you last have the boiler checked? It's broken down and there are several taps dripping."

"Only to be expected in an old house," he replied, smiling.

"Yes." Pru had hit her stride. "But it's nigh on twenty-five years since you and Mummy renovated the old place. Don't you think it's about time it had a bit of an overhaul? Maybe some decorating too — it's looking rather dated."

Dorothy arrived with coffee and mugs on a tray, which she banged down on the table. "Dated? It's perfect."

"Of course, of course," soothed Connie. "But a lick of paint would brighten it up."

"Who for?" said Henry. "The only people who come to the house are you lot. Are you saying we're not up to your standards?"

Connie blushed. "No, Daddy. It's wonderful and we love coming down. Really, it's only the hot water that needs looking at."

Henry sat back in his chair. "So get it looked at."

As the girls left The Bungalow, the light drizzle developed into a cloudburst. They ran across the squelching grass and through the French windows of Atlantic House's kitchen.

Greg and Francis were reading their respective papers.

"Careful," said Greg crossly as Connie shook her dripping cardigan. "You'll get my paper soggy."

"Never mind that," said Pru, handing her wet sweatshirt to Francis, who carefully draped it on the Aga. "You two need to find a plumber. Daddy's quite happy for us to get the plumbing system overhauled."

"Who's paying?" asked Greg suspiciously.

"Well he hasn't said as much but Daddy, of course! We're just supervising," said Pru, sitting down. "Right, Connie. You and I shall spend the day in Truro looking at paint. Maybe some new cushions."

"We could do with new loo brushes," Francis chipped in.

"Good idea." Pru smiled. "Connie, make a list."

Truro was wet and grey. Holidaymakers shuffled about staring into shop windows before sitting in overcrowded cafés with their anoraks gently steaming.

The sisters found a parking spot in Lemon Street and made a dash for Marks and Spencer. They enjoyed their browse round the store and then went on to a very smart interior design shop where they chose several cushions and collected some paint and wallpaper samples. Then they drifted through a couple of boutiques, each buying small holiday essentials that neither husband need know about.

Over a late lunch at Mannings restaurant, their conversation turned to their parents and Atlantic House.

151

"The whole place could do with redecorating. It hasn't been touched since Mum did it up all those years ago." Connie took a sip of her Pimm's.

"That's the trouble with older people: they get so stuck in their ways," Pru replied through a mouthful of focaccia.

"Mummy's still quite with it. She's not seventy yet. Mind you, Daddy is starting to show his age. Have you noticed how he's slowed down? And he can't hear anything."

Pru sipped her red wine. "Yep." She tapped at the side of her head. "Still all there though. But I'm worried about him driving."

"Me too."

The waitress came with their food and they dived in. Sharing each other's dishes and enjoying their own company. As the plates were cleared away, and the atmosphere grew warmer, Pru felt it was a good time to bring up the subject of their parents' will.

"Now, Connie," Pru dabbed the corners of her mouth with her napkin, "when Mum and Dad are no longer with us, I want you to know that you can come to Atlantic House, and stay in The Bungalow, whenever you want. It'll still be your home."

Connie looked up sharply. "I beg your pardon?"

"You and Greg and Abi will always be welcome. I don't want any awkwardness between us." Pru beamed at her.

Connie felt cold inside.

"Has Daddy or Mummy told you they are leaving Atlantic House to you?"

"No, not in so many words. But I am the elder child — and you have Greg, who's virtually running the family business. I shan't be interfering in that."

Connie shook her head a couple of times. "Hang on. You think you're getting the house *and* The Bungalow, outright, while Greg runs the company yet doesn't own it?"

"Well, the shareholders own it, of course. But I'm sure Daddy will hand his shares over to Greg at some stage, so you'll be set up."

"Set up?"

"Yes. Comfortably off, with a Cornish bungalow that you can holiday in at any time."

"No, no. Not this time, Pru. You always want what's mine, but you are not taking Atlantic House from me."

Pru sat back in her chair and looked at her sister contemptuously. "I have two words to say to you, Connie. Grow. Up."

Connie raised her voice, causing other diners to turn and stare. "Oh, not this again! Grow up? Let me remind you, *you* were the childish one, always taking the best of everything. Always wanting whatever I had. The blue bedroom, for instance."

"Yes. And you, Miss Bloody Self-righteous, you're not so squeaky clean yourself, are you? We all know what you're capable of when 'poor baby sis' can't get what she wants," spat Pru.

"Oh! Now who needs to grow up! We were barely more than kids — I did you a favour!"

"A favour? How dare you!"

"I'll tell you one thing, you are not having Atlantic House, I shall make damn sure of that. And if you think I'm going to let Daddy spend good money putting in new curtains and getting the old house up to scratch for you to enjoy, you have another think coming."

The journey home was frosty, to say the least. Both women were on the edge of a precipice where their relationship was concerned. Neither of them wanted to acknowledge that the appearance of Merlin might have had something to do with it.

As soon as they got back to the house, Connie went in search of Greg. She found him playing with his bloody emails again. He hurriedly put the laptop lid down and smiled innocently.

"Darling! Cup of tea? How was Truro?"

Connie ran into his arms and started to sob.

"I love this house." She rubbed her dripping nose on Greg's shoulder and turned her face towards his. "Pru can't take it away from me."

Nonplussed, Greg kissed her nose and reassured her. "Course she's not going to take this house from you. In fact, do you want the good news, or the good news?"

She stopped crying and held his hand tight. "The good news, please."

He smiled. "I've found a plumber. And he's here right now, looking at the boiler."

Connie became demented, shouting, "Stop him, stop him!" She ran into the hall and on to the stairs. "We are not doing any repairs until we've sorted out who is going to get this house."

154

Greg ran after her and pulled her back. "It's too late."

A Cornish voice sounded from the top of the stairs: "I've done a temporary job on the thermostat. I'll be back tomorrow to put the new parts in and then I'll make a start on the rest of the house."

A familiar, sunburnt face leaned over the banisters. "Hello, Connie. I'm working as a plumber now. Greg and I have been having a good old chat about the old days."

Connie watched aghast as Merlin descended the stairs.

Greg was beaming. "Top man, Merlin."

"My pleasure, G." Merlin took his phone from his pocket and checked the time. "Is that the time? Beer o'clock already. Fancy a pint?"

Greg's face lit up with the offer and he picked up his keys from the hall table. "Great idea. Where are we going?"

"Bar up the road — the Dog House."

Connie stood aghast for a moment then, gathering her senses, she stepped forward. "If you go, *you'll* be in the bloody dog house, Greg. I'm warning you."

Merlin laughed. "Still the little firecracker, eh! Come on, Greg. See you later, Connie."

It was past eleven and supper had long since been eaten and washed up when Greg finally arrived home. Connie, waiting for him in the kitchen, could smell the beer on his breath as soon as he walked into the room.

"Nice chap," said Greg. "Very fond of you, Connie."

Connie froze. "What did he say?"

"That you and Pru and he had had a terrific summer when you were all young, and that I was a lucky bloke to have you." He put his arm round Connie. "Mind you, he clearly had a soft spot for Pru too. From what he was saying she was a bit of a goer in her time."

Connie pushed her chair back noisily and crossed her arms and legs. "Really? Well that's something he'd know all about."

"Hey hey, Con. You weren't jealous of old Pru and Merlin, were you? Did he fancy her more than you?" Greg walked towards her and knelt in front of her. He steadied himself on her knees. "My poor little Connie." He put his finger to his lips and blew a beery "Sshh" through his teeth. "Better not tell old Francis, eh?" He tapped the side of his nose and heaved himself back on to his feet. "I think it's time to go up the wooden hill to Bedfordshire. Come on, my poor old girl. At least I fancy you."

Connie gave Greg a mean look and without saying a word marched upstairs to the blue room. On reaching the sanctuary of her bedroom, she slammed the door and fell on the bed sobbing.

CHAPTER
THIRTEEN

Connie woke the following morning to the sound of Greg's alcohol-induced snoring and the pounding of footsteps on the landing.

Doing up her dressing gown, she opened her bedroom door to find Francis tearing down the stairs two at a time.

"What's happened?" she asked.

Francis had already arrived in the hall, where he was barged out of the way by a furious Pru, who was marching towards the telephone. Picking up the receiver she tapped in a number from a business card in her hand.

She waited while it was answered. "Bloody answer phone," she hissed, then screeched into the receiver: "Merlin, this is Pru Meake at Atlantic House. The kitchen is under six inches of water. If you don't get here within the next half-hour I am going to sue the arse off you. DO YOU HEAR!" And she slammed the phone down.

Merlin, blissfully unaware of the chaos he'd left behind the night before, was driving along the lane towards Atlantic House and congratulating himself on getting a

157

job at last. Greg was a good lad. They'd had a laugh together. Might take him out for another pint or two, or maybe fishing. It had been fun winding him up about Connie and Pru. One thing was for sure, that family had money and he could screw a sizeable chunk of it out of them.

He'd only recently returned to Cornwall after a spell in Wormwood Scrubs. Three years for a bit of dealing. He'd been properly stitched up. Nevertheless, while being detained at Her Majesty's pleasure he'd served an apprenticeship in plumbing. As soon as he was released, he'd gone to North Devon to work with an old mate. Everything had been going well, until he'd got a bit too friendly with the old mate's missus. So, a couple of weeks ago, he'd made tracks back to his old stomping ground, Treviscum Bay. What a stroke of luck that he'd bumped into the Carew girls. Was it really twenty-one summers ago that he'd managed to seduce her? She had been a lovely little maid. Lovely body, but lacking her sister's fiery passion. He'd soon warmed her up though, when he got her to the fuggee hole. Nice spot that. Warm, dry, romantic and hidden from prying eyes and ears. He wondered whether he could still find it.

As he turned his battered van into the drive of Atlantic House he noticed a woman with rosy cheeks, twinkly eyes and golden curly hair worn in a careless up do hanging her washing out in the garden of Dairy Cottage. The thing that really captured his attention was that she was topless. He gave her a long look and pulled the handbrake on stiffly. At the sound she looked up and with no embarrassment smiled. He killed the engine and nonchalantly stepped out on to the gravel. "Mornin'." He nodded his head and then ignored her as he opened the creaky back doors of his van. He made sure his bottom looked taut and muscular as he reached inside, and when he came out again, slowly peeled off his tight T-shirt to reveal tanned pecs and abs.

"It's going to be a hot one today," he said, loud enough for her to hear. "Things could get rather steamy."

He allowed himself a glance in Belinda's direction. She was holding a towel over her breasts flirtatiously. "One can only hope," she replied, then raised her eyebrows and grinned before turning her back on him and walking towards Dairy Cottage, wobbling her dimpled, bikini'd bottom to great effect.

Suddenly the front door of Atlantic House was thrown open and the sound of raised voices filled the air. As Merlin turned to the source of the noise, Belinda crept back out into the garden and concealed herself behind the dividing hedge so she could watch and listen.

Greg was marching towards Merlin. "Where the hell have you been? I've turned the stopcock off, but it's like the bloody *Poseidon Adventure* in there."

Merlin looked bemused. "What's happened, G, mate?"

"Don't you 'G mate' me. The whole house could have flooded, thanks to your incompetence."

159

"You should have called."

Pru had rushed out now and was squaring up to Merlin. "I did, you moron. Don't you answer your phone?"

"Terrible coverage round here. Sometimes I don't get my messages for a week or more." He smiled ruefully and started to roll a cigarette. "Why don't we all calm down and I'll take a look at the damage."

Pru looked daggers at him and gave a kind of guttural growling sound before turning tail and storming into the house.

Like the figures in a weather house, as she went in, Connie came out. She launched into a tirade aimed at Greg.

"Greg, we are not spending a penny on this house. Not a *penny*, or we'll be paying for Miss High and Mighty and Little Lord Fauntleroy's future home and seeing no return on our investment."

"All I did was what you bloody asked me to do. 'Find a plumber,' you said. So I did."

"I didn't mean Merlin Pengelly," Connie hurled at him.

Pru had come out of the house again, brandishing a mop and bucket. She rounded on Connie.

"How dare you call me Miss High and Mighty. And my son is nothing like Little Lord Fauntleroy."

"Actually, I was describing your poor henpecked husband," screeched Connie.

"Girls, girls, that is below the belt," said Greg. "Connie, darling, apologise."

"I will not apologise, and thank you so much for backing me up as a husband should," Connie replied sarcastically. "Furthermore, don't you 'darling' me, you thoughtless ape."

As Connie was clearly losing control of herself, Pru attempted to claim the moral high ground.

"Greg, dear, please try to keep your wife under control. She's always had these temper tantrums. It's so pathetic."

Connie rounded on her. "You're the pathetic one. Pretending you have a bad back, getting Francis to do all the dirty work for you, sucking up to Mum and Dad to steal my inheritance."

As the girls continued venting grievances they'd been storing for decades, Francis appeared on the doorstep with two full buckets of soapy water.

Standing stock-still, listening to the unusually colourful language being employed by his wife and sister-in-law, he looked to Greg for help. Greg shrugged his shoulders.

"Come on, old man. Leave them to it. This has been brewing all week."

"We can't just leave them." Francis put the buckets down and went towards Pru. His timing meant that he walked straight into her hand as she raised it to slap Connie. "Ow." He fell to the grass on his knees, stunned.

Belinda could take no more. Francis needed her. In seconds she was in their garden and had drenched both women with one of the buckets of water. Before they had a chance to recover, she pushed Connie towards Greg and Pru towards Francis. Standing with her hands

161

on her hips, she gave the sorry-looking, sopping-wet group a disappointed stare. "Do you want your kids to hear you airing your dirty laundry in public? Now shake hands, the pair of you."

The sisters looked at each other with undisguised aggression. Had they been cats, their tails would have been lashing the air.

"I said, shake hands," growled Belinda.

The men let their women go and the sisters managed the briefest of hand contact.

"Good," said Belinda. "That wasn't so bad, was it? Now, I don't want to hear another word from either of you."

She turned towards the men. "And what are you gormless chumps gawking at? Never seen a woman break up an argument before?"

Merlin took a long draw on his cigarette. Francis stared at his feet, his cheeks colouring. Greg gave a suggestive laugh and said, "Oh, many times, Belinda. But never topless."

An hour later and a composed Belinda had showered and was pouring herself a deserved glass of perfectly chilled white wine in the kitchen of Dairy Cottage.

There was a knock at the door.

"Hi, kids. Come in."

"Hi, Mum," said Emily. "Can Abi and Jem come in too?"

"Absolutely. More the merrier." Belinda kissed them all and directed them to the parlour. "What'll you have to drink, Jem? Abi? Glass of wine?"

162

"Yes, please," said a hopeful Emily.

"Not you," replied her mother.

Grabbing a couple of extra wine glasses, the chilled bottle, a family bag of Twiglets, and a tin of Coke for Emily, she settled down with the kids.

"What you been up to today?"

Emily, her mouth full of Twiglets, told her mother all the places that Jem and Abi had taken her to during their walk to the village. "I got a tattoo, look." She rolled up the sleeve of her T-shirt and at the top of her arm was a small mermaid coloured in pink and green with a dusting of glitter over it.

Belinda played the game. "Is it a real one?"

"Don't be daft — you have to be eighteen."

"How long does that one last then?"

"A week."

"It's very cool."

"Yeah. And afterwards we got ice creams and went and sat on the beach, then we had a swim and went rock-pooling."

"Really?"

"Yeah, and Jem, like, catches fish with his bare hands!"

"Does he now? Clever boy." She gave him an appreciative look and noticed his glass was empty, "Pass me your glass for a little top-up."

He held his glass out readily. Abi frowned at him and put a hand over hers.

Belinda set the bottle back down on the floor. "So, who taught you how to fish? Your dad?"

"No, it's not really his thing. It was Poppa, my grandfather. He loves all that stuff. Have you seen his speedboat yet?"

"No," said Belinda, raising her eyebrows. "Sounds fun."

"Oh, it's wicked. Abi and I are qualified to drive it — soon as we were old enough, we did the course and passed the test and everything. But we only go out when the weather's good."

"Of course. Where does he keep it? Trevay?"

"Oh no, it's under the house." Jem told Belinda and Emily all about the hidden cave.

"Coool," said Emily. "Can I have a ride in it?"

"Yeah," said Jem, "but I'll have to check with Poppa and Mum first."

"OK, but best not bother them today," said Belinda, swirling the wine round her glass. "Leave it till tomorrow."

"Why?" said Abi. "Has something happened?"

Abi and Jem sat astonished as Belinda gave them a sanitised account of what had happened earlier.

". . . I'm sure they will have sorted things out by now," she finished. "I wouldn't let it worry you."

The children didn't know whether to laugh or cry.

"But why were they arguing?" asked Jem.

Belinda shook her head, "Family business, from the sound of it. Let's not talk about it any more."

Abi felt she had to apologise. "I am so sorry. How embarrassing. God. It's freaking me out just thinking about it."

"Don't be silly — I'm a grown woman who has seen it all. Families can be so complicated. But your mums love each other. Trust me, they'll work it out."

Jem and Abi looked at each other. They weren't so sure.

The next morning, Henry and Dorothy were sitting in their warm conservatory sharing a crossword. Henry was in his comfortable armchair and Dorothy was calling out the clues.

"Fifteen down, 'Impossible to ignore or avoid.'"

"How many letters?"

"It's three words. Two, four, four. We've got the first letter of the second word, Y."

"Y for Yankee?"

"Yes."

"Hmm. Try another clue."

"OK. 'Sheets and pillowcases.' Starts with a B."

"P?"

"No. B for Breast."

"Ah . . . Bedlinen?"

"Yes. Good."

"Another one."

"'Silly fool.'"

"I am not."

"No, that's the clue: 'Silly fool.' Four letters starting and ending in T."

"Doesn't start with a C, does it?"

"Behave yourself!"

"Twit?"

"That'll do."

A knock on the conservatory glass disturbed them. It was Abi and Jem.

"Hello, kids! Lovely to see you." Dorothy stood up to welcome them in, smoothing down her halter-neck sundress.

Abi went to kiss her. "Hey, Granny. You look pretty groovy."

"Thank you, darling. I try to stay with it. I was about to get our mid-morning coffee and biscuits. Care to join us?"

"Yes, please," the kids chorused as they sat on the huge wicker sofa.

Dorothy looked pointedly at Abi's bare thighs, revealed by her micro shorts. "No biscuits for you, Abi."

"Don't be so ridiculous, woman!" Henry frowned. "She's skin and bone."

Dorothy tutted and continued on her way to the kitchen.

Henry looked at his two grandchildren with perceptive eyes. "So, what do you want? It's not just to say hello, is it?"

Jem laughed. "No flies on you, Poppa."

"Never have been. Never will be, my boy. So what is it?"

"Have you taken the boat out for a run yet this year?"

"A couple of months ago. Got it serviced. Hasn't been out since. Why?"

"Can we take it out one day? Belinda and Emily want to have a ride."

166

"And where will you go?"

"Just along to Trevay and then up the river for a picnic. I won't go mad."

Henry looked at Jem for a couple of moments, considering the request. "OK — as long as I can come too. You can be skipper though."

"Fantastic!" Jem's face split into a huge grin.

Henry continued: "How about we take your parents, too? There's room for everyone."

"Ah," said Abi. "That was the other thing we wanted to talk to you about."

Jem and Abi told Henry about the argument. "We don't know what it was about, but the atmosphere today is awful."

"Hmm. And how are Greg and Francis?"

"Dad's got a red mark on his cheek to match the bruise he got when he knocked himself out the other day. Apparently Mum accidentally hit him when he tried to stop them arguing," said Jem.

Henry sat for a moment, deep in thought. "And you have no idea what this is all about?"

Both kids shook their heads.

"I'll have a word and see if I can't get to the bottom of it." Henry sat forward in his chair. "Now bring that table a little closer — Granny's here with the coffee."

Dorothy poured the coffee from the cafetière and handed round the mugs. "Do you know what you want for your birthday?" she asked Abi.

"Yes. There's something, I really, really want . . . but I don't think I'll be allowed to have it."

Dorothy passed the plate of shortbread to Jem, bypassing Abi.

"Oh yes? What's that?"

"A party on the beach. All my friends. Boys and girls. Barbecue. Some wine. Music. But Mum and Dad want to do the usual thing in the garden."

Henry and Dorothy both chuckled. "I'm sure they do," said Henry. "Would you like me to work on them? No promises, mind."

"Would you?" pleaded Abi. "I would love you for ever!"

Henry laughed again. "I'll do my best." He picked up the plate of biscuits. "Here, Abi, have one of these."

"Thanks, Poppa."

Jem and Abi left looking much happier than when they'd arrived.

Dorothy waved them off from the front door then rejoined her husband. "The trouble with you, Henry Carew, is that you are a soft touch."

"I can't have my grandchildren made miserable. It's her seventeenth birthday, for God's sake." He winked at his wife. "Now then, give me that last clue."

"Fly into Portugal. Four letters. First letter F for —"

"Faro."

"Well, it fits."

CHAPTER
FOURTEEN

Back at Atlantic House, sitting round the breakfast table were four, unwashed, sullen adults. They were waiting for Merlin and the return of hot water, to arrive. He was not answering his phone. Connie made an effort to be cheerful.

"Well, at least we've got electricity!"

Greg was ostentatiously working at his computer, tapping noisily on the keys. He replied absently, "Hmmm?"

"I said at least we've got electricity," repeated Connie with what she hoped was a relaxed smile.

Francis, who was writing out one of his endless shopping lists, picked up her tone and agreed. "Yes. We're lucky, really."

Pru, who was sitting as far away from Connie as possible, gave her sister and husband a scathing look before returning to her paper.

The silence lingered on until Francis cleared his throat. The rest looked up expectantly.

"I have noticed that we need some more loo rolls. Any preference in colour?" he asked.

Pru rattled her broadsheet pages and spoke very clearly. "No."

Francis bent back to his list. "OK, I'll get the white then."

The silence returned. Only the scraping of Francis's chair as he stood up to stock-take in the larder disturbed them.

This was how Henry found them when he knocked on the patio doors.

Pru leapt up before Connie and hurried to welcome him in. "Hi, Dad." She kissed him.

"Good morning," he said sternly, surveying the four of them with a look that the girls remembered from childhood. All four felt a chill in their stomachs. They were in for a telling off.

"Morning, Daddy," Connie said in a small voice.

"I hear you two have been arguing —" he studied Francis's sore face — "and Francis has come off worst, by the look of things. Mind telling me what it was about?"

The sisters looked anywhere but at each other or their father.

Henry bellowed at them, "I am going to remain here until this is sorted out. What's been going on?"

Connie leapt in: "Pru said that you and Mummy would be leaving Atlantic House to her instead of sharing it out between us. And then Greg got that idiot Merlin Pengelly to look at the boiler and we had a flood and now we're waiting for Merlin to come back with the spare parts because we still don't have any hot water."

Henry pursed his lips. "Let's deal with the plumbing first. Merlin Pengelly — is he that bugger who made a mess of our summer twenty-odd years ago?"

"Yes," said Connie. "And now Greg's got him to mess up the plumbing as well."

Greg spoke: "Come on, I was only doing my bit. You asked me to find a plumber and I did."

"How did you manage to come up with that waste of space? He's not even a plumber!" boomed Henry.

Greg reached across to a pile of discarded newspapers and pulled out a copy of the parish magazine. "Here, it says: 'Merlin's Magic Plumbing Services. No job too big or small.'"

"Oh," said Pru nastily, "it wasn't too onerous a task for you to track him down then? All you had to do was read through the recycling. Well done."

Greg clenched his hands. "I can do without your sarcasm, Pru. And if it wasn't for you plotting to con Connie out of her inheritance, we wouldn't be in the situation we find ourselves in. Would we?"

"Exactly." Connie threw a spiteful look at her sister and then laid her hand on Greg's. "Well said, darling."

"I see," said Henry. "Tell me, Pru, what is this about you inheriting Atlantic House?" He looked her straight in the eyes.

She dropped her gaze under his scrutiny and whispered, "That's not quite what I said."

Connie shot back, "It's exactly what you said."

Henry raised his hands to silence them both.

"Did you say that, Pru?"

Pru squirmed. "In a way, but —"

"But what? Since when do you decide how I divvy up my home and worldly goods?"

Pru, shame-faced, didn't answer.

Connie chipped in: "Exactly, Daddy. She wants all the good stuff and she's trying to cut me out."

Now Henry's stony gaze turned on Connie.

" 'All the good stuff'? What do you think the firm is? I made your husband managing director. Carew Family Board Games has made me what I am today, what Greg is today and what you are today. Without the factory and the business, there would be no Atlantic House."

Connie opened her mouth as if to say something, but Greg caught her eye and shook his head, so she closed it again.

Henry placed his hands palms down on the table. "So, my two venal, selfish daughters, you want to know how much you'll be worth when I'm dead and gone?" He waved away their vehement protests. "Yes, you do. And the answer is that I don't know. Your mother and I intend to go on living for a while yet. And we may as well indulge ourselves a little, since neither of you have done anything to deserve Atlantic House or the company."

Greg, looking aggrieved, protested, "Hold on, Henry, I'm keeping the money coming into the firm."

"True. But I would expect nothing less, you are a salaried managing director with a generous annual bonus, a pension scheme and a family home bought and paid for by the firm. You are not — I'm sorry to be blunt here — my son. You are my daughter's husband. Two different things."

Greg looked with fury at his father-in-law and chairman, but wisely kept his temper under control and fought the urge to respond.

172

Henry continued: "In all the years you've been coming here, have you ever helped your mother prepare the house for these long, *free* family holidays? Have you ever offered to pay for the fuel or water bills that you run up so profligately? Or chipped in to help with running repairs?"

He looked around at the guilty faces before him. "No. So, if Dorothy and I decide to sell up, go to Las Vegas and put all the money on red, we shall."

A silence so dense you could see it, fell upon them.

"I'm sorry, Daddy," said Connie, clearly shaken.

"What can we do?" asked Pru.

"You can all start pulling your weight around here and not expecting it to land in your lap. I worked hard for everything you enjoy in life. And my father worked hard before me. I've been too soft on you all. I suggest you begin by sorting out the plumbing — which, by the way, you will pay for as a sign of goodwill. Do I make myself clear?" Henry saw their nodding heads and then turned to leave. When he reached the French doors, he paused and said sadly, "You have really disappointed me."

The four adults felt very small indeed.

Francis, who'd been doodling on his shopping list, lifted his head and said quietly but firmly, "If we're not careful we're going to ruin this holiday for your parents and our children. Henry has a point. We do all take this house and Dorothy's hospitality for granted." He looked around the table. "I propose we make a concerted effort to smarten the old place up. And pay for it too. All those in favour, raise their hands."

Pru sniggered, "You're not at a PTA meeting now, Francis."

"Are you saying you are not in favour?"

"No, I'm —"

"Then raise your hand."

Three hands went up and Francis added his. "Motion carried. Excellent. Greg? Where's yesterday's maintenance list? You and I will do an inventory of work that needs to be carried out on the exterior of the building. Connie and Pru, you go through each room inside the house, noting if anything needs repairing or repainting, and then give everything a good spring clean. OK?"

Everyone nodded, stunned at the transformation in Francis.

"Yessir!" said Greg. "But let's have a brew first."

"Did I hear you're making a brew?" Merlin walked into the kitchen looking rather rough and undeniably handsome in his overalls.

"Ah, morning, Merlin." Francis got up. "I could think of one or two other elusive figures you might more aptly have been named after. Houdini for one and the Scarlet Pimpernel for another."

"Is that an up-country joke?" said Merlin with a short laugh.

"No. You are a West Country joke, Merlin. You are not leaving this house today until you've repaired the boiler, fixed the leak under the sink — which was second only to Niagara Falls last night — and replaced the washer in the dripping tap of our en-suite. Do you understand?"

"Handsome. No worries," responded Merlin, the insults rolling off him like mercury on glass.

Pru, glass of cranberry juice in hand, edged her way past Merlin, saying, "I'm off to make a start in the drawing room." Merlin goosed her as she went by. She scowled at him and called her sister. "Come along, Connie."

Connie hurried past an innocent-looking Merlin. He goosed her too. She gave him a cold glare, but he merely smiled his beatific smile and turned to Greg and Francis. "Right, chaps. I'll start on the bottom and work my way up, shall I?"

In the drawing room, Connie and Pru finally spoke to each other.

"I haven't seen Dad that angry for a long time," said Pru, running her fingers through her hair.

"I can't believe Greg got Merlin in to do the work!" exclaimed Connie.

"A horrible coincidence," agreed Pru.

"Ghastly," replied Connie. "And, Pru . . ."

"Hmm?" Pru was gazing around the room, taking in the faded curtains and stained rug.

". . . I'm sorry about yesterday."

Pru stopped her mental inventory and looked at her sister. "Me too. I didn't mean it to come out that way."

"It did, though. And it made me angry."

"I know."

"So, we're back on a level playing field? For the house and everything."

"Yes."

They gave each other a short hug, but a residual resentment remained — simmering away under the surface.

"Mind you," said Pru, "there'll be bugger-all left if we don't look after it."

Connie smiled, trying to shake it off. "Help me shift this sofa, would you?"

The castors hadn't been moved for years and it took an effort to budge them. Eventually they dragged the sofa out, revealing a dusty but cleaner patch of carpet.

Pru surveyed the floor.

"God, this is filthy. Look at the difference!"

Connie bent down to pick up two old biros, a marble and a rubber band from among the balls of fluff that had lain under the sofa for decades.

"We'd better hire a carpet-shampoo machine. Do you suppose Mr Pomeroy's in Higher Barton would have one?"

Pru wiped her hands on her I'D RATHER BE SURFING apron and threw the bits of rubbish into a black bin liner. "Bound to. Old Pomeroy does everything from Alka-Seltzer to wellingtons via sunbeds and lipgloss, as far as I can remember."

Connie picked at a dead moth stuck in the brocade of the heavy curtains. "If I take these down, you could pop them into the dry cleaners. I think the one next to Pomeroy's is still there. Oh look, a fifty-pence piece."

She stooped to pick it up. "We can use that for parking."

She flipped it to her sister, who caught it neatly.

"Which reminds me," continued Connie, "how are we going to share the cost of all this spring cleaning and renovation?"

"Keep the receipts, give them all to me and I'll tot them up and split the bill down the middle."

"But suppose Greg and I spend more than you and Francis?" Connie queried.

Pru tightened her lips, "Well, write your name on each receipt so I'll know who's paid what. OK?"

"OK."

Pru straightened up and put her hands on her hips. "I'm not trying to do you out of anything, Connie. I'm not going to get Daddy drunk and make him sign a will giving me everything."

"Hmm," murmured Connie as Pru turned away. She turned back quickly.

"What did you say?"

"Nothing," trilled Connie. "Just pass me a bin bag and I'll pop the curtains into it."

For the next fifteen minutes neither of them said a word. While Connie balanced on a kitchen chair to unhook the curtains, Pru busied herself removing the loose covers from the sofas and armchairs.

When they had everything bundled up into seven or eight bin liners, they carried the first couple to Pru's car.

Outside the front door, Francis and Greg were doing something with the guttering.

"Let's start with the roof and clear the gutters," Francis had suggested earlier. "A sound roof is the best basis for a sound house."

"Is it?" said Greg. "What about good footings, a damp-proof course and solid brickwork?"

"Well, of course, those are all important too, but they need to be kept dry by a sound roof."

"OK," said Greg, who knew as little about building as Francis but couldn't be bothered to argue the point. "Who's going up the ladder? You or me?"

"I'm not good at heights," admitted Francis. "I'll keep the bottom steady for you."

"Righto. Here I go."

At the top of the ladder, Greg had a breathtaking view of the rolling fields and the rolling flesh of Belinda, who was in her garden, hula hooping in a bikini, with Emily.

Her invitingly wobbly bosoms and folds of comely stomach and hips were much more appealing than listening to Francis, who was standing at the foot of the ladder wittering about cracked slates.

Greg's pleasant reverie was interrupted by Connie calling from below: "Greg, would you help me carry these bags into the car, please?"

"No can do. I'm busy."

"I'll help," said Francis.

Greg felt the ladder give slightly as Francis let go.

"You'll be all right up there, won't you? I'll only be a mo."

"Of course, old man," he called down.

He waited until the tops of his wife and brother-in-law's heads had disappeared into the house, then seized his chance.

"Morning, neighbour," he called from his perch.

Belinda, very aware that he had been watching her for the last ten minutes, pretended not to know where the voice was coming from, and turned her head from side to side before looking up and feigning surprise. She caught her hula hoop and let it fall to her ankles.

"Ah! Hello again. You're looking busy."

"And you're looking hot."

She gave him an impish grin. "Cheeky!"

He hurriedly continued, "I mean, hot doing all that hula hooping."

She smiled again and in a faux Cornish accent replied, "Ooh, sir! Thank you."

"You look as if you could do with a cold glass of something."

Connie, coming out of the house with another heavy bag, peered up at her husband and said, "I'd love a cold glass of something, darling. That's thoughtful of you. But since you're busy up there, I'll sort it out. Fruit juice OK?"

She dropped the bag by Pru's car and went back inside.

Belinda giggled. "You're a naughty man," she said in a stage whisper.

Connie returned minutes later with a jug of juice and a tall glass with several ice cubes in it. Greg began whistling nonchalantly, giving the guttering his undivided attention.

Connie called up to him, "I'll put the jug here for you." She was setting it down on the bench under the rose arbour when Francis came staggering out with two more bags. "Put those on the back seat, would you?" she instructed him, and then walked back into the house.

Belinda had now left her garden and was standing in the drive. "Hello, Frankie." She moved forward and embraced him. "Greg was just saying I looked hot. And could do with a cold drink. I was about to make up a jug of Pimm's. Want some?"

Pru came out now and elbowed her way past Belinda and Francis with the last of the bags. "Not for the boys, thank you. Alcohol and ladders don't mix."

She got into the car and with a small wheel spin, accelerated up the lane in a cloud of sand and grit.

"God, I wish she wouldn't drive like a maniac," muttered Francis.

"If you change your mind about the Pimm's . . ." Belinda winked at both men, "I'll be next door."

Connie came out again with another bin bag. "Has Pru gone?"

"Yes," said Francis, tearing his eyes away from Belinda. "You just missed her."

Connie shrugged and set the bag down. "Oh, hi, Belinda."

"Hi there. Want a Pimm's? I've asked the boys, but Pru said they weren't to have any alcohol."

Connie laughed. "That's my sister, all right. I'd love a Pimm's!"

"You're my kind of girl. Come on over and I'll make you one."

"I should be getting on in the house. We've got loads to do. Especially since the flood."

"Then why don't I bring the jug to you and give you a hand?"

"Thanks!"

Connie darted back inside the house and Belinda smiled wickedly at Greg and Francis. "What a lovely family you are! I can see Connie and I will get along famously."

The two women worked well together. It wasn't long before, tongues loosened by the Pimm's, Belinda began questioning Connie about Pru and Francis.

"They're a bit of an odd couple," she said.

"You're telling me!" Connie laughed. "My sister, much as I love her, is a total control freak. If things aren't done her way there's hell to pay. Poor Francis."

"He's such a lovely man," said Belinda. "Whereas she seems a bit . . . forceful."

"God, yes!" Connie took another sip of Pimm's. "Do you know, she told me that having sex was immature. She hasn't given Francis any in *years*."

Belinda thought about this for a moment. "Really?"

Connie nodded her head vigorously, her eyes wide and shocked.

"Poor Frankie. We all need affection, don't we?"

"Oh quite." Connie was hitting her stride. "I make sure that Greg has no need to go elsewhere."

Belinda thought about the Greg she had observed. Very flirtatious and with a definite twinkle in his eye. "So neither of you has ever been tempted?"

Connie shook her head vehemently. "Absolutely not. I'm a very lucky woman."

"You certainly are. What about Frankie? Has he ever strayed?"

Connie, mid swig of Pimm's, spluttered a laugh, "Good God no! He's lovely and all that, but he's not exactly sexy, is he?"

Belinda frowned. "Oh, I don't know."

Connie looked at her with widening eyes. "Do you fancy him?"

"I think he's a nice bloke."

"Oh wow! How hilarious. That would put the cat among the pigeons. Poor old Pru. What would she say if you and Francis were to have a passionate affair! Hilarious!" Connie burst into peals of laughter and Belinda tried to join in.

CHAPTER
FIFTEEN

A couple of hours later, after the pair of them had sobered up a bit and finished the drawing room and rumpus room together, Belinda took herself and her empty jug back to Dairy Cottage.

Connie, realising she had used the last clean duster and was running low on bleach and wood polish, gathered up her handbag and car keys and walked out to the drive. She called to the boys, who had by this time made their way round to the stretch of guttering at the far end of the house.

"Right, boys. I shan't be long. By the time I get back I want to see all those gutters clear and empty. OK?"

"Jawohl, mein littlen Battenburg cake," said Greg, with a pantomime salute.

Connie looked unamused. "It frightens me to say it, but you are in charge till I get back. Keep an eye on Merlin, too. I heard him opening the door to the loft."

"No problem, my love. Everything will be fine. Toodle-oo." And he waved Connie off.

"Right, old man. Look out below!" Greg tossed down two great handfuls of foul-smelling detritus that had been clogging up the guttering.

Francis, steadfast at his post holding the ladder, barely had time to duck before the murky mess landed at his feet.

"Careful, Greg. You nearly got me."

"Hmm? What?" Another avalanche of brackish dead leaves was tipped out on to the lawn.

"How am I going to get this off the grass?" Francis called up. "Should I fetch an old sheet or something for you to throw it on to?"

"No, no, we'll rake it up later," said Greg dismissively. "Hang on, there's a couple of tiles loose here."

Francis looked up and got a face full of slate chippings.

"Stop! I've got something in my eye," he yelled, blinking painfully. But Greg wasn't listening.

"I'll climb up the roof a bit and check how much of a problem it is," he shouted down.

Francis, unable to see through his blurred and teary eye, felt the weight of Greg leave the top rung and guessed that he had climbed on to the roof.

"Careful, Greg. You don't know whether the beams are strong enough."

"I'm fine, old man. Just a little bit furth —"

Francis heard rather than saw his brother-in-law fall, knees first, through the roof.

"Aaargh . . . God help me . . . my arm . . . arrgh."

Francis let go of the ladder and, half-blind, ran indoors and up towards the attic.

Merlin, who had been making up some hours lolling against a roof truss with a comfy pile of old dust sheets under his bum, was snoozing with the *Daily Mirror*.

184

The sudden noise gave him a fright and he leapt up, banging his head on a wooden crossbar. Once the dust had cleared, through the shaft of sunlight pouring through the new hole in the roof, he saw Greg, lying prone on the rafters and swearing.

"'Ello there, boy," he chuckled. "Nice of you to drop in."

"Help me up, you idiot. I think I've broken my arm."

Merlin lifted Greg easily and hooked his arm under Greg's shoulder. "D'ye reckon you can make the loft ladder?"

Wincing, Greg replied through gritted teeth, "I'll give it a try."

"Hellooo?" Francis was on the landing below. "Greg. Can you hear me?"

"'E can hear you, all right. It's 'is arm that's hurt, not his ears."

Slowly Merlin eased Greg through the loft hatch and on to the ladder.

When the three of them finally made it to the kitchen, Merlin assessed the damage. Greg's arm was looking misshapen and his face had gone very pale with a tinge of green.

"Does that hurt?" Merlin asked, trying to straighten the arm out.

"Aaaarrrggghhh! What the hell do you think?" shrieked Greg.

"Stop screamin' like a girl and sit quiet a minute while I look at Francis's eye."

Francis's eye could barely open and was all raw and red.

"I'm not going to touch that," shuddered Merlin. "Might make it worse. I'd better get you both down the hospital. Your eye could do with washing out and you'll need an X-ray on that arm, G."

"Is there a Bupa clinic nearby?" moaned Greg.

"Nope. But we've got very good vets in Cornwall."

"I cannot for the life of me understand how you managed to make such a mess of everything."

Connie had no sympathy for the two wounded soldiers sitting in the drawing room on the coverless sofas.

"I mean, look at the pair of you. One with an arm in plaster, the other with an eye patch. Together you could go to a fancy-dress party as Nelson!"

Greg smiled ruefully. "That's rather good, old girl."

"It's not a joke, it's a bloody disaster," huffed Pru. "A disgrace. You were supposed to be clearing the gutter — instead you go and make a bloody great hole in the roof."

Greg was defensive: "I was trying to help you and your family. And look where it got me: an NHS casualty department with a brutish male nurse and an arm broken in two places. And not so much as a thank you!"

"Thank you for what?" Pru rounded on him. "Thank you for half-blinding my husband? You should have left the roof to the professionals. Surely you could have found the phone number for a roofer in the parish magazine?" Greg felt the arrow of her sarcasm fully pierce his ego.

Francis spoke, "Pru, be fair, it wasn't Greg's fault. We were trying to help."

"And you've been left with a severe laceration to the cornea. You have been very lucky, Francis. Very lucky indeed." Pru swept her hands through her short dark hair and looked at Connie, who was trying to figure out how to work the carpet-shampoo machine.

"There's nothing else for it, Connie. You and I will have to take the maintenance work while the men look after the children and the cooking."

The following days saw Connie and Pru working from dawn till dusk, cleaning the house. Woodwork was washed, curtains and windows cleaned, every nook and cranny vacuumed and dusted. From time to time Dorothy would pop in to annoy them. One morning, while the girls were shampooing the stair carpet, Dorothy called up to them from the hall:

"Whatever you do, don't touch this chandelier. It needs professional cleaning."

Connie turned off the machine and gritted her teeth. "Mum, all it needs is a quick rub with some wet wipes to get it sparkling again. We don't need to spend a fortune on a professional cleaner."

"Wet wipes?" Dorothy pointed indignantly at the chandelier above her head. "That's Venetian glass, I'll have you know."

"Yes, we do know, Mum. We were there when you bought it, remember?" grumbled Pru, recalling the oppressive heat of an Italian August. She and Connie had pleaded to go on a gondola ride, but Dorothy had insisted on dragging them around the glass factories of Murano instead. Visiting the furnaces had been like stepping into an inferno. She shuddered at the memory.

Dorothy sniffed. "In that case, you'll remember how much money Daddy paid for it. The chandelier *must* be cleaned professionally."

"OK, whatever you say," sighed Connie. "Who do you use? I'll give them a ring."

"I have never had it cleaned," Dorothy replied breezily. "I'll have a look on Daddy's computer web net thing. You can find anyone on there, you know."

Pru and Connie smiled fondly at their mother. "Yes. We do know."

"Right. Well. I'll go and do that now then."

"OK, Mum," the girls chorused.

As soon as she had gone, Connie said to Pru, "Pass me the wet wipes."

While the girls did their chores, Greg and Francis kept their heads down and tried to run the domestic side of things as smoothly as they could. The kitchen became their domain. Francis was in his element, taking charge of all the cooking.

"What do you fancy for supper tonight, Greg?" he asked. "How about some lobsters?"

"Where will you get them from, old man?"

"Down in Trevay at the fish market."

"And how do you propose to get there when neither of us can drive?" Seeing his brother-in-law's shoulders slump in defeat, Greg tried to make amends for his sharp tone. "I know. Give me a moment and I'll sort you out a taxi."

Minutes later he was back, smiling broadly. "Francis, your chariot awaits! Be at the front door in five. Belinda said she'll be only too happy to have you to herself for a couple of hours."

Francis blanched. "No — no need. I'll call the mini-cab place in town. Go and tell her no."

They heard the front door creak open and Belinda's voice calling, "Yoo-hoo."

"Too late!" Greg gathered up Francis's horseshoe-shaped leather purse and a bundle of jute sustainable shopping bags, and in a low voice said, "Come on, old man, give yourself a treat. Take her out for lunch."

"But Pru and Connie — what will they think? I'm supposed to be fixing their lunch," Francis whimpered.

"I'll cover for you." Greg dropped his voice further still. "Strictly *entre nous*, I'm expecting a call from Janie shortly, so I could do with the privacy." He pushed Francis out into the hall. "Ah, Belinda! This is so very kind of you," he gushed, propelling them both towards the front door. "Francis says he's going to treat you to lunch as a thank you. Off you go now. Don't do anything I wouldn't do! Ha ha ha. Bye!"

As he slammed the front door shut behind them, the phone in his pocket began to vibrate.

Belinda insisted on taking Francis's arm and helping him into her 2CV. In the footwell, his feet rested on several cardboard coffee mugs and a carpet of chocolate-bar wrappers.

"Sorry about the mess. It's Emily and her mates. I haven't had time to clean it out. Now, let me just do up your seat belt."

Francis sat, helpless as a toddler, as she leaned across him, smothering his face with her magnificent breasts. He breathed in her musky, sun-warmed smell. She really was extremely attractive. As she clicked his seat belt into place and moved back out of the car, he flicked his one good eye nervously up towards the windows of the house. Thank goodness Pru and Connie were cleaning the bedrooms on the other side this morning.

Belinda eased her sun-tanned flesh into the driver's seat and started the engine. She laid her hand on his knee and patted it. "How's your poor eye today?"

"A little better, I think. The doc says the patch can come off in a day or two."

"That's good." She smiled at him. "Pity, though: you look very dashing with a patch."

She gave him a wink and started up the engine. "Trevay here we come!"

Although the day was sunny, there was a cool breeze as the 2CV, its soft-top rolled down and its engine chugging away like a sewing-machine motor, carried them into Trevay. Holidaymakers were strolling along the streets, oblivious to traffic, stopping and starting as they wished, licking ice creams and window-shopping. The main car park was full, but Francis directed her to a sneaky space — one of the few not covered in double yellow lines — behind the main street. They were lucky. It was empty.

Belinda was delighted. "Frankie, you clever man!" And she leaned over and planted a warm kiss on his cheek. Gathering up a couple of his jute bags from the back seat, she said, "Right — where's this fish market?"

Ambling arm in arm with Belinda as they made their way to the fish market was a revelation to Francis. Pru had never taken his arm; on the one occasion he had taken hers, she had shrugged him off. Belinda's arm was comforting in its fleshiness. Her chubby wrists and tanned fingers made him feel powerful and . . . well, male. As they walked he found himself smiling at strangers and enjoying the sound of Belinda's inconsequential but amusing chatter. Her golden curls kept blowing across her face and on to her lips. He didn't hear much of what she said. He didn't need to. He felt happy. Naughty, but happy.

Together they chose six lobsters, which the fishmonger packed into a polystyrene cool box.

At the trendy food market next door they got asparagus, new potatoes, lemons and — for home-made mayonnaise — eggs and good olive oil.

"Look at those raspberries! My favourite!" cooed Belinda.

"Do you like Eton Mess?" asked Francis, carried away by her foodie enthusiasm.

"Who doesn't?" She smiled at him, twinkling her blue eyes.

"Right. I'll make meringues with the egg whites left over from the mayonnaise."

"Are you inviting me to supper, Francis Meake?"

191

Francis took a grip on his destiny. "Yes, I am. You and Emily. Come and have dinner with the family. Pru would love to have you share it with us." He was less sure about the last part, but this new shot of courage in his veins kept him from buckling.

Once they'd paid for everything, they returned to the car, which was sitting in the shade of the narrow street.

"I'll put all this in the boot — there's no danger of it spoiling, here in the cool — and then we can go and have some lunch," twinkled Belinda.

There was a small café across the road that served huge bowls of moules marinières and chips. Francis couldn't remember ever having such a relaxed lunch with a woman. The way Belinda chatted, laughed, enjoyed her food and drank her glass of perfectly chilled wine was fun.

". . . So, my husband walked out eighteen months ago and moved in with Steve. I had no idea whatsoever that he was gay. It's always the wife who finds out last, isn't it? Anyway, Steve is a lovely guy and Brett's happy. We're all good friends now. Emily is pretty cool about it, as she gets to go clothes shopping with a dad who really likes fashion." She leaned across and dipped a hunk of her French bread into Francis's white wine and garlic sauce. "I do get a bit lonely, though. I don't want to be single for ever . . . Still, there's always tomorrow, right?" She laughed and wiped her lips on her napkin. "How about you? Are you and Pru happy?"

Francis coughed as he took a gulp of wine. "Yes, yes. Very happy. Well, as happy as two people who've been married for almost eighteen years can be."

192

"She looks a bit of a ball-breaker to me," said Belinda with candour.

Francis was horrified. "No, no. She's strong and kind and a good wife and mother. We look after each other."

"Hmm." Belinda gazed deep into his eyes until he looked down at his wine glass. "I notice you didn't mention the word love."

"Well, of course. That goes without saying."

"So, say it."

"What?"

"That you love your wife."

"I . . . I love my wife."

"Good. When was the last time you told her?"

"Good lord. I mean, after all those years together, one doesn't need to."

"Yes, you do. When was the last time she told you she loved you?" Belinda fixed her blue eyes on him. "If she loved you, she'd tell you every day."

Francis was getting very uncomfortable, "Well, we're all different, aren't we." He beckoned the waitress. "I think we'd better get going."

He spent the journey back to Atlantic House in deep thought. Belinda, beside him, chattered away as if blissfully unaware that he wasn't listening.

She had awoken something in him that he'd managed to suppress for a very long time. Years. He thought the world of Pru, but what did she think of him? Was he just faithful old Francis, chief cook and bottle washer? Where was the passion? He felt the vibrant heat emanating from this buxom and attractive woman by his side and realised how much he missed the physical joy of love-making. Could he take Belinda as a lover in the way Greg had taken Janie? The thought thrilled and terrified him in equal measure.

"So, shall I come over at about six thirty? I'll bring a couple of jugs of Pimm's."

He forced his mind back to the present.

"Yes. That would be lovely."

Belinda helped him out of the car and then helped carry the bags to the front door of Atlantic House.

"I'll take them to the kitchen for you, shall I?"

"That's very kind, but just leave them on the step. I can manage from here," he said. He pushed the heavy oak door open. The hall was cool and smelled of lavender polish. His ears strained to hear Pru. He didn't want her to catch him like this, in Belinda's company and smelling of wine.

"OK." Belinda straightened up and kissed his cheek for the second time that day. "Thank you for a lovely morning and for lunch. Any time you need a driver, you know where I am."

"Thank you."

"See you at six thirty."

"Six thirty. Yes."

"And, Francis . . ."

"Yes?"

"Those things we talked about over lunch? I don't mean to stick my nose in, but you are a lovely man and deserve to be appreciated."

"Oh well, erm, I'll see you later . . ."

Francis watched as she manoeuvred the 2CV back on to the drive of Dairy Cottage, then he quietly closed the front door and carried the bags to the kitchen. While the kettle was boiling for the calming cup of camomile tea he so badly needed, he fished in his pocket for a piece of extra-minty chewing gum.

CHAPTER
SIXTEEN

Francis unpacked the shopping and put the lobsters in the salad compartment of the fridge to quieten them down. Then he made a large pot of tea and went out into the hall. "Anyone for tea?" he shouted up the stairs. "It's in the kitchen. Come and get it."

Greg came out of the rumpus room looking sly. "Hello, old man. How did lunch go with B?" he whispered.

Francis, not liking this subterfuge, said, "Fine. How was your phone call?"

Greg rolled his eyes in rapture as an answer.

"Did Pru wonder where I was at lunchtime?" asked Francis.

"No. I told her the truth. Belinda had taken you shopping for supper."

"Why did you tell her that?" Francis hissed.

"The truth is always best." Greg looked up as Connie and Pru descended the stairs. "Hello, girls. Golly, you look as if you could do with a cuppa."

Connie pushed her fringe out of her eyes with the back of her rubber-gloved hand. "Pru and I have finished upstairs. The last lot of clean curtains are up. How did your phone call go with Janie?"

Francis looked sharply at Greg, who seemed completely relaxed.

"All fine. She wanted to run a few things past me and there were plenty of things I needed her to do for me."

Connie gave him a hug. Over the top of her head, Greg gave Francis a wink as he mouthed, "The truth, see."

Pru walked through the middle of them all, clanging her bucket and mop. "Good of Belinda to take you to the shops, Francis. Did you get everything we need?"

"Yes. Sorry I wasn't here to prepare lunch."

"No problem. Greg did pretty well as a one-armed sandwich maker. Cheese and pickle."

Greg winked at Francis again. "See, old man. Nothing to it."

Francis relaxed. "Well done on completing the spring clean, girls. I see you've managed to get a tarpaulin on the hole in the roof."

"Yes," said Pru. "The weather forecast is looking a bit iffy, so I had to ask Merlin to do that. I'll find a proper roofer tomorrow."

They moved into the kitchen and helped themselves to tea and slices of shop-bought Madeira cake.

Dorothy appeared at the back door with Henry's iPad in her hand. "How do I turn this on?"

Connie laughed. "Mummy, I showed you the other day."

"No you didn't. I would remember if you had."

"I did. But, anyway, if it's to find a chandelier cleaner, I think you'll find we don't need one. Come into the hall and look."

Connie got up and escorted Dorothy into the hall. The afternoon sun was slanting through the mullioned windows either side of the front door and glinting on the glass drops. The hall was lit with the refracted sparkles of light.

"Oh, darling!" Dorothy clasped her hands in front of her chest. "You've beaten me to it! Doesn't it look wonderful? Who did you get to do it so quickly?"

Connie smiled. "A marvellous company: Johnson and Johnson. They have all the specialist gear. I've some left over, if you want it."

"Ooh, yes please, darling."

"They're in the kitchen."

On the kitchen table lay the packet of wet wipes. Connie handed them to her mother. "Here you go."

At six thirty, Belinda came round with a large jug of Pimm's and Emily. Henry and Dorothy were strolling over from The Bungalow at the same time.

Dorothy smiled a welcome and said, "Pimm's! My favourite. Good evening, Belinda. Hello, Emily." The women greeted each other with kisses and Henry followed suit.

He spoke to Emily. "Now, young lady, have you any idea how an iPad works?"

"Yes, of course. I haven't got one, but I've used my friend's."

"Ah. Could you help me with it? My daughter, Connie, tried but she's not much better than me and she gets so impatient. Would you give me a lesson or two?"

"Of course!" Emily smiled.

"Thank you. Oh, I say, look at the firepit and the table. Doesn't that look nice. Would you sit next to me?"

The entire family were gathering round the table and Henry chose his seat at the head with Emily to his left. "We can watch the sunset from here. We might even see the green flash."

She turned and stared at him. "Do you believe in the green flash? I mean, does it exist?"

"Oh yes. Cornwall is full of myth and legend, but the green flash is real enough. It's a trick of the light that sometimes happens at sunset. We might be lucky tonight."

Francis staggered out of the kitchen and on to the terrace with an enormous bowl of cooked lobsters.

"Frankie, why didn't you call me. I'll help you with that."

Belinda was up on her feet and following Francis back to the kitchen. Pru, who was stoking the firepit, looked at Jeremy. "Jem, go and help your father . . . and you, Abi."

The kitchen was steamy from the enormous pan of water in which the lobsters had been cooked. Francis was busy pouring his mayonnaise into a sauce boat. A small drip landed on the worktop. Belinda and he both reached for it with their tasting fingers.

"Great minds, eh!" laughed Belinda. She dipped her finger in and licked it lasciviously, rolling her eyes in ecstasy at the same time. "You are the King of Sauce,

Frankie." Her cleavage jiggled as she laughed again at her own joke.

Abi and Jem arrived in time to witness Francis and Belinda with arms looped round each other's shoulders, shaking with mirth.

"Hey, Dad," said Jem, "I haven't seen you laugh like this for ages."

"Yeah, unc. It, like, suits you," agreed Abi.

Belinda let Francis go and flicked her tea towel at Abi and Jem. The kids started laughing and a chase ensued round the kitchen table. As soon as Belinda got round to the sink, she dipped her hand in the sudsy water and began flicking them all with bubbles. Abi and Jem retaliated by picking at a bunch of grapes and chucking them at Belinda and Francis.

Pru, hearing the laughter from the garden, came to see what the joke was. They were having such a good time with their playfight, no one noticed her. Standing at the French windows, however, Pru noticed the way Francis seemed so relaxed in Belinda's company. A tremor of fear and — jealousy? — blew into her heart. She coughed loudly and walked in. "Hi, guys. Having fun?"

The noise stopped and they all stood awkwardly.

"You sort of had to be there," said Jem. "Belinda's been splashing us."

Pru looked at Belinda. And said flatly "Well, that does sound hilarious. Any chance of supper?"

Between them they loaded the garden dining table with dishes of buttery new potatoes, asparagus, salad and mayonnaise.

200

"Tuck in, everyone," said Francis. And they did.

Slowly the sun sank lower in the sky until it was almost touching the horizon. Henry wiped his fingers clean of lobster juice and nudged Emily. "Keep watching the sun as it slips further down." Emily had never seen or noticed how quickly the sun travelled. In a few minutes there was only half of it left, then a quarter, then, at the moment it finally slipped from view, there was a definite green blink of light.

"Oh my God! The green flash! Was that it?"

"Yes, my dear. That was it."

"Wow. Cool."

"As you say," Henry chuckled, pouring her a small glass of rosé with which to celebrate. They toasted each other quietly and Belinda, watching from the other side of the table, smiled to herself.

The firepit was sending tracer sparks into the warm night air and the moon was playing peekaboo with the racing clouds.

Henry turned to Pru and raised his glass. "May I say, Pru, what a fine choice of husband you made all those years ago. Not only has he put up with you . . ." he paused for the gratuitous laughter, ". . . he cooks like a dream. This lobster was delicious." He raised his glass. "Here's to Francis the chef. Cheers!"

"Cheers!" echoed the assembled throng.

"Uncle Francis, would you help me with the food for my birthday party?" piped up Abi.

"Ah!" said Henry. "So the parents are letting you have the party on the beach, are they?"

"What's this?" Connie, slightly tipsy, tuned in.

"My party, Mum. My birthday's only a week away. Jem and I have invited some people —"

"How many people?" Her mother tried not to slur.

"A few friends, that's all. For a tin of beer on the beach and some food, some music."

"Did I say yes to this?" Connie tried to focus on Greg. "Did you say yes to this?"

Greg, in an expansive mood following his lengthy and erotic call with Janie, said, "What the hell, you're only seventeen once. Yes, she can have her party. *But* . . . she'll have to fund it herself."

"Oh, Daaaad." Abi's face had fallen from triumph to tragedy. "I haven't got any money."

"You have your monthly allowance."

"I've spent it."

"Then you'll have to get a job."

"Where?"

Belinda butted in, "I'd be more than happy to help with the organisation. It needn't cost a fortune."

"Would you?" asked Abi hopefully.

Pru leapt in, "Well, that would be very kind, Belinda. Thank you. Connie and I simply won't have the time to help as we are full on with finding a roofer and watching Merlin like a hawk while he fixes the plumbing. And, of course, neither Greg nor Francis are able bodied enough to cart party things up and down the path to the beach. So, are we all agreed? Connie?"

Connie had her head flat on the table. Greg tried to wake her, but she was in a deep wine-induced sleep.

Belinda beamed. "I'll be your Uncle Francis's kitchen helper."

A frown crept onto Pru's brow — had she just scored an own goal, she wondered?

Abi, however, was delighted.

"Mum's out for the count! Good, she won't remember that she didn't say yes!"

"Don't be disrespectful to your mother. She's exhausted with all the cleaning she's been doing," said Greg, filling up his own glass.

Dorothy surveyed her unconscious daughter with a curl of her lip. "Doesn't know her limit. Never did. Remember that summer, Henry? We found her in a terrible state. She'd been at your brandy."

Henry thought for a moment, "That was Pru, wasn't it?"

"No." Dorothy was quite definite. "Connie." She turned to Pru: "What was it all about? A row over some boyfriend, as I recall."

Pru looked into her own glass and said quietly, "I really don't remember."

"Yes, you do," said Dorothy. "You and Connie didn't speak to each other for months."

"God, yes," Henry breathed. "It was over that boy — Merlin."

Greg sat up, suddenly attentive. "Merlin? He told me you two girls had had a falling out. Don't tell me you got in a fight over that no hoper!" Greg waved his glass at Pru. "Come on, spill the beans. Did he break poor old Con's heart? Or yours?"

Pru stood up and started to collect the dirty plates. "It was a summer of parties and friends and Merlin was just one of the gang." She reached across the table. "Pass me your plate, Daddy."

Registering Pru's discomfort, Belinda leapt to her aid. "Gosh, Look at the time! Come on, everyone, let's get this lot tidied up so we can head off to bed. Emily, you wait here — I'm just going to give Pru a hand clearing up."

As they busied themselves in the kitchen, Belinda chatted away brightly.

"Frankie and I had a wonderful morning in Trevay, today. He's such a lovely man." She put the last of the dinner plates on the worktop. "Did he tell you we had lunch?"

"Yes, he said you had been kind enough to give him a lift." Pru reached for an apron.

"How did you two meet?" asked Belinda, loading cutlery into the dishwasher.

Pru told her the story. "And he has looked after me, and then Jeremy, ever since," she concluded.

"So you're very good friends?"

Pru ran the hot tap into the sink and squeezed in a measure of Fairy Liquid for the larger bowls and pans. "Yes, that's true. We are very good friends." She gave Belinda a gimlet "back-off" stare. "We are an excellent team." She emphasised the last word.

Belinda smiled to herself and picked up a tea towel. "That's nice."

Pru lifted a soapy saucepan on to the draining board. Belinda picked it up and started drying it. "So, tell me about Merlin. I've seen him working on the house."

204

"Nothing to tell," said Pru, scrubbing a pot. "We were all friends. It was years ago."

"You and he together?"

Pru looked at Belinda steadily. "No, me *and* Connie, and a large group of friends."

"One of whom was Merlin?"

"Yes."

"And . . .?" pushed Belinda.

"And, nothing," said Pru.

"Strange. Outside just now, the way you were talking about him, it sounded as if you and Merlin and Connie had a bit of a history."

Pru gave her a withering and bemused look. "*Puh-lease*, as the young ones say."

They continued washing up for a few more minutes, then Belinda said, "He's a good-looking man."

Pru pulled out the sink plug and dried her hands on her apron. "Yes. Merlin was always rather handsome."

"I meant Francis," drawled Belinda.

Greg had somehow managed to steer Connie up to bed. His one good arm was still strong enough to hold her, even though on every stair tread she stopped and kissed him. She had always been an amorous drunk, and tonight was no exception. Greg, fired up with thoughts of Janie, was quite happy to oblige. He swiftly got his wife undressed and comfortable on the bed.

Afterwards, he kissed her and held her and told her how much he loved her. It was possible she was asleep and couldn't hear him, but he felt a pang of guilt all the same. He promised himself that, as soon as the summer was over, he'd cool it with Janie. Maybe.

Connie, meanwhile, had been quite aware of what was happening to her but she'd chosen to close her eyes and imagine that it was Merlin in her bed. His beautiful face, his lean, tanned body, the mischievous charm of him. He had first made love to her in this house. He'd come one day when everyone else was out. Connie had poured him a shandy — the most grown-up drink she could think of. He had teased her and said he couldn't drink it alone, she'd have to have one too. After a couple, she'd been desperate for him to kiss her. They'd sat talking, head to head, almost nose to nose. He'd told her about the sea, and what it was like to grow up in Cornwall, and he'd told her how good she looked in her bikini when she came to the beach. When he finally moved in for a kiss, she closed her eyes and let him do what she wanted. Just as she had let Greg do this evening.

She smiled when he told her how much he loved her. He was sleeping now. Once again she thought how lucky she was to have a husband she could trust. It had taken a long time for the pain of Merlin's betrayal to fade.

Pru watched Francis as he got himself ready for bed. She tried to see him with fresh eyes. He had strong legs and only a tiny bit of belly. His face was pleasing. His kind eyes were large and well set, his nose of average length and straight. His teeth were good and his hair, although slightly receding, was otherwise thick and cut well. Handsome? She supposed he was, but that wasn't what had attracted her. It was the man inside that mattered. She knew they were a team. A partnership. They could rely on each other. She looked again at his familiar face.

"Francis?"

"Hmm?" He was concentrating on applying athlete's foot powder to his toes.

"I think you have an admirer."

He froze but managed to say, "Oh yes?" in a tight voice.

"Yes — Belinda! How funny is that!"

CHAPTER
SEVENTEEN

The following morning found Abi, in her pyjamas, lolling on Jem's bed.

"Like, it's so *unfair*. Mum and Dad have always paid for my birthday parties. Why won't they pay for this one? They know I haven't got any money." She sighed, twirling her hair round her finger and then picking at the split ends.

Jem was trying to sleep. He hadn't moved since she'd come in a couple of minutes earlier. Drool had made the pillow wet under his open mouth.

She continued: "Where am I supposed to get a job? This is my holiday. I'm supposed to be relaxing after my ASs and building my strength for the A2s."

"Uh," Jem managed.

"It's so mean of them. I've worked hard at school and everything and I'm tired. I really need my holiday. They just don't get it."

Jem turned over and grunted again.

"It's not like I can ask people to bring their own food and drink, is it? So-o-o not cool. I'm seventeen, for crying out loud." She tossed the lock of hair behind her shoulder and started picking at her chipped nail polish. "I can't wait to be eighteen and outta here."

"Uh."

"So what should I do?"

Jem rubbed his eye and farted.

"Go and look for a job?"

"Oh, you're so gross," said Abi, wafting a hand under her nose. "And anyway, where am I supposed to look for a job?"

Jem knew she wouldn't let him sleep any longer, so he gave in and opened his eyes. "We'll go to Trevay and ask around."

"Will you come with me?"

"Yeah."

"When?"

"When you've left me alone so I can get up and get dressed. Go and put the kettle on and I'll be down. Put some toast on too."

Abi gave him a hug. "Thanks, Cuz."

In the kitchen she found her father.

He smiled at her. "Good morning, darling daughter. You're up early this merry morning."

"Stop with the sarcasm, OK."

"Well, it is only ten forty-five."

"Stop having a go at me." She glared at him and he continued typing one-handed on his laptop. "I'm, like, gonna look for a job . . . to pay for my birthday party, since you won't, 'cos you're too mean."

"Correction: I'd happily pay for the usual party in the garden. I'm not happy to pay for a load of drunken teenagers I don't even know."

"I've told you I don't want party games in the garden eating your horrible barbecue sausages. I want a proper party on the beach."

"Then you must pay for it." Greg snapped shut his computer, stood up, ruffled her fringe and went off towards the garden.

"Arsehole," muttered Abi after him.

Greg reversed through the kitchen door. "I heard that." He turned to face her. "Tell you what — any money you manage to raise, I'll match it. OK?"

"Really?" asked Abi.

"Yes. Really. That way you'll learn the value of hard-earned cash."

"I know the value of money." She sighed theatrically.

"No you don't. But you soon will, once you've worked eight hours for a tenner."

Trevay was humming with holidaymakers, holiday-makers' kids and holidaymakers' dogs. It was just after midday and the cafés and takeaways were doing a roaring trade.

Jem and Abi tried to ask about casual work in three or four places, but the harassed staff simply shrugged their shoulders and either told them that there were no jobs or to come back when it was quieter.

They walked up to the Starfish Hotel but didn't get beyond the receptionist, who directed them to the hotel website where job vacancies were advertised, but warned that there was nothing going at the moment.

They wandered limply down to the harbourfront and sat on a bench.

"Fat lot of good that was," huffed Abi.

They sat and watched the boats in the harbour. Several motor yachts had strings of washing tied to the rigging, others were languishing empty, waiting for their owners.

There was a brisk trade in speedboat trips. Apprehensive children with eager dads were queuing up to take the high-speed trip around the coast, leaving exhausted-looking mums on the quay, keeping an eye on their over-packed buggies.

A bigger boat, the *Puffin Boy*, slowly entered the harbour and tied up, disgorging its sunburnt passengers.

One of the crewmen was helping some elderly ladies and a woman with a baby in a pushchair, on to the safety of dry land. Once everyone was off, he put out a sandwich board on which were the departure times and details of the next sailings.

He started calling to passers-by: "One-hour trip around the bay. You don't come back, you don't pay!"

A young couple and their two children stopped and had a conversation with him. After a few moments, they climbed aboard. The crewman started again.

"See the dolphins and the seals round our beautiful coastline. One hour's trip. Refreshments served on board." A large family group stopped, spoke to the man, then embarked, smiling, making their way to the open seats at the back of the boat.

Jeremy and Abi watched with fond memories. "Remember that trip we took on *Puffin Boy* when we were little? I was sick all over Dad," laughed Jem.

211

"God, yes! Mum and I threw up over the side, but only because Dad held our heads down so we wouldn't vom on his new deck shoes," Abigail remembered, giggling.

"I'd never do it to my kids," said Jem.

"You'll have the *Dorothy* by then, though, won't you," Abi stated.

Jem looked at his cousin's sad face. "Look, whatever Mum and Auntie Connie inherit from Poppa, we'll share. Shake?"

He put his hand out. Abi smiled at him. "Do you mean that?"

"Yep. Let's you and I make a pact that when they've dropped off the perch and we are grown up, we'll share everything out between us." He put his hand out to Abi, who took it and shook.

"Deal."

Jem stood up. "I wonder if there are any jobs going on *Puffin Boy*."

The crewman was only too pleased to hear that Jem wanted a job. "Got any experience of being at sea?"

"Yeah. My grandad has a boat: the *Dorothy*."

The crewman was impressed. "You mean the Riva? Mr Carew's boat?"

"Yeah."

"She's a beauty. Worth a fortune. And he lets you drive her?"

"Since I was twelve, yeah."

The crewman considered this.

"Can you shout loud enough to call the punters in?"

"Er, yeah, I'll, like, try."

"Give it a go then."

Jem cleared his throat: "Roll up, roll up for the adventure of a lifetime. The good ship *Puffin Boy* is patrolling for pirates, dolphins and mermaids. Can you help us find them? Roll up, roll up."

Abi was pink with embarrassment for her cousin but couldn't stop giggling.

"Right," said the crewman. "My name's Robbie and you've got yourself a job. Thirty quid a day. Take it or leave it."

Jem didn't hesitate. "I'll take it."

"OK. See you first thing tomorrow. Eight thirty sharp. Time and tide wait for no man."

To celebrate, Abi and Jem cycled back to Treviscum, where Jem scraped up enough cash to buy them a big bag of chips from the burger van in the beach car park.

"How come you find a job first go and I, who really need one, can't find one?" Abi licked her salty fingers.

Jem was in too good a mood to let Abi bring him down. "We'll get you one too, don't worry. And my birthday present to you will be two days' pay towards your party."

"Would you really do that?"

"Yep."

"How much cider will sixty quid buy?"

"Almost enough for you. Don't know about the others though," laughed Jem. Balling up his chip paper and searching in his shorts pockets for some more coins, he asked, "Want an ice cream for pudding?"

On the sand dunes above the beach was perched a gaily coloured caravan with an awning advertising *Pearl's Ice Creams*.

Pearl was one of many young women who'd fallen in love while on holiday and decided to stay. Over the long winter, she and her coastguard lover had secured the rental pitch above the beach and invested two hundred pounds in a thirty-year-old caravan.

Gone were the Formica pine-effect worktops and the sofa and pull-out bed.

The interior now housed a state-of-the-art freezer and tea- and coffee-making equipment. Everything was painted white, apart from the ceiling, which was covered in Friesian cow sticky wallpaper. An old but comfy armchair in the corner had a small puppy curled up on it.

The outside was painted in pink-and-white stripes and had wind chimes and driftwood hanging from the sun blind.

A hand-painted menu offered many delicious flavours of ice cream.

At least a dozen hot holidaymakers were queuing.

Pearl was busy: "A double rum and raisin with fudge sauce and a chocolate flake for you," she said, passing the cone to a middle-aged mum.

"Two large 99s with extra clotted cream for you," she said, handing them to a couple of kids. "And a strong coffee for you." She poured one for the dad of the family. He took it and handed her a ten-pound note.

"Keep the change."

"Ah, thanks, sir." She put the cash in a small pot on the counter and looked at Jem and Abi. "Yes, my loves. What can I get you?"

"Two 99s, please. And would you like a paid helper?" Jem steamed straight in.

Pearl grinned. "Why? Do you want a job?"

"No, but my cousin Abi does."

Abi blushed furiously as Pearl laughed with delight.

"How fabulous! Can you keep an eye on the dog, look after any stray kids, watch the deckchairs and make a decent ice-cream scoop?"

Jeremy nudged Abi into answering. "Er. Yes. Well, I mean, I, like, have never done it before, but I'll try."

"Fair enough. You turn up tomorrow, nine thirty, and I'll show you the ropes. If you're no good, I'll pay you what I owe you — thirty quid — and we'll part friends. However, if you are any good, the job's yours till the end of the season. Do you have to go off to college or anything?"

"I go back to school at the beginning of September."

"Perfect." Pearl passed them their ice creams. "On the house. Be here in the morning, on time, and don't let me down."

Abi smiled up at this warm and lovely young woman. "Thank you. I won't."

They skipped up the path to the back gate of Atlantic House chanting, "We've got j-obs. We've got j-obs."

In the garden, Greg, Connie and Dorothy were gently snoozing. They woke as soon as the gate swung on its hinge.

215

"We've got jobs!" shouted Abi, running towards her father and falling on to his prone body.

Greg struggled to catch his breath. "Have you? Doing what?"

Abi told them all about it.

"Fantastic!" said Greg. "I am very impressed."

"Well done, darling," said Connie.

"Don't eat the profits," said Dorothy, peering over her sunglasses and looking pointedly at Abi's thighs.

CHAPTER
EIGHTEEN

Jem and Abi were almost late for their first day at work. Completely out of practice at waking up to an alarm, they didn't even remember to *set* an alarm.

Francis woke Jeremy at seven forty-five and made him eat some cereal before handing him a packed lunch and waving him off on his bike, bleary-eyed and with shorts drooping dangerously from his hips and exposing an unfortunate amount of pants and buttocks.

"Bye, son. Good luck," Francis called. Back in the kitchen he cleared the Weetabix crumbs from the table, unstacked the dishwasher and restacked the dirty cereal bowl and spoon. He made himself a cup of coffee and thought about Jeremy. He was full of paternal pride for this young man, sixteen, taller than he, but with his father's kindness and his mother's brains. Francis would have loved a large clutch of children. He had been an only child himself. At least Jem had Abi.

Abi? He looked up at the clock. Eight thirty-five. He'd better get her up.

Holding a steaming cup of tea in one hand, he knocked gently at her bedroom door.

"Come in," called a sleepy voice.

He opened the door and saw a body shrouded in bedclothes.

"Abi, it's eight forty-five. You'll be late for work."

A small hand with green-painted fingernails poked out of the duvet and pulled it down, revealing a dozy Abi.

"Oh," she managed as she watched her uncle move various makeup-stained tissues, her phone, and a dirty hairbrush to one side of her bedside table in order to find a place for the mug.

"Why didn't anyone wake me?"

"Well, everyone is still asleep. Did you forget to set your alarm?"

She sank back on to the pillows, closing her eyes with a small frown. "Oh. Yuh. Thanks, Uncle Francis."

"Get up quickly and I'll have some breakfast ready for you."

When she came down, Francis had made her a fried-egg sandwich and a packed lunch.

"Thanks, Unc. You're, like, the best."

They hugged one another and she set off across the lawn and through the private gate to the beach. He watched her go. Hair piled up in a bird's nest, caught with a tortoise-shell comb, walking with a rumpled, exhausted pace. Lovely Abi. His favourite niece. Technically, his only niece, but he thought that even if there were other nieces she'd still be his favourite.

"Hiya!" Pearl was opening the caravan for business. Her large friendly smile welcomed Abi. "Take that broom and sweep the inside of the van, would you. Last night I had some kids in here with sandy feet, playing with Blue." The little dog lying on the armchair looked at her mistress and thumped her tail on the floor. "Yes, Miss Blue. They loved you, didn't they?" Pearl said.

"Right, Abi. The forecast is a good 'un today. Slightly overcast, a little breeze and getting warmer as the day goes on. Perfect ice-cream weather. Exactly the way we like it. The tea urn needs filling up and heating. Ollie brought down the water containers, but I need you to keep topping it up through the day. OK?"

"Yes. Have you got a dust pan and brush?"

"What for?"

"This sand I've swept up."

"Bless you, no. Sweep it straight out of the door and back to where it belongs."

Abi swept everything out, filled up and turned on the tea urn, then sat down with Blue and tickled her ears.

"What are you doing down there?" asked Pearl, hands on her hips. "I don't pay you to tickle the dog, not when there's newspapers waiting to be collected."

Abi struggled to her feet. "Sorry. Where do I have to go for the papers?"

"The village shop in Higher Barton. They'll have my order ready. Oh, and get a couple of extra puzzle books: crosswords and sudokus. Those always sell well. There's a rucksack on the floor, carry them in that. My bike's parked outside."

"I've got a bike at the house."

"OK, use your own. But wear a helmet, please!" Pearl gave Abi a mock-stern look, then added, "I'm serious. These holidaymakers drive like maniacs with their big cars and roof racks."

"Don't worry, I will."

"Good. And no hanging about in the village. I'll see you in half an hour."

Abi was back with a couple of minutes to spare and found Pearl already four-deep in customers.

"Here she comes. Our newspaper girl. Abi, a *Sun* for Terry, please."

Abi pulled out a copy of the *Sun* and passed it to the man at the head of the queue. Pearl handed him a paper cup of tea at the same time. "There you are, Terry. D'you want a deckchair? Abi, get Terry a deckchair, please."

And so the day went on. Pearl knew everyone on the beach. If someone came along that she didn't know, she'd be on first-name terms with them by the time they left. Abi was amazed at how much information people were ready to give. Their address, here on holiday and back home; who they were with; their state of health; names of children, grandchildren and dogs . . . everything.

In a short lull, Abi asked Pearl how she did it. "I'm interested, that's all. The more special and important they feel, the more they'll come back and spend their holiday money." Pearl laughed. "I like them, they like me, *and* it's good for business. Make me a cup of tea, will you — and have one yourself."

The afternoon got hotter and sunnier and the trade for ice creams got brisker. Abi started to master the art of scooping the ice cream and balancing it perfectly on its cone.

Children flocked to the caravan to tickle Blue and take her for walks up and down the beach. "Take one of my plastic bags in case she does a poo," instructed Pearl. The kids loved hearing her say "poo" and diligently collected the steamy little bags and brought them to Pearl for inspection.

"Bless their little hearts!" said Pearl. Each child was given a Flake as a reward for their help.

By six o'clock, Abi's legs and jaw muscles were aching from standing and smiling all day. Pearl was as fresh as a daisy, her lipstick freshly applied and her glowing face tanned but never shiny.

"Right, young Abi. How do you think you've done today?"

Abi was surprised by the question. "Uh, I don't know. I hope I've done OK. I really enjoyed it."

"Which bit did you enjoy the best?"

"Serving the ice cream and talking to the kids."

"Good. Do you reckon you could do that every day till the end of August? Because, my girl, the job is yours if you want it."

"Oh, yes please." Abi hugged Pearl.

"Excellent. Tomorrow I want you here by eight forty-five, with the newspapers. By nine I want the tea urns on and the floor swept, ready for me at nine fifteen. I'm having a lie-in. I'll push the keys through your letter box when I close up tonight. OK?"

"Yeah. Great!"

"Off you go then, and I'll see you tomorrow."

Abi walked into the kitchen and flopped on a chair, yawning.

"Hi, darling. How did it go?" asked Greg, who was pecking at the keys on his laptop, having become quite proficient in the art of one-handed typing.

"S'all right. Knackering." Another theatrical yawn. "I'm going to have a bath."

On the stairs she met her mother. "Hi, darling. How was it?"

"It was OK. I'm so tired I'm going to have a bath."

"Oh, right. Supper's at seven thirty."

"What are we having?"

"Granny's done one of her shepherd's pies."

"Oh yum. Is Jem back yet?"

"I haven't seen him."

Connie went to the kitchen to find Greg, who, on seeing her, quickly pressed a button that made his computer go to screen saver.

She ambled over and put her arms round his shoulders.

"You seem to be working so hard this holiday. I've hardly spent any time with you." She kissed his head.

He flapped his broken arm in its cast. "It's this thing. I feel absolutely bloody useless. You and Pru have been so busy with the house. How's the roof looking?"

"Not bad. The roofer seems a nice man, even if he is a friend of Merlin's." She perched her bottom on the table and faced Greg. "He says it'll be finished tomorrow."

"What about Merlin? Any news on the boiler?"

"He says he's ordered it and it'll be here at the end of the week. In the meantime, the old one is at least giving us hot water and the leak under the sink has stopped." She ran her fingers across her neck and shoulders. "Fine holiday this is turning out to be. Your arm, the house . . . I could do with a day away from this place. Just the two of us. Can we do that?"

Greg looked at his wife. She looked exhausted. It was true: she had been working non-stop while he and Janie had been enjoying virtual sex via email. Maybe she deserved a bit of a treat.

"What would you like to do?"

"Nothing too complicated. A drive along the coast. Find a nice pub for lunch and sit in the sunshine. Hmm?" She moved off the table and sat in Greg's lap. She kissed him warmly. He put his good hand on her bottom and gave it a squeeze.

"Why not. My wife and I are going to have a day out tomorrow." They kissed again, more passionately this time.

"Get a room, can't you?" Abi came in with her hair wrapped in a towelling turban and wearing shortie silk pyjamas covered in pink hearts.

She picked up a magazine from the worktop and went out to the verandah where she collapsed, groaning, on to a sun lounger.

Her parents watched her. Connie giggled. "Drama school, do you think?"

"They couldn't teach her anything," smiled Greg.

"Hi, guys." Jem walked in and swung his shoulder bag down on to the table. "Does my face look red?" He crouched to examine his reflection in the toaster.

"A bit," replied his aunt. "Did you forget to put sun cream on?"

"Yeah. It didn't look that sunny."

Greg reopened his computer and started typing. "That's because the sun's rays bounce off the —"

"— sea. Yes, I did that at school. Well, now I've done the control experiment and can confirm that the sun's rays do indeed bounce off the sea and burn your bloody face to a crisp."

"Language, Jem." His mother appeared with dark circles under her eyes and a laundry basket under her arm. "Connie, are you making tea?"

"Yeah." Connie got off Greg's lap and stretched. "I'll put the kettle on."

Pru walked to the washing machine and began loading it. "I'm exhausted. What with Francis's eye and the house and everything, I shall need a holiday to get over this one." The washing machine started whirring happily and Pru yawned before sinking into a chair. "If you don't mind, I think I'm going to take a day off tomorrow."

Connie tightened her lips imperceptibly. "Tomorrow? The roofer is coming to finish off tomorrow and someone needs to be here to make sure he does."

"What about you?"

Greg came to the rescue. "Connie won't be here. I am taking my darling wife out for the day. She deserves a rest and a treat."

"And you think I don't?"

"No, Pru. Of course you do. Perhaps you and Francis could go out the day after tomorrow?" Greg was at his most charming. "Maybe even go away for the night? Mousehole or Sennen?" Then the clincher. "You really deserve it."

Connie bridled. "I'd like a night away too. God knows I could do with it."

"While you lot are making your social arrangements, is there any tea for a hard-working man of the sea?" Poor Jem, his face glowing like a red Christmas bauble, was still standing waiting for attention.

Francis came in from the garden with a selection of herbs. "Hi, Jem. Golly, your face looks red. I'll get you some after-sun. Lamb chops with fresh mint sauce and redcurrant and rosemary gravy, everybody?"

Ignoring this, Pru dived straight in: "Francis, we are having a day off tomorrow. We are going for a drive and lunch out."

"Are we?" he replied, opening the kitchen drawer where the first-aid kit was stored. "That's nice. Here, Jem, put this on." He handed Jeremy some calendula cream. "I'd love to have a day out with you."

"No, no," Connie said quickly. "It's our turn tomorrow. Yours the day after."

Greg saw his mother-in-law coming across the garden from The Bungalow and had an idea.

"Tell you what. Why don't we all have tomorrow off and ask Dorothy to babysit the roofer?"

CHAPTER
NINETEEN

Nothing ever goes according to plan with families. The following morning, Connie, who had got Abi and Jem out of the door and off to work, was looking forward to her day out, alone, with her husband. But her plan was to be thwarted.

Once she'd got the kids off she called Greg down for breakfast and spread a coastal map over the kitchen table. They were calculating how long it would take them to drive to Polperro and Fowey when Francis walked in, rubbing his hands together and saying, "What a great idea this is. Just the four of us out for the day. Like old times, eh? So, where are we going?"

Greg smiled, "Nice try, old man. Very funny. This is a day out for —"

But Francis wasn't listening. Pru had swept in, in a new Diane von Fürstenberg blue multi-print chiffon dress which, even Greg had to admit, made her look pretty good. He gave her an appreciative wolf whistle and got a punch on the arm from Connie.

"Thank you, Greg," Pru said condescendingly while glaring at Connie. "I felt the need to make an effort after looking like a charlady for days on end." She glanced at Connie's rolled-up jeans, Trevay T-shirt and fleece wrapped around her shoulders. "I see you've gone for comfort over style, Connie. Good for you." Connie glowered. Ignoring her, Pru continued, "Are we ready for our magical mystery tour? Let's get going. Greg, you can sit in the front and navigate. I'll drive."

Connie, looking horrified, gave Greg a poke. "Tell Pru what we have planned."

"Ah, well," said Greg. "You see, Connie and I were hoping to head to Polperro and have lunch in a little place that's rather special to us."

"That's a marvellous idea," said Pru. "Francis and I haven't been to Polperro for years. Let's go." And she was out in the hall collecting her keys and bag before they could stop her.

Dorothy twitched her net curtains. "They've gone. Pru's driving. She always reminds me of Cruella De Vil when she gets behind the wheel."

Henry laughed. "They deserve a day out. Weather's looking fantastic for the next few days. I hope it holds for Abi's party."

"Me too. I'm amazed she's found herself a job. And Jem too."

Henry nodded. "Good for them, I say. Character building. Children have it all handed to them on a plate these days. They'll know the value of a five-pound note after this summer."

Dorothy moved away from the window and sat opposite Henry in a matching armchair. "This is a different world to the one we grew up in. The grandchildren think we had dinosaurs for pets."

"Oh, I'm old-fashioned, I know. But those values still hold good."

"Not so old-fashioned . . ." She hesitated. "After all, isn't making an honest woman of me one of those values?"

Henry looked uncomfortable, the pattern on the carpet suddenly catching his interest. "Don't start that again. Besides, it's a bit late in the day now, old girl."

"Maybe." Dorothy twisted the ring on the third finger of her left hand. "I would have liked to arrive at the pearly gates with everything settled, though."

"Don't you worry, St Peter will have you down as just that in his ledger."

"Mmm."

They both sat and looked at each other.

"I'm only glad neither of us will be around when the girls find out," said Dorothy.

"They're mature women. They'll take it in their stride."

The doorbell gave a cheerful ding-dong. "Now who the hell is that?" sighed Henry.

Dorothy stood up. "I'll get it."

Henry listened. He could hear a woman's voice and Dorothy saying, "Come in, come in. I'm about to make coffee. Henry's in the front room. Go on in and say hello."

Henry moved his eyes to the door as Belinda poked her head in. He liked Belinda. Fun, uncomplicated and rather sexy. He got to his feet. "Hello, my dear. Please, take a seat."

"Hello, Mr Carew. I've just popped in to see if you or Mrs Carew want anything from the shops. Emily and I are going up a bit later." Emily came into the room. A tall and pretty but self-conscious teenager. "Hello, Mr Carew," she said in a quiet voice.

"Hello, Emily. No need to be so formal. Everyone calls me Henry or Poppa. Which do you prefer?"

"How nice," said Belinda. "May we call you Poppa?" She caught Dorothy's eye as the older woman elbowed her way through the door bearing a tray of coffee and shortbread. "Emily never knew her grandfathers."

"I'd be honoured." Henry smiled at Emily, who was taking a biscuit from the plate offered by Dorothy.

"And you can call me Dorothy or Granny."

"Isn't that lovely, Em?" Belinda beamed at Emily, who was looking embarrassed.

"Yes. Thank you."

"It's an honour, young lady. Tell me, have you ever played Lawyer, Lawyer?"

"No."

"Oh, Henry, don't be a bore. Emily doesn't want to play board games, do you, dear?"

Emily, embarrassed, murmured, "I don't know."

"Of course you want to play," said Belinda. She looked at Henry, "You invented it, didn't you?"

Henry laughed self-deprecatingly. "As a matter of fact, I did. Who told you?"

"Francis did, ages ago. From what he said, you saved the family business from going under."

"Something like that," said Henry, getting to his feet. "So, Emily, do you fancy a game? I'll teach you how to beat anyone."

"OK," said Emily, not exactly brimming with enthusiasm.

Henry got up and went to the conservatory, Emily trailing after him. "Come along then."

Once the doors were safely closed, Dorothy smiled and said to Belinda, "They'll be gone for at least an hour." She plumped up the cushion behind her back and settled down. "So, Belinda, tell me all about yourself."

Belinda stirred a large spoonful of sugar into her coffee. "There's not much to tell. Forty-something single mum. Struggling a bit to make ends meet. My cup's always half-full, though — I try to focus on the positive."

"Quite so." Dorothy watched as Belinda helped herself to a biscuit. "What happened to Emily's father?"

"Oh, Brett's still around. We're good friends, as a matter of fact. But when he met Steve, he met the man of his dreams."

It took a superhuman effort for Dorothy to prevent her carefully drawn eyebrows from going into orbit. "Steve?"

"Yeah." Belinda took another biscuit. "It was a shock, naturally. I'd had no idea Brett was gay. I'd always counted myself lucky that I had such a kind husband with tremendous empathy." She wiped the crumbs from her bust so that they bounced off her skirt and on to Dorothy's carpet. "And now I have Brett *and* Steve, so I am lucky, when you think about it."

"Oh dear." Dorothy was bemused. "Did your family help?"

230

"Well, my mum was very understanding. My dad had abandoned her when I was a baby. Only in his case it was for another woman. We never heard from him again."

Dorothy tutted. "How can men be so feckless when a child is involved?" She leaned forward to offer Belinda the plate of biscuits.

"Oh, thank you. These are delicious. It's my breakfast."

"Would you care for some toast?"

"No, no. This is lovely." Another crumb fell, but this time into Belinda's cavernous cleavage. Dorothy wondered if, when Belinda stood up, it would work its way past her knickers and join its friends on her carpet.

"So, how do you know my son-in-law, Francis?"

Belinda popped the last piece of shortbread in her mouth and wiped her fingers on her skirt. "At school. When Em joined year nine, last autumn, I thought I'd help out with the PTA. I'm good at organising and it's a nice way to make friends. Frankie is a brilliant committee member. Organised and generous with his time. A lovely man."

"When you say 'Frankie', you are referring to Francis?" Dorothy queried.

"Oh, sorry — yes. It's a name I started calling him and now a lot of the committee do too. I think it annoys him a bit."

Dorothy raised her eyebrows. "Surely not?"

"It's my little joke. Anyway, he and I have got really friendly and when he told me he was coming down here for the summer and that there were cottages to rent next door, I thought, why not? Em deserves a break. I spoke to Big Ben yesterday and it looks as though we can stay right through August; he's had a late cancellation and has reduced the rent down to almost nothing."

Belinda drained her coffee cup and placed it on the tray. "Which is great, because it means I can get stuck in helping Abi with her party. Which reminds me, I'm going into Trevay to have a look for party inspiration round the shops. Is there anything I can get for you while I'm there?"

"If you're sure you don't mind, there were a few items — I made out a list earlier. It's in the kitchen." She stood and, picking up the tray, headed for the kitchen. Belinda fell in behind her.

Dorothy put the tray down on the spotless work surface and found her glasses, pen and notepad. After adding *Shortbread biscuits x2* to the list, she passed it to Belinda. "Now then, where did I put my purse . . ."

"Don't worry, we'll settle up when I get back."

"Thank you, Belinda. That really is most kind. You've certainly saved me a trip. Now, let's find Emily and Henry."

The Lawyer, Lawyer board and pieces were all laid out on the conservatory table, with Henry and Emily hunched over it. Emily was placing a black cap on her head while reading from a card: "You shall be taken from this place and hanged by the neck."

Henry's laugh rumbled from his chest. "Hold on, I only got a parking ticket!"

232

Emily started to giggle too. "It's the sentence card. I can't help picking it up. It was at the top of the pile."

Henry spotted Dorothy and Belinda by the door. "Well, the law is an ass. We all know that to be true."

"Come on, Em. We've got things to do," said Belinda, holding out her hand.

Emily put the card and black cap down reluctantly. "Can we play again, Poppa?" she asked Henry.

"Oh, rather. You just come right over, any time you like."

CHAPTER
TWENTY

As they watched Belinda's car disappear down the lane, Dorothy found the spare set of keys to Atlantic House.

"Come on, Henry — we're going to check on the roofer and take a look at what they've been up to next door."

The moment they unlocked the door, the smell of fresh polish and washing powder hit them with a pleasing strength. They wandered from room to room, Henry checking that the television was still working and that the woodwork was being rubbed down and properly prepared for painting. Dorothy went into every corner, trying to spot anything that had been missed by duster or vacuum. When the downstairs passed the inspection with flying colours, she made her way upstairs. The curtains in one of the bedrooms were missing, still at the cleaners, but the carpets were newly shampooed and pristine.

Dorothy checked her old en-suite bathroom, now used by Pru and Francis. The basin tap was dripping.

"Henry?" she called. "Has that bloody plumber finished? Only the tap is still dripping up here."

Henry's muffled voice came from somewhere downstairs, possibly outside. She caught the words "boiler" and "leak" and "damn cowboy" and went to find him.

He wasn't in the kitchen, but the back door was open. As she walked through it and out into the garden, she found him coming out of the top cellar that led down to the cave.

"That useless bugger! Look in here." He went back through the old fortified door and she followed.

"Oh my God!" she said. The floor was six inches deep in water.

"Quite. That stupid idiot hasn't tightened the joints on the piping. Well, I hope he's not expecting to be paid for this."

They heard the sound of whistling outside. Henry moved faster than a man half his age.

"That's the bugger now! Let me deal with him."

Merlin took Henry's furious rant with annoying calm, rolling a leisurely cigarette all the while. When Henry had run out of steam, Merlin lit up and asked, "What would you like me to do to make it all better?"

Henry returned to the boil again. "It's bloody obvious, isn't it?"

"Righto, Mr Carew, I'll see to it directly. I'll have to turn the water off at the mains for now. Then I'll be back Monday."

Henry stood aghast at the brass neck of the man. "Monday? It's Wednesday today. We can't go without water for that long!"

"Ah, but I'm a busy man. Got a job on at Higher Barton, see."

"Buggering up their plumbing too?" blasted Henry. "In that case, I'll get a proper plumber in to sort this out. Don't bother sending me any bills as I shan't be paying them."

Dorothy, worried that they might not be able to find a plumber, stepped in. "Merlin, please. Whatever it costs, do it today."

"Well, now, that'll be double time and cancellation of my other job, so . . ."

"I'll give you two hundred in cash, provided it's done by tonight." Dorothy held her hand out for Merlin to shake.

He hesitated for a second then took her hand. "You drive a hard bargain, Mrs Carew."

Henry walked away before he blew his top at his wife's profligate waste of money.

Dorothy continued: "I see your friend hasn't repaired the tiles on the roof."

"He'll be here directly, and he'll do a proper job up there. Just one or two bits to tidy up in the attic. I was going to attend to them today, but I can do them next week an' all. OK?"

Not waiting for an answer, Merlin jumped athletically into the cab of his van and drove off as if he hadn't a care in the world.

Dorothy turned to Henry, who was staring in horrified fascination at the retreating van, and said soothingly, "Now then, I'm taking you out to the pub for lunch. You could do with a drink."

The beautiful historic pub restaurant, built to lean over the small river that ran through Polperro, was cool and

236

welcoming. Pru chose a table for them, and called for the menus.

"I'll have the deep-fried brie with gooseberry marmalade, please," said Connie, handing her menu back to the young waiter.

Pru gave her order: "Dressed crab with a plain green salad, thank you. And the same for my husband."

"I was thinking about the courgette soup and chargrilled quorn burger," said Francis.

"You'll prefer the crab." Pru looked over Francis's head to Greg. "Greg, what'll you have?"

"When did pubs stop serving proper pub food?" Greg grumbled, "I'll have the steak, very rare, with chips, fried mushrooms and grilled tomatoes, please."

"Very good, sir. Would you like your French fries chunky or skinny?"

"I don't know. What do I like, Con?"

"Chunky."

"Chunky, please."

"Very good." The waiter made a note on his pad — probably something insulting, thought Greg — before enquiring, "And to drink . . .?"

When the small party was finally settled and the drinks had arrived, Greg raised his pint to Pru and Connie. "Cheers, girls! Thank you for looking after the house and two old crocks of husbands."

They all chinked their glasses.

"Lovely spot," remarked Francis.

"Isn't it," said Connie fondly. "Greg brought me here when we were first together."

"How did you find it?" asked Francis, curious.

"The old AA book recommended it."

"It's amazing you made it here at all," sniffed Pru, "if your sense of direction was as bad then as it was today."

"That junction said Tadcombe left," protested Greg. "I can't be held responsible for the mysteries of Cornish signposting."

"OK, children. Stop now," pleaded Connie, anxious to quell any further debate on the subject.

The food arrived and was eaten in near silence. The sound of the river running playfully outside and the view of its fern-lined banks was enough to keep them occupied with safe topics of conversation to the end of the meal.

As Greg paid for the meal, which Pru noticed went on his Carew company credit card, Connie asked him, "Would you come with me down to the harbour? We can take the cliff path and look at the view, the same as we did all those years ago." She snuggled against his cast as he used his good arm to put his wallet back into his trouser pocket.

Connie's intention was to spend a bit of time alone with her husband, but once again she was to be thwarted.

"OK," sighed Pru. "As long as it's not too far."

The view from the cliffs was worth the walk. To the left was the open sea and to the right the ancient fishing harbour. They found a bench and sat watching the sea as it curled over itself and sent wisps of spray flying like smoke in the wind. Then they turned their attention to

238

the harbour and watched as a woman and a teenager, presumably her daughter, drove a Land Rover towing a small motorboat down a slipway. At the water's edge the Land Rover reversed to the water and the daughter jumped out. In a few minutes, she had detached the boat and eased it into the waves.

"Abi's party is going to be great fun," said Francis. "Belinda is taking her role as party organiser very seriously."

"Isn't she just?" Connie winced, then continued: "My baby — seventeen. She wants to learn to drive, but I'm not keen on encouraging that."

"She'll have to one day," said Greg.

"I know. But seventeen is too young. I mean, the roads at home are so busy and narrow."

They were still watching the girl and her motorboat. The older woman had driven up the slipway and off down the road. Meanwhile the girl climbed aboard and started the boat's engine. Within minutes she was heading confidently out to sea.

"That's very cool," said Greg. "What a nice little boat."

"And a beautiful day to take it out," said Francis.

Connie watched her husband with pursed lips. "No. You are not having a boat."

"Not for me! A birthday present for Abi. Give her some adventure without the dangers of the road. It'll be fun for us all."

On the journey home from Polperro, Greg and Connie bickered over the proposed new boat.

"What would she do with a boat?" Connie argued.

"She'd use it for fun and water skiing with her friends."

"She doesn't water ski."

"Precisely. Now she can learn."

"She's got the *Dorothy* if she wants a boat."

"You know what Henry's like about that thing. He won't let anyone take it out without him. She needs some freedom."

"But I don't want her to have that sort of freedom."

On and on they went while, in the back, Francis read his Kindle and Pru gently snored.

"Helloooo!" Belinda was bellowing from the front door.

"In the kitchen," called Connie, noticing Francis scuttle out to the garden.

Belinda pushed her way into the room with armfuls of bags. Her bracelets were tight on her podgy wrists, the buttons on her shirt mostly undone, revealing her tanned bosom and a pink bra. Her tiny mini skirt was riding up over freckled thighs.

"Where's Francis? I have some ideas on the party food."

Catching sight of Francis scampering across the lawn towards the beach gate, Connie summoned him in a loud voice: "Francis! Belinda is here and would like to speak to you."

He stopped running and turned towards the house, knowing when he was defeated.

"Look at all this lovely stuff Belinda has bought for the party, Francis!"

He could see a lot of shimmering net fabric and boxes of fairy lights bursting out of the carrier bags Belinda was dumping on the kitchen table.

Plucking some of the netting out of the bag, she walked towards Francis and wrapped it around his shoulders. "You'd make a wonderful sea nymph, Frankie."

He tried to smile and shrug the fabric off himself at the same time, but he wasn't quick enough.

"Uh-uh. Stay there. Let me find . . ." She dug in the bag again. "Ah, here we are!" She pulled out a necklace made of winkle shells and put it round his neck. "There we are! Give us a kiss."

"Francis, what are you doing?" Pru had come in from the hallway.

Belinda threw her arms round Francis's neck and chanted, "I am under the spell of the mighty sea god, Frankie. There is nothing I can do . . ." And she slid down Francis's thighs and draped herself about his knees.

Connie hooted with laughter.

Pru felt that peculiar draught catch her heart again. Noticing the change in her expression, Francis quickly took off the shells and stepped over the prostrate Belinda towards his wife. "Pru, Belinda is just showing us some of the stuff she got for Abi's party."

Belinda stood up.

"I've decided on a sea-fairy theme. Green, blue and pink. Wait till you see the lights and candles and costumes I've bought!"

"Abi's not keen on pink," Connie ventured.

"Not keen on pink!" Belinda shook her head disbelievingly. "Every girl loves pink. Get me a cold drink would you, Con? It's so hot. Is Abi in?"

"Connie was at the fridge, pouring a beaker of juice. She put it into Belinda's outstretched hand.

"Oh, that's better. Thank you."

"Abi's not home yet. I'm expecting her around six-ish."

"Right, I'll wait for her. What's for tea? I'll help you make it. You don't mind me and Emily joining you, do you?"

Connie had no say in the matter. Before she knew it, Belinda was knocking up a bolognese sauce and leaving a trail of saucepans for Connie to wash up.

"Belinda! I love it! It's going to look amazing. Isn't she clever, Mum?" Abi had come in from work more animated than Connie had seen her in ages. All the family were watching as Belinda pulled out one extraordinary thing after another.

"Yes," said Connie, wanly, trying to clear the table and lay it up for eight. "So clever. I didn't think you liked pink."

"Pppffff! Of course I like pink! Who doesn't! Honestly, Mum, where did you get that idea from!"

"Oh, you know your mother," said Greg, standing over Belinda and topping up her glass while trying to get a good gander down her cleavage. "She's very good at getting the wrong end of the stick."

"I am not," huffed Connie.

"Yes, you are," chorused Abi, Greg and Pru.

242

Connie felt crushed. She had to dig the nails of her right hand into the palm of her left to stop herself from crying.

"Can I help you dish up, Con?" asked Francis kindly.

Eventually everybody was seated and munching their supper.

"This spaghetti bolognese is delicious," said Francis, smiling at Belinda.

"One of my own recipes, Frankie. Glad you like it," shrieked a wine-filled Belinda. "I'll give it to you, if you like?" she leered.

Greg laughed raucously. "Ooh, now that's a promise I couldn't turn down, Francis! Ha ha ha."

Connie turned to him. "Sit down, Greg. You've had too much wine."

"Yes, and you, Francis. I think you've had quite enough." Pru looked sternly across the table at him.

"I've only had one glass."

"Yes, but after all that fresh air today, it's gone to your head." Pru stood up decisively and put the bottles of open wine away. "Thank you, Belinda, for a lovely supper. I'm sure you need to get Emily to bed."

"But it's almost nine . . ."

"Quite," said Pru determinedly.

"Oh. I see." Belinda stood up, "Come on, Emily. We need to leave the family to themselves and get back to Dairy Cottage."

"I was going to watch TV with Abi and Jem." Emily couldn't hide her disappointment.

Belinda was gathering up bags and bits. "You must always leave people wanting more. Never overstay the hospitality of others. Now come on."

They left and the room was instantly quieter.

Pru started to stack the plates. "Thank God she's gone."

CHAPTER
TWENTY-ONE

"Storms are still battering the Eastern Seaboard of the United States," said the breakfast television newscaster. "Several hundred families have been evacuated from their homes after a second night without electricity. This report from our Washington correspondent . . ."

Henry and Dorothy watched the footage of distraught householders, looking on helplessly as their houses and possessions were swept away by the raging torrent.

"They should be grateful they don't have Merlin as their plumber," said Dorothy. "Poor devils."

"They keep promising us a hooley blowing in on this side of the Atlantic, but we've been lucky so far."

Dorothy smiled at him. "It's been a pretty good summer, hasn't it? Apart from the flood next door and the various injuries sustained by the boys."

Henry chuckled. "Bloody useless, the lot of them. Still, they have got the house back in order. And the moron Merlin should be finished by the end of today."

"Are you really going to make the kids pay?"

Dorothy and Henry always referred to their grown-up daughters as "the kids".

"Well, I might chip in. I'll nip over later and take a look at what kind of job Merlin's made of it."

"He'll know you're checking up on him."

"I have a plan." He tapped the side of his nose. "I'm taking the iPad — that way I can pretend that I need the kids to help me with it."

"Very good, Sherlock."

"I want an email address. Where do you get one from?"

Dorothy gave a dry laugh. "How should I know? Ask Jem or Abi. They've got good brains on them. They'll get you one."

"Hey, Poppa!" Abi had reached the cliff-path gate and was letting herself into the garden.

"Hello. How was work today?"

"Knackering!"

He ruffled her sun-streaked and untidy hair. "Poor old you." He kissed her and she nestled herself into his warm, navy-jumpered chest.

When he let her go, she put her hand in her shorts pocket and pulled out a wodge of folded notes. "Pearl's paid me, though."

"Good stuff. Shall we run away to Penzance and catch a boat to Spain? Don't tell Granny."

Laughing, they arrived at the French windows just as Greg and Merlin emerged from the kitchen, the latter carrying his tool bag.

"I'll put the invoice through the door as soon as I've worked it out," Merlin was saying, shaking Greg's hand.

"Thank you for everything, old man. Obviously, if you can sharpen your pencil, I'd be grateful. I can pay cash, if you like."

At that moment he noticed Henry. "Oh, hello, Henry. Merlin's finished. Done a great job. The roof, new boiler and pipework. All excellent."

Henry gave Merlin a long look then slowly said, "It had better be good. And the price had better reflect the ridiculously generous cash payment my wife gave you the other day."

Merlin outstared Henry. "Oh yes. I always do a good job for the price."

Greg, eager to get Merlin off the premises, clapped him on the back. "Well, thanks again, old man. Don't forget, if cash helps . . ." He winked. "I'm off to have a hot bath. Ha ha ha." He laughed insincerely and steered Merlin to his van.

Henry's gimlet eyes followed them.

"You don't like him, do you, Poppa?" said Abi.

"I'll like him a lot more once I've checked his work and found it satisfactory."

Henry took his time checking all the upstairs taps for leaks and loos for flushes. Then he turned on all the radiators and checked the boiler's thermostat.

Greg dogged him. "It's OK. Merlin's done a good job."

Henry refrained from passing judgement. "While the heating comes on, I'm just going to make sure the outdoor cellar room is dry."

He pushed open the heavy old door and stepped into the ancient, cold store room. The flood had left behind a smell of damp, but other than that the floor was dry enough. He opened the door that led to the underground cave and flicked on the lights. The steps were a bit slippery, but nothing out of the ordinary. He climbed down them and into the natural boathouse beneath. The tide was low and the *Dorothy* was resting on the shingle. Shrouded in her cover, he knew she was perfectly dry.

Tomorrow morning, weather permitting, he would take her out. Maybe get Dorothy to make a picnic.

Which reminded him. He must get one of the grandchildren to set his iPad up. Internet, email, Skype, apps — he wanted the lot.

Back inside Atlantic House, the radiators were warming up nicely. Greg was looking pleased with himself.

"Good as new," he told Henry. "All the rads are toasty warm."

Henry felt the radiator in the hall and had to agree it felt fine. "OK, let's see what the bill is."

Greg turned away from Henry and threw his eyes to heaven while walking back into the kitchen. Henry followed him.

Jeremy was home from work and pouring himself a cold drink. "Why's it so hot in here?"

"The heating's fixed and your grandfather and I are checking it. I'll turn it down now."

"Good. Hey, Poppa."

"Jem, just the fellow! I need your help with my iPad . . ."

★ ★ ★

248

"There you are, Poppa. All sorted."

"Marvellous! Would you mind showing me again how I send an email."

Patiently, Jem showed him again.

"And my email address is . . .?"

"I'll write it down for you, here." Jeremy wrote *henry.carew@carewfbg.com*. "I've connected you to the company email system so you'll get all the messages that Dad gets."

"Excellent. Will you send me my first email?"

Jeremy tapped out a message on his phone and within a few seconds Henry's iPad went "ping". Following Jem's step-by-step instructions, he managed to open and read the message:

Hi Poppa. Here is your first mail. Love Jem.

"That's wonderful, my boy. Your grandmother will be amazed that I've joined the twenty-first century, at last."

As he carried the laptop over to The Bungalow, Henry heard a succession of pings. He couldn't wait to read them.

Settling himself in the conservatory with the first Scotch of the evening, he opened them up. They were all addressed to Greg. Assuming this was something to do with sharing online access with the entire Carew company, Henry opened the first one with interest.

It was an invite addressed to Greg, for a corporate golf day in the autumn. He read three or four emails from the sales and marketing team, all reporting positive interest and figures. Next was an email from Greg's secretary, Janie, with the subject heading "Bloomers". He clicked on it. It took him only a few lines to realise that his son-in-law was cheating on his daughter.

For a moment Henry sat, unmoving, absorbing the ramifications. His instinct was to go next door, grab Greg by the throat and sling him out. His second was to keep this to himself until he'd thought it through.

He poured himself another whisky. Greg had a good marriage and a loving wife in Connie. Didn't he? Henry clenched his fist, fighting the urge to march over there and smash it into Greg's face.

Henry was no stranger to the misery of an unhappy marriage, but he'd hoped his daughters would never have to go through what he'd endured. How could Greg do this to Connie and Abi?

Much as he hated Greg at that moment, preying on his mind was the knowledge that he hadn't exactly been a model husband himself.

CHAPTER
TWENTY-TWO

Henry hadn't slept a wink. All night he'd been tossing and turning, trying to decide what to do. Should he confront Greg? Tell Connie? Upset Abi before her birthday? Early the next morning he got out of bed and put on his dressing gown. His slippers made track marks in the dewy grass as he walked across the garden to Atlantic House. He managed to catch Jem before he went to work.

"Ah, Jem. Just the chap. I appear to be picking up your Uncle Greg's emails on my iPad and I wonder if you could show me how to stop that?"

Jeremy, swallowing a large glass of orange juice, wiped his mouth with the back of his hand.

"Yeah, no worries, Poppa. Can it wait till tonight? You can delete anything you don't want." He grabbed his bag and packed lunch. "Drag the arrow to the dustbin icon and left click." He gave his grandfather a quick hug. "Laters."

Back in the solitude of his bedroom, Henry did as instructed and removed the incriminating email, along with all the others addressed to Greg.

Then he snapped closed the iPad cover and hid it in his wardrobe.

Dorothy was still in the shower. He didn't want to face her until he'd come up with a solution to the Greg problem, so he slipped out of the house to go and get the boat ready.

As he walked across the lawn to the fortified door that led to the cave, he saw Greg and Connie waving to him from the kitchen. Greg was looking pleased with himself, standing there with his arm draped round Connie. It was all Henry could do to stop himself running over there to confront his philandering cheat of a son-in-law. His hand clenched into a tight fist as he imagined landing a punch that would wipe that smirk off Greg's face. Instead he smiled grimly and walked on.

Opening the door into the old stone room, now used as a store for household detritus, he took in the familiar smell of sea damp and the sound of the water lapping at the bottom of the rough flight of rock steps ahead of him. He often thought of the young girl who had died down here. Such a tragedy. How would any parent recover from that? A painful stab of loss made him catch his breath, and he was aware of a lump forming in his throat. God, what was this? He put his hand out to the damp wall to steady himself. Tears stung his eyes and he swallowed hard. He fumbled for an old stool and sat on it. He told himself that what was past was past. He had Dorothy and Connie and Pru. He was blessed. But what should he do with the knowledge he had about Greg? If he told Connie, it would kill her marriage. Could he do that to her? He didn't know. He hoped the answer would come to him. Standing up, he

252

switched on the boathouse lights and descended the steps to the cave.

The *Dorothy* was resting in her hammock hoist, suspended above the water. He checked the boat's bottom and twin propellers and ran his hand along the sleek curves of the hull. Satisfied that everything was in good order, he lowered the hoist and eased the boat into the rising tide.

Forty-five minutes later, he was putting away his cleaning cloths and thinking about turning on the engine, when he saw Dorothy enter the cave with Belinda. Belinda was carrying a large cool box.

"Hi, Poppa." She waved to him. "Dorothy asked if I'd like to join your little cruise, so the least I could do was to pack a picnic."

"Well, you are very welcome, my dear." He got off the boat and stepped on to the rock floor that doubled as a harbour wall. "Let me help you aboard."

The women got themselves settled and Henry gave them each a life jacket, untied the ropes securing the boat to the wall and turned on the engine. The deeply pleasing throb bounced around the cave.

"OK, girls, duck your heads as we go out. The ceiling is a bit low." Henry confidently manoeuvred his pride and joy round to face the cave entrance. Belinda couldn't see the outside world yet. The narrow passageway took a twist to the left and then to the right before she could see daylight ahead of them.

Coming out into the warm sunshine they surprised a basking pair of seals, who flopped from their rocky ledge into the sea.

"Seals!" Belinda laughed.

Dorothy patted her hand. "We might be lucky and see the dolphins."

"Really?"

Dorothy nodded as she tied a cotton spotted handkerchief over her hair. "If we're lucky!"

Now that they were clear of the rocks, Henry gently opened the throttle. Within moments they were bouncing over the waves with the wind in their faces.

Belinda trailed her hand overboard so that her fingers were in the water. "This is heavenly!" she shouted above the engine.

Henry was in his element. The *Dorothy* always had this effect on him; it was as if all anxious thoughts were whipped away by the breeze and scattered in the turbulent wake behind him. He took them out to sea and round a small island that was home to a reasonably large seal colony. He slowed the engine and let it idle as Belinda foraged for her camera and took photos.

The weather was fine and the sea flat. "Would you like to pop across to Trevay?"

Dorothy shook her head. "No, let's go to Shellsand Bay. We can eat Belinda's picnic."

"Righto, Number One." He pushed the throttle on again and for the next twenty minutes they raced and bounced the waves to Shellsand Bay.

He dropped anchor just offshore and the three of them sat in the comfortable leather seats munching the houmous salad wraps and sticky slices of flapjack that Belinda had made.

"I love the sea," she said. "I grew up on the South Coast and loved going on day trips with my mum. Brighton was my favourite; it was always so busy and full of life. The pier scared me, though. I didn't like seeing the water between the planks."

"Is your mother still alive?" asked Dorothy.

"No, she died just over a year ago. She'd suffered a massive stroke that left her almost paralysed. It meant she had to go into a nursing home, because she was unable to do anything for herself. But she still had all of her marbles, which made it so much harder to bear."

"I'm sorry," said Dorothy.

"Not your fault," said Belinda, taking a bite of flapjack.

"What about your father?" asked Henry.

"I don't remember much about him. He walked out when I was a baby. I found some bits and pieces about him in Mum's papers. I've been wondering about tracking him down."

"What did he do for a living?" asked Henry, reaching for his second piece of flapjack.

Belinda looked at him steadily. "Mum never told me."

"Where did you grow up?" asked Dorothy.

"Pevensey Bay. We had a little flat just off the seafront. My mum was very beautiful. She had a few boyfriends in her time. They helped her with money, I suspect, but she worked in T J Hughes, the old department store. On the cosmetics counter."

"Where was her nursing home?"

"Oh, in Eastbourne — God's waiting room." Belinda gave a rueful smile and started to pack up bits of sandwich bag and tinfoil.

Dorothy thought about her own family. "It must have been horrible for you all."

"Yeah. It was . . . Is." Belinda shrugged and put on a smile. "But life is what it is. Me and Emily, Brett and Steve — we're OK." She gave a laugh. "And get me: sitting on a swanky speedboat with one of the most handsome captains in Cornwall! Can it get any better?"

Connie was reversing into a perilous parking space on the edge of a quay next to the River Fal. Greg was blocking her view as he turned to see what she might hit.

"For God's sake, woman, there's a bollard behind us."

"I know, and I could see it better if you sat back in your seat and let me park. That big head of yours is not see-through, you know."

She moved forward a little and then slid back into the space.

"Bloody hell, Connie, there's a thirty-foot drop behind us!" Greg yelled, making her jump.

She stamped on the brake and shouted back: "I'm doing you a favour, you stupid man. I don't want Abi to have a bloody boat for her birthday, but I have brought you here because you have a broken arm and I'm trying to be nice! OK?"

A youngish man in faded red cotton shorts with a navy blue jumper was coming towards them. They both immediately plastered on their best fake smiles.

Connie got out. "Hello! You must be Peter. I'm Mrs Wilson and this —" she waved vaguely to where Greg was struggling to get out of the car — "is my husband."

"Nice to meet you." Peter shook her hand and that of the advancing Greg. "I've got a super little boat for you. Perfect for your daughter. Come and have a look."

The small grey RIB was bobbing gaily on the water. Peter handed Connie and then Greg into it.

"You sit here in the front seat, Mrs Wilson and your husband and I will sit behind the console while I take her out."

The men discussed torque and trim and engines and stuff while Connie enjoyed her comfortable seat and view of Falmouth from the water.

"Why's it called a rib?" she ventured.

Greg tutted and said impatiently, "Rigid Inflatable Boat. It's got a rigid hull and blow-up sides. I thought you'd know that."

Peter added more kindly, "Many people ask the same question, don't worry. It makes the boat very light and easy to handle."

"What happens if you get a puncture?" asked Connie.

"You have to be careful of barnacles and such, but you can get it fixed."

Connie would have liked to ask more, but Greg was monopolising Peter's attention again.

Later, as they left the sales office with their invoice and a promise that the boat would be delivered in time for Abi's birthday, Greg was buoyant.

"What a little corker we've got there. Perfect for the family."

"It's Abi's, not the family's," said Connie, opening the door for Greg and helping him in.

"Of course it's Abi's," he snapped. "But while she's at uni it'll need to be taken out and used." He fixed his seat belt in place. "Great name, though, eh? Am I genius or what?"

"It's OK," said Connie, starting up the engine.

"OK?" It's genius. *Abi's Gale* — she'll love it."

"What shall we get for Abi's birthday?" Dorothy asked Henry over a lunchtime prawn sandwich in their local pub.

"Money. That's what she wants."

"Too boring. I'd like to give her some jewellery. It's a custom for grandmothers to pass their engagement rings to their granddaughters."

Henry ignored this and continued eating.

"If I had an engagement ring to give. Or a wedding ring," needled Dorothy.

"Good God, woman. You are my wife. There has never been anyone can hold a candle to you."

Dorothy rounded on him. "Oh, I'm your wife, am I?"

Henry put his hand to his forehead and winced. "You know what I mean. In every sense that matters, you are my wife."

"Except in the sense that *really* matters."

Henry tilted his head towards the nearby tables that were filled with lunchtime diners.

258

"Dorothy, lower your voice. Do you want the whole pub to hear? This isn't the time or the place."

"When exactly would be a good time for you, Henry? It's been more than forty years and you still haven't told me when would be a good time. You never want to talk about it. I've had enough — and I don't care who bloody well knows about it!"

Henry raised his hands in a gesture of conciliation. "Darling. Why all this now? Let's finish lunch and then I promise we will talk about this later."

Eyes brimming with tears, Dorothy pushed aside her plate. "I'm not hungry any more." She picked up her bag and got to her feet. "You may not want to discuss it, Henry, but the fact remains: I am not and never have been your wife. Susan is your wife."

Henry watched helplessly as she stood and fumbled with her handbag. Finding her sunglasses, she did her best to make a dignified exit.

CHAPTER
TWENTY-THREE

"I can't believe our baby is going to be seventeen in two days' time, can you?" Connie was sitting in bed, completing her nightly routine of creaming her feet and hands. She was rubbing vigorously at her cuticles as Greg sat on the bed and lifted his legs under the covers.

"No. I can't. Where did the time go? We're lucky that she's got this far without doing anything illegal."

"That we know of," said Connie, screwing the lid back on to the hand-cream tube.

"Well, she hasn't got a boyfriend, so we know she's still innocent in that sense."

Connie gave a quiet laugh.

"What's that supposed to mean?" asked Greg.

"Nothing." She turned to face him. "But teenage girls are very good at having private lives that remain private."

"I would know if she'd been up to anything. I could tell just by looking at her," said Greg smugly.

"Really?"

"Yes."

"OK." Connie reached for the bedside light and turned it off. "Good night."

"Good night."

In the darkness, with the house settling around them and the dull shush of the unsleeping sea outside their bedroom window, Greg began to worry about Abi and her purity. Connie, on the other hand, smiled a secret smile and closed her eyes, reliving once again her own seventeenth birthday.

She'd been alone in the house — she couldn't remember why — when there was a knock at the front door. She opened it to find Merlin leaning casually against the porch wall, looking very desirable.

"Hey, birthday princess. I hear you've got the key to the door today?"

"Not quite," Connie had giggled. "I'm only seventeen."

"Shame — I was going to take you for your first legal drink." He had stepped into the hall, uninvited, and closed the door behind him.

Connie felt a shiver of anxiety. "Pru's not here."

"It's you I've come to see, birthday girl." He leaned in and gave her a peck on the cheek. "It's very hot outside. Can I have a cold drink?"

"Yes. Sorry. Come into the kitchen."

He stood behind her as she opened the fridge door. "I've got some Coke or orange juice . . . Milk?"

Laughing, he reached his hand in and pulled out a tin of shandy. "This is more like it. But I can't drink alone — will you join me?"

Connie had tasted a sip of her father's shandy and wasn't keen on the flavour, but wanting to appear sophisticated she agreed and got out two glasses.

He took the tins and walked with them into the big drawing room. "Quite a house." He opened one tin with a hiss and offered it to Connie. She poured it into a glass and then did the same with the second tin. "Come and sit on the sofa next to me."

Connie did as she was asked and he sat down next to her, very close.

"Cheers."

"Cheers." They clinked glasses.

Connie wasn't sure what to say next, but it didn't seem to matter. Merlin started talking.

"Like your sister you're a very 'andsome woman. Different, mind, but I bet you've got plenty of admirers an' all."

"Have I?" She took a quick mouthful of the bittersweet shandy.

"Don't pretend you haven't seen the boys lookin' at you on the beach."

Connie, who had hoped this was the case, shook her head. "No."

"Yeah, an' some of them 'ave been asking me to put in a good word for them."

"Have they?"

"Oh yeah."

Connie took another sip and felt its unfamiliar alcohol warmth hit her tummy. "Who?"

Merlin laughed and drained his glass. "I'll get us each another one of these, then I'll tell you."

When he came back, with two more tins, he sat down next to her and turned his sleepy, sexy blue-green eyes on her. "Where were we?"

262

"You were going to tell me who had asked about me."

"Oh yes." He looked from her eyes to her lips and then seemed to shake himself and come back to the question. "Well now, there's all the lifeguards for a start, and there's . . . well . . . there's someone else."

Mesmerised by the thickening of the atmosphere between them, Connie murmured, "Who else?"

In answer he turned his head slowly to one side so that his nose wouldn't squash hers and his lips kissed her mouth very gently. As he broke away, he said quietly, "Me."

Connie had never been kissed by a boy before. This was unlike any practising she'd done on her hand or her mirror. This was warm and responsive and sensual and she wanted more.

After a while, Merlin lifted his hand and very gently cupped her breast. As his thumb stroked her nipple, she understood why girls at school were obsessed with discussing sex. She'd felt something similar reading the odd adult book borrowed from a friend, but this was real. A man was kissing her and touching her and wanting her. He took her hand and placed it on the zip of his trousers. He groaned as he pressed her hand down. She realised somehow that this was the point of no return. Either stop now or step into the unknown.

He lifted her hand and pulled her up. "How about we go upstairs?"

Her legs felt weak and her breathing was quickening. What should she say? She knew she shouldn't be doing this. He kissed her again so that she couldn't speak and

263

when he stopped kissing her, she led him up to her bedroom. It wasn't long before all thoughts of how wrong this was left her completely.

The memory had reawakened Connie's libido and she turned in the bed to face her husband. "Darling, are you asleep?"

His eyes were closed but his mouth moved. "No."

"Would you like a cuddle?"

"Don't I always?"

Next door, Pru and Francis were in bed reading a Kindle and a pamphlet respectively. Francis turned to the back page of the pamphlet. "I think we should give Abi a cookery course at the Starfish. It'll stand her in good stead at uni, when she goes."

Pru, deep in her Kindle, didn't reply. Francis tried again: "Darling, did you hear me?"

Pru laid her open Kindle on her lap and turned to look at him with rather dilated pupils. "Oh, yes, yes." She shifted her body to face his and touched his lips with her fingers. "It's been a long time, Francis."

"Since what, Pru?"

"Since I made love to you."

"Oh, er, yes. Must be . . . quite a long time now."

"Shut up and let me kiss you."

"Let me clean my teeth first."

"Don't worry about that. Kiss me."

"I'm a bit tired, actually."

Pru stopped advancing on him. "It's Belinda, isn't it?"

"What?" Terror gripped Francis.

264

"You fancy Belinda. Are you having an affair with her?"

"NO!" he almost shouted.

"Do you want to have an affair with her?"

"NO."

"I'm not blind, Francis. I saw you in the kitchen with her that day, playing with the kids, chucking grapes at each other. And then that time you let her dress you up as a sea fairy."

Pru moved to sit on the edge of the bed and hugged herself. For the first time, Francis saw her vulnerability. He moved towards her and put his arms round her shoulders.

"I love you, Pru. I may not have said so often enough. But I do."

She turned and looked at him, her eyes shining with tears. "I love you too. You're not going to leave me for Belinda, are you?"

"God, no!"

Then Pru's mouth was on his. As she lifted herself on top of him, her Kindle slid to the floor. In the dying light of the screen a passing moth may have read the title: *Fifty Shades of Grey*.

Over in The Bungalow, Henry popped his head round Dorothy's door to say good night and found her weeping.

"What's all this, old girl?" He walked to the bed and sat beside her. She sniffed. "I can't stop worrying about the girls and Abi and Jem. What's going to happen to

265

them? If you die first, I'll be left with all the mess. They'll be furious that you never made a will . . ."

Henry felt a twinge of guilt and sighed. "What do you want me to do?"

"You know what you should do. Find out if Susan is still alive. Do what you should have done forty-odd years ago. Even if you have to pay through the nose, it will be worth it for the peace of mind. Please . . . for the children's sake if not for mine?"

Henry kissed the top of her head. "I'll get on to it tomorrow. I promise."

Dorothy took his hand and gripped it tightly. "We're old, Henry, and time won't wait. Do the right thing, for the children and for me."

Henry padded back to his own room, deep in thought. He knew he was being an old fool. Dorothy meant the world to him and he had let her down. He lay in his bed, looking at the cosy clutter around him: old copies of *The Times*, books that had belonged to the children when they were young — he spied a copy of *Five Go to Smuggler's Top* and remembered Connie's addiction to Enid Blyton. As his eyes roamed the shelves, they settled on something that he had barely noticed for a long time, though it must have been there since they moved into The Bungalow. It was a battered but still intact box containing the first prototype of Lawyer, Lawyer produced by the factory. Henry threw the covers off and went over to the shelf, removing the game from beneath a *Wisden Cricketers' Almanack*. So much of his life was down to this game, he mused. Work, Dorothy, the house . . .

Henry thought back to the first time he laid eyes on Dorothy. More than forty years had gone by, yet it seemed as if it were only yesterday . . .

Henry had just returned from lunch on a dreary, overcast Wednesday when his father's secretary appeared, summoning him to the old man's office. He knocked on the half-glazed door and went in without waiting for a reply.

His father was sitting behind his big old desk, silhouetted against the Crittall windows, which looked out on to the factory car park. He was wearing his usual office clothes of loose tweed trousers, twill shirt, knitted tie and sleeve garters.

"Ah, Henry, come in. Are you busy this afternoon?"

"Nothing too important. Why?"

"I'd like you and Miss Danvers —" he waved to the corner of the room just behind the open door — "to join me for a meeting about advertising. Apparently we're not doing enough."

Henry turned to where his father had pointed. Miss Danvers, the cool typist who'd joined the firm a month or two ago, was smiling at him warmly but without any hint of flirtation. She took a couple of steps towards him, juggling her shorthand book and pencil into her left hand and offering him her right. He shook it and asked rather pompously, "Do you have advertising experience, Miss Danvers?"

That smile again. "Yes, a little. I worked for the *Surrey Advertiser* after leaving secretarial college.

Occasionally I'd be roped in to help with the classified ads."

"So, not an advertising executive then?" he asked.

She laughed. "No. Sorry."

Henry's father coughed and indicated that they should take a seat. "Now we've established that *neither* of you have advertising experience, perhaps we can get this meeting under way. I propose starting an advertising department for the company. Just a small team at first: you two."

"Really, Dad?" Henry was excited. "When? What's the plan? What's the budget?"

The three of them had spent the rest of the afternoon devising an advertising strategy. Carew Family Board Games was viewed in the industry as a relic of the fifties and sixties; while tradition and the cosy family image remained important to the brand, they needed to show that board games still had a place in the seventies.

"Times may change, but the fact remains: the family that plays together, stays together," declared Henry's father, Clarence. "Nothing can beat the fun of a family sitting round the table playing Ludo."

Henry looked up under his eyebrows to see if Miss Danvers was familiar with his father's favourite catch-phrases. She gazed steadily back at him with a small curve of her lips.

He returned his attention to his father: "Absolutely, Dad."

"I've an idea," said Miss Danvers. "How about redesigning the Snakes and Ladders board? Instead of the usual nursery rhyme figures, how about having some more modern faces pictured on the board? Maybe pop stars? David Cassidy and the Partridge Family, or the Jackson Five."

"Good idea," said Henry warmly.

Mr Carew senior looked bemused. "I don't know who the hell they are, but why don't you ask Sylvia in the art department to mock something up? Anything else?"

Dorothy, confidence growing, spoke again. "Supposing I contact Thames TV and the BBC and ask if we could have the franchise to use their popular programmes? In Ludo, for instance, each of the four teams could be a children's programme: Blue Peter, Dr Who, Crackerjack and Catweazle?"

Henry's father leaned back in his chair and placed his hands firmly on the desk in front of him. "Genius! Why haven't you thought of this, my boy?"

Henry was still gasping in awe at the brilliance of Miss Danvers. "I've got some catching up to do, I agree." He turned to her: "Are you sure you need me as a colleague?"

She laughed and looked down at her unused notepad.

His father got to his feet. "Right! That's the new department up and running. Henry, your office is now the HQ of Carew advertising."

He ushered the two fledgling advertising executives to the door and rang through to his secretary to order his afternoon cup of tea. "And, Elsie — I'll have a couple of Bourbon biscuits, too."

"Yes, sir," replied Elsie before putting the receiver down. Bourbons! He must be having a good day.

The following months had seen the blossoming of the advertising department and the blossoming of a love affair between its two members. Everything about Dorothy Danvers appealed to Henry. She was upfront and honest, she was attractive but didn't spend hours on her appearance or feel the need to flirt with every man she encountered. Dorothy wore little makeup and treated men as equals. She was all the things that his life had been lacking.

One evening in her small one-bedroom flat, stomachs replete with Henry's home-cooked spag bol, they lay on the sofa together watching *The Goodies*.

Henry turned off the TV, stroked her hair and kissed the top of her head.

"I love you, Dorothy."

She gazed up into his eyes. "I know. I love you too."

A lump formed in his throat and his eyes shone. She reached up and brushed the unformed tears away. "Whatever's the matter?"

He swallowed hard and, finding her hand, kissed the fingers and the palm.

"I want every evening to be like this. I want to live with you and be with you every day and every night. As man and wife."

It was her eyes that filled with tears now. "Oh, Henry. So do I. I want to be Mrs Henry Carew so very much."

Henry paused. He knew this would the hardest thing he would ever do; there was so much at stake here. "Dorothy . . . there is something I have to tell you. Something . . ." he gulped. "I'm afraid you might not love me after you hear this."

He let her sit up and face him. Clutching her hands in his, he told her, holding nothing back.

When he had finished, she looked at him, eyes wide with shock and disbelief. "This is a cruel joke you're playing on me." She stared at him, willing him to laugh. "It is a joke, isn't it?"

"I wish it were."

Hearing this, she buried her face in her knees.

"Do you hate me?" he ventured.

"I am disappointed in you." Her voice was muffled by her skirt. "I think you'd better go now, Henry. I need to think."

He thought about falling to his knees to plead with her, or sweeping her up and carrying her into the bedroom. But in the end he walked to the door in silence and let himself out.

Dorothy stayed as she was for some time. Her brain was trying to make sense of the enormity of the mess she'd found herself in. Who was Henry? Her Henry had vanished and this other man who could keep such an enormous secret from her had taken his place.

She realised that her feet were getting cold. Rubbing her hands together to warm them, she slowly stood up. Her legs felt as if they didn't belong to her. She went to the bathroom and ran a bath. The little pilot light leapt into action as she turned the Ascot water heater on and the gas jets hissed with heat.

Dorothy caught sight of her drained face looking back at her from the clouded mirror above the basin. She didn't cry. She wasn't sick. Although she felt like doing both.

Instead she came to a decision. In the bath she washed her hair and afterwards towelled herself dry and applied Nivea crème to her skin. Then she cleaned her teeth, got into bed and slept soundly.

In the morning she got to work half an hour earlier than usual. By the time Henry arrived she was surrounded by cardboard boxes, packing up her things.

He threw down his briefcase and rushed to her, pleading, "Don't go. Please, Dorothy."

She looked at him, astonished. "I'm not leaving. I'm reorganising the office, that's all. I think our desks should face each other in the centre of the room. Much more practical, and it'll mean I get a bit of the natural light from the window."

He gawped at her. "Oh. OK."

She moved towards his desk. "And another thing: book a taxi for six o'clock tonight. We're catching the Caledonian Sleeper to Scotland. I have reserved us a room in a nice hotel for three nights. When we come back we shall return as Mr and Mrs Henry Carew."

Henry placed the tatty box containing Lawyer, Lawyer back on the shelf.

Dorothy was right. It was time.

CHAPTER
TWENTY-FOUR

"Morning," breezed Pru as she popped a wholemeal bagel into the toaster.

"Morning," replied her sister, who was gazing out into the garden, still basking in the afterglow of memories of Merlin. She looked at her watch. "Blimey, sis, you're up early — it's only seven thirty."

"Well, I don't want to waste such a glorious day. I was thinking, is there anything I can do to help with the party preparations?" asked Pru.

Connie gave her sister a suspicious look. "Why? That sort of thing isn't usually your bag."

"Well, she is my only niece." Pru opened the cupboard containing the mugs. "Would you like a tea? Or coffee?"

"Tea." Connie frowned. "What's going on? Who are you and what have you done with my sister?"

Pru gave an uncharacteristic peal of laughter. "I'm only offering to make tea, dear."

There was a sound in the hall and Francis appeared in a pair of rumpled pyjamas, looking as perplexed as Connie.

Pru shot him a beaming smile. "I thought I told you to stay in bed. Go back and I'll bring your breakfast up to you."

Francis hesitated, not quite knowing what to do. He liked making his own breakfast. He'd grown accustomed to making his own breakfast.

Pru shooed him out. "Go. Upstairs. I'll be there in a minute."

"Oh." Francis gave a nervous smile. "OK."

Connie stared at Pru's back as she busied herself with slices of salmon and cream cheese for the bagel.

"Come on, Pru. Tell me. What's got into you?"

Pru smiled coyly and in a hushed voice told Connie about the book she'd been reading.

Connie's eyebrows shot up into her hairline. "Oh. My. God! Poor Francis! You've been practising on him, haven't you?"

Pru nodded gleefully.

"I thought you told me you didn't like sex?"

"Well, I've woken up again."

"Blimey. I bet Francis doesn't know what hit him: nothing for yonks and now you're going to wear him out!"

Pru leaned with her back against the worktop and gave Connie an earnest look. "It was something Belinda said the other day. I think she's got her eye on Francis."

Connie gave a hoot of laughter. Pru held up a hand.

"Honestly, Con! And a couple of days later I read a review about this book and how it had transformed one woman's love life, so I thought I'd see what all the fuss was about. You should read it."

"I did. I skipped to the first couple of dirty bits and found it rather dull. But then I don't need anything to

274

improve my love life. Greg and I satisfy each other very nicely."

"Well, bully for you."

"Oh, Pru, I'm sorry," exclaimed Connie, seeing the hurt expression on her sister's face. "I didn't mean to pooh-pooh your new lease of life."

Ignoring her, Pru carried the breakfast tray out to the hall in silence.

"I'm pleased for you," Connie called after her, "truly I am."

Pru met a sleepy Jem on the stairs and gave him a smacker of a kiss. "Morning, my darling boy."

He rubbed his cheek where her lips had left a damp impression and then scratched at his unshaven throat. "Not so loud, Mum."

"Oh, poor little boy. Working hard for his living?"

"Yeah, and I've got to see Poppa before I go. He wants me to do something on his iPad for him."

Pru laughed and gave him another kiss, which he tried to dodge.

"Muuum."

"See you later, darling. Bye." And she continued up towards her bedroom.

With a sigh of contentment, Jem wiped the bacon sandwich crumbs from his lips.

"Can I make you another one, Jem?" queried Dorothy, poised with the frying pan in her hand.

"No, you're all right, Gran." He got up and collected his canvas bag, which he slung over one shoulder.

"Gotta go now. Tell Poppa his iPad's all sorted now. Laters!"

Dorothy saw him out of the door and waved as he rode off to Trevay on his bike. She spied her husband coming up the path on his way back from Higher Barton where he'd collected some milk and his newspaper.

"He's a good lad," said Henry, as he watched Jem disappear into the distance.

"And growing. I reckon he's shot up another two inches this summer. Must be over six foot by now." Dorothy shut the front door. "Won't be long before he's ready to take on the family firm . . . assuming it's still in the family."

"I'd be happy to have Jem and Abi in the family firm after uni, but . . ." Henry frowned. "I don't think it's fair to burden them with that sort of decision at this stage. They may not want to be part of it."

"So sell up and share it all out between Pru and Connie."

"I can't sell the company — I'd feel I was letting Dad down."

"Now you're being silly."

Henry looked steadily at Dorothy. "I just don't want to make the decision."

"Better to give them the whole lot — the company, Atlantic House, the *Dorothy* — while we're still alive to see them enjoy it. If nothing else it would put an end to the tension between them."

Henry gazed out of the window to the garden and the ocean beyond, saying nothing.

Dorothy tried again: "It'll save any misunderstandings when we're gone."

He turned and looked at her with a heavy heart.

"You mean Susan."

Dorothy hesitated, then said, "Yes, I mean Susan."

"If she wanted anything from me, she would have found me long ago."

"Maybe she's been abroad and doesn't know what a success the company is?"

Henry smiled ruefully. "Darling, Carew Family Board Games is an international brand. She'd know."

"So she'll also know that she could be entitled to a share . . . unless she's dead?" Dorothy brightened at the thought. It was one that always brought a glimmer of hope. "If we only had confirmation, that would solve all our problems."

"And how would we explain it to the girls?"

"We'd find a way — times have changed, they'd soon get over it. Please, Henry. I need to know where I stand."

"What do you want me to do?"

"Find out if Susan is alive. Maybe we can start by searching the Internet. Jem said he'd sorted out your iPad so we can get online again. I'll do it, if you show me how."

They got out the iPad and logged on to Google. Dorothy immediately tapped in SUSAN CAREW.

Up popped many Susan Carews. A dozen or so in America, some on Facebook, others on LinkedIn. There was no way of telling whether one of these many Susan and Sue and Susie Carews was the person they were looking for.

Dorothy was disappointed. "I thought you could find anyone on this thing."

"Let's put it away, shall we? I was thinking of paying a visit to the jeweller's in Trevay — I'd like you to help me choose something nice for Abi's birthday."

Francis was breathless. "How was that?"

Pru could barely speak. "Amazing."

"Good."

"Very good."

"No. I meant good as in I'm pleased it was all right."

"I am pleased."

"Good."

"Don't start that again."

Francis stepped out of bed feeling better than he'd felt for a long time. He was astonished at how the floodgates of no desire had lifted to reveal a dam of sexual energy. And he hadn't thought of Belinda once.

"Helloooo!"

Oh God. Talk of the devil. That was Belinda calling from the hall. The bloody woman never knocked. She just walked right in.

Francis met Pru's wide eyes and they stayed perfectly still, listening for further sounds. They heard Greg saying something and then the sound of Belinda's cork wedges squeaking towards the kitchen. Pru started to giggle.

"What are you laughing at?" said Francis, frowning.

"Her. She definitely fancies you. Watch out while she's around."

"Gosh, no, Pru. Never." Francis was blushing horribly. "I'd never do anything like that."

Pru took his reaction at face value. "Well, of course you wouldn't." She got out of bed and put her dressing gown on. "You haven't got it in you."

Francis was on the verge of defending himself but decided that no answer would be the best answer. "I think I'll have a shower," he said, and disappeared into their bathroom.

Greg's voice shouted up the stairs. "Coffee, anyone? Belinda's here to talk 'party'."

Pru studied herself in her wardrobe mirror and saw a woman who needed to comb her hair and brush her teeth. A woman who had just had very satisfying sex. A woman who was going to go downstairs and flaunt her sexual satisfaction in the enemy's face.

"Hi, Belinda," Pru greeted her with a Cheshire cat grin.

Belinda was put on the back foot. She'd never seen Pru in any other guise than uptight businesswoman in designer holiday casual wear. Pru in satin robe and clearly no underwear was hard to adjust to.

"Hi, Pru," she replied, unconsciously slipping a shirt button undone to reveal a little more freckled bosom.

Greg noticed immediately and hurried over with her mug of coffee, seizing the opportunity for his customary appraisal of her cleavage. "Belinda's come to discuss party food with Francis," he said.

"Has she?" said Pru, raising an eyebrow and smirking. "How fabulously kind of you. He'll be down in a moment. We had a . . . lie-in," she purred.

Belinda shook her curls and rattled her bangled wrists. "Really? I'm so full of energy I need very little sleep."

"Hmm," murmured Pru, psyching Belinda out. "How fascinating."

Greg chewed nervously at a fingernail, realising that he was watching some kind of predatory female haka, the opening gambit in what could turn out to be a full-on catfight. "I'll get Connie. So you girls can do whatever you girls do." He darted into the hall and they heard him go upstairs.

Moments later there was the sound of two pairs of running feet. The news that Pru and Belinda were about to do battle over Francis had Connie and Greg racing down the stairs in an unseemly scramble so as not to miss the sight of fur flying.

Much to their disappointment, the two women were sitting calmly at opposite ends of the kitchen table, discussing the weather. "I love getting a suntan, me," Belinda was saying.

Pru narrowed her eyes. "Yes, I noticed there was some sun damage to your neck."

"Belinda!" Connie burst out, making everyone jump. "Great of you to come over! I've had an idea about how to hang the fairy lights and things. Have you had any thoughts on how to use the pink stuff you got?"

Pru laughed softly. "Still using the pink, are you? How delightfully outré. Ah, here's Francis." She reached an arm out to clasp his hips as he stopped beside her chair. "Belinda's here to help with Abi's party. I think she wants to know what you plan for the menu." She turned again to Belinda. "This is definitely the man to satisfy any hungry appetite, aren't you . . . Frankie!"

Belinda could read the startled look in Francis's eyes. Licking her lips, she replied, "Oh yes. Of that I am quite certain."

Pru flashed a look of pure ice towards her adversary. Then she rose from the table, kissed her husband full on the lips, and slunk, catwalk style, out of the room.

It was way past lunchtime by the time their meeting finished, but now the menu and theme of the party were agreed.

Belinda went home with a notebook full of to-do lists and Francis set about writing up his shopping list. Pru was working on something that looked like a spreadsheet and Connie was heating up some soup. Greg was on the phone.

"Come all the way down the lane and you can't miss us . . . Atlantic House . . . on the right . . . just before the beach . . . OK, OK, I'll stand on the drive now and look out for you. Bye." He put the phone down and headed for the door, saying to no one in particular, "Abi's boat will be here any minute. I've asked Henry if we can put it round the side of The Bungalow so that she won't see it. I'm going to stand on the drive to wave him in . . ."

Connie carried on stirring the soup. Francis looked up quizzically. "Did Greg just say there was a boat coming for Abi?"

"Yep," said Connie. "He's called it *Abi's Gale*. Please remember to laugh when he tells you."

"Good afternoon, Mr Carew," said Mr Carter of Carter's Fine Jewels. "Long time no see. Tom, fetch a seat for Mrs Carew, would you?"

A spotty young man with an enlarged Adam's apple scuttled into a back room to collect a bentwood chair. As soon as Dorothy had settled herself, Mr Carter beamed at them and asked, "Now then, how can we help today?"

"We're looking for a gift for our granddaughter who'll be seventeen tomorrow."

"I see. A watch, perhaps?"

Henry looked at Dorothy for her reaction.

"A watch would be very suitable," she agreed. "It would leave us with the option of giving her a nice ring or something," here she stared pointedly at Henry before continuing, "for her eighteenth."

"Quite so," said Mr Carter, heading for a large cabinet full of watches. He pulled a key from the chain in his pocket and opened the door. "Here we are. These are very popular with young ladies at the moment. Pretty, waterproof and reasonably priced."

Henry left Dorothy to do the choosing. While she was engrossed in consultations with Mr Carter about the merits of the various watches, he stepped to one side and surreptitiously glanced at the trays of diamond rings on display. The small diamond on Dorothy's finger was over forty years old and the gold band was rubbing thin. It had been the very best he could afford at the time. He put his glasses on and peered at the tiny price tickets. How much? He put a steadying hand on the glass counter top and reminded himself that, of the promises he'd made to Dorothy, this was the only one he was in a position to fulfil.

"An excellent choice, Mrs Carew," announced Mr Carter. "And if your granddaughter doesn't like it, we can always change it."

"She'll like it!" said Dorothy firmly.

Henry drifted back towards them and admired the small, elegant watch. "Lovely," he said. "And now would you mind showing us a selection of your diamond rings — for Mrs Carew."

"A special birthday? Anniversary?" enquired Mr Carter.

"Nope." Henry smiled at Dorothy. "Purely because she deserves one."

CHAPTER
TWENTY-FIVE

Woken by a loud and tuneless rendition of "Happy Birthday", Abi buried her head under the duvet to drown out the noise.

"Go awaaay," she mumbled from under the covers. "Oww! Get off me, Dad!"

Greg had put all his weight on top of the form of his sleepy daughter and was attempting to squash her the way he used to when she was little.

"Come on, my little Abi-Wabby," he said in a high baby voice. "You used to love a lickle tickle from your daddy."

"I said get off me. Oww, you're hurting me."

Greg lifted his weight from her and waited for her head to surface. One hand appeared from the depths of the duvet and pulled it down just enough for him to see the mascara-smudged eyes of his beloved child.

"Hey, Dad," she managed.

"Hello, you." He kissed her nose. "We have breakfast for you and a surprise."

"What time is it?"

"Eight o'clock."

"Why so early? Pearl has given me the day off."

"Too early for birthday surprises?"

Abi groaned. "Yes. No. Can't I just have another half-hour?"

"OK, but if you're not down then, I shall come and squash you again." He threw his weight on top of her and tried to tickle her squirming body.

"All right all right," she laughed, "I promise. But my presents had better be good."

Greg was like a cat on hot bricks. He was so excited by the boat that was lurking on the other side of The Bungalow that he couldn't sit down. He'd also had a few hot emails from Janie. He was missing her. He'd told her about the party and *Abi's Gale* and she'd jokingly threatened to come and join the celebrations. What a hoo-ha that would make!

"Is she up?" Connie was beating some eggs.

"Yep. On her way."

"Lay the table for me, would you?"

When Abi eventually made her entrance, the entire family were waiting for her. "Happy Birthday" they shouted together. She was lost in a blizzard of hugs and kisses for a few minutes before being ushered to her place at the table. There were two balloons tied to her chair. One said "17", the other "Birthday Girl".

"They're from me," said Jem. "I got some funny looks cycling home with them yesterday."

"That wasn't the balloons, Cuz," replied Abi drily, and everyone laughed.

Dorothy placed a narrow box wrapped in silver paper and tied with a purple ribbon, on her table mat. "This is from me and Poppa."

Abi ripped apart the paper, opened the box and was suitably pleased with her gleaming new watch. "Cool, Granny. Thanks, Poppa. It's lovely."

"Don't lose it," said Connie.

Abi ignored her. "Next present please."

Francis handed her a smart-looking envelope with *Starfish* written on it. "What's this? A weekend away from you lot, in luxury?" She opened it up and read: *A one day cookery course in the preparation and cooking of fish dishes*. Abi looked at her aunt and uncle with a small bright smile. "Lovely."

"And here is the antidote," said Pru, handing her another Starfish envelope. Abi opened it in trepidation. Her face lit up when she read the slip of paper inside: "A pamper day at the Starfish spa! Thanks, Auntie Pru!"

"My pleasure," said Pru, clasping Francis's crestfallen hand.

Connie plonked a huge dish of bacon, sausage, fried bread and scrambled eggs in the middle of the table. "Here we go — eat up. Toast is on its way."

"What about my present from you and Dad?" asked Abi.

Greg, hampered by the cast and sling, did his best to clap his hands together and rub them joyfully. "After breakfast, miss!"

Greg had fashioned a blindfold out of a tea towel and had wrapped it over Abi's eyes. He led her out into the garden and round to the side of The Bungalow. The rest of the family followed.

"Are you ready?" he asked Abi.

"Yes."

"OK. Here we go. One, two, three —" He whipped off the tea towel and Abi saw in front of her the boat tied with pink ribbons and balloons with *Abi's Gale* in large gold letters on the back and side.

"Oh my God!" she squealed, running towards it. "Is it mine? Mine alone? No one else's?"

"All yours." Her father put his arm round her skinny shoulders and hugged her. "Mum wouldn't let me buy you a car."

"Shut up, Greg," responded Connie. "Do you like it, love?"

"I adore it! Poppa, will you take me out in it and teach me how to drive it?"

"Of course. You'll be a natural," said her grandfather. "Haven't you been skippering the *Dorothy* since you were little?"

"Can we go now?" she pleaded.

"Get dressed first," said Henry, looking at her standing in her shortie pyjamas.

"OK! See you in fifteen!" She turned and raced back to the house.

"See. Told you she'd love it," crowed Greg to Connie.

"Well, if nothing else it'll keep her out of the way of the party preparations," Connie replied.

Connie was standing on the garden terrace of Atlantic House watching Abi skimming across the waves in her new boat, with Henry sitting next to her and bending his head away from the stinging spray they were whipping up and Greg sitting up front, posing with his sunglasses on his head.

"Look at her. Poppa never let Pru or me touch the *Dorothy*, but he's happy to take his life in his hands for his granddaughter."

Belinda looked up from where she was sitting with a pile of pink tulle in front of her. "She's having a ball. Come and sit down and help me with this stuff. It'll take your mind off her." She passed Connie a quantity of pink fabric. "All you have to do is make a little froufrou skirt and put some gathers in for the waist. We'll sew the pink ribbon on as a waistband and *voilà!*"

Connie sat and took hold of the proffered netting. "How many do we have to make?"

"As many as we can. And then we have the turquoise blue." She nodded towards a plastic bag at her feet.

Connie threaded a needle with pink cotton and together the women sewed in silence. After a few minutes, Belinda said, "It must be a great feeling to have a sister. Pru seems so much fun."

"Really? Well, we have our moments," replied Connie.

"You can share so much. Secrets and laughter."

"Mmm."

"I'd have loved a sister."

"Are you an only child?"

"Yes. And I grew up wishing for a family. You see, it was just me and Mum. I didn't even have a father, let alone brothers or sisters."

288

Connie didn't know how to reply. She wasn't really in the mood to hear about Belinda's deprived childhood. The best she could manage was a subdued, "Oh," as she kept on sewing.

Belinda did a few stitches more and then looked up at Connie. "You're so lucky to have the family you have. A loving dad. Money. This house."

"Mmm." Connie had turned to look out to sea to watch Abi and Henry again.

Belinda changed tack. "Frankie is a sweetie, isn't he?"

Connie turned back with suspicion. Was Pru right? Did Belinda fancy Francis? "Er. Yeah. I suppose so. He's a very good father."

"I think he'd make a wonderful partner."

On Pru's behalf, Connie became defensive, "Really?"

"To be honest, a lot of the mums at school have a crush on him."

Connie could not conceal her disbelief. "*Francis?*"

Belinda nodded her head and bit through a piece of cotton. "Oh yes. I'm not sure Pru knows what she's got."

Connie decided that Belinda needed to know her sister's marriage was sound. "Oh, I think she does. They've been like a couple of honeymooners these last few days."

Belinda's eyes clouded over. "What do you mean?"

"Just that this holiday seems to have relaxed them both. They're enjoying each other's 'company', shall we say, more than ever."

Belinda twisted her mouth to one side. "Oh. I see. You surprise me. I thought they had quite a . . . cold marriage."

Connie laid her sewing in her lap. "What makes you say that?"

Belinda tried to bluff Connie into divulging more information. "Something I sort of picked up. Pru doesn't seem the passionate sort and . . . well, quite frankly, Frankie is a very sexy man."

"Is he?" said Connie, taken aback.

"You should hear the women at the school gates."

"What do they say?"

"That if his wife doesn't want him, there are plenty who do."

Connie was both astonished and furious on Pru's behalf. "Well, you can tell them that my sister and Francis are very happy and have a healthy, passionate marriage — not that it's any of their business!"

Belinda said nothing but bent her head to her sewing.

It occurred to Connie that she might be hiding tears. "Are you OK?" she asked.

Belinda added the finished skirt to the pile and stood up, keeping her face turned away from Connie.

"Oh, gosh yes! Talking of Frankie, I promised I'd help him with the trifles," she said. "Any problems with the rest of those skirts, give me a call." And she walked across the paving and through the kitchen doors.

Francis was stirring an enormous pot of chilli mince.

Belinda sniffed appreciatively. "Something smells good," she said, sidling close to him.

He gave her a quick look and carried on stirring, "Hi. You're just in time. Would you make a couple of bowls of couscous? There's some coriander, parsley, dried apricots and oranges and limes to squeeze into the mix over on the side."

She put her arm gently round his waist and squeezed him. He felt her warm breast on his arm and shamefully remembered how that feeling had aroused him until this week's surprising revival of his sex life with Pru.

He made a casual movement away from her so that she had to let go of him.

"Right," she said. "I'll get on with this, then make the trifles, shall I?"

He didn't even look at her. "Yes please."

She busied herself with boiling the kettle and emptying couscous packets into a couple of large bowls.

"Where's Pru?" Belinda asked quietly.

"In Trevay, getting her hair done."

"When will she be back?"

"Not for an hour or two. Why?"

"It's nice to spend some time together. You know. Chatting. No interruptions."

Francis felt nervous and slightly guilty that he might have inadvertently led Belinda on.

"Oh."

Belinda put down her wooden spoon and came towards him. Two fat tears had finally been released and were meandering down her cheeks. She put her arms around Francis's stiffening neck and kissed him on the lips.

"I have some very strong feelings for you, Frankie."

"I'm awfully sorry," he said, nervously wiping her kiss from his lips.

"Tell me you don't have any feelings for me."

"Oh golly, Belinda. You're a lovely woman and I treasure our friendship, but I don't feel . . . You see, I love Pru."

Belinda's tears dripped on to his hands, which were clenched close to his chest in order not to accidentally stray towards her breasts. She let him go and dipped her head to wipe her eyes on her cardigan.

"Well! I've made a fool of myself, haven't I? I'm sorry. Please don't tell anyone about this."

"Of course I won't." He moved slightly towards her but then thought better of giving her a consoling hug.

Belinda took a deep breath and plastered an over-bright smile on her face as she looked out of the window to the sea.

"Looks as though Abi's enjoying her birthday present."

Not knowing quite what to do, Francis dipped a teaspoon into the chilli ready for tasting. "Yes."

"What did you give her?"

"Erm, sorry. What? I'm trying to remember if I put the cumin in."

Belinda scanned the worktop in front of her and found an open cumin pot. "I think you did." She showed it to him.

"Ah good. Well, I think that's done. I'll crack on with the guacamole."

The two of them continued to work with the minimum of conversation. Belinda's heart was heavy. Here was another man who was abandoning her. It was odd how, with age, these pains of loss were getting worse. Her father leaving, gentle Brett walking out for Steve, and now Frankie. A wave of anger and self-pity hit her. *Come on, Belinda,* she admonished herself. *You've come a long way. The end is in sight.*

The door knocker sounded in the hall. "I'll go," said Belinda, bustling out.

When she came back, she was followed by a willowy blonde in her mid-twenties. "Hi." She walked straight up to Francis with her hand out. "I'm Janie — Greg's PA. I'm here for the party."

Francis, having barely recovered from Belinda's shock confession, now stood gulping as if he'd swallowed one of his fresh chillies whole. "Janie?" His wide eyes slid to the outdoor terrace, where he knew Connie was sewing in all innocence.

"That's right!" said the blonde, tossing a glossy mane of hair over one shoulder.

"Greg's PA?"

"The one and only."

"He . . . he didn't mention you were coming."

"Well, it's kind of a surprise," she said in a conspiratorial tone. "Is he in?"

Belinda was intrigued. Greg had been sufficiently flirty with her that she sensed immediately this girl spelled danger with every tap of her stiletto-booted foot. Here was mischief to be made. "No, he's out on the boat with his daughter."

"*Abi's Gale?*" said Janie.

"You know the name of the boat?" gasped Francis.

"Sure. I was the one who came up with it," Janie preened.

"Belinda, I've finished the pink and I'm on the blue now . . . Oh, hello." Connie, having spotted Janie, was looking at her curiously.

Francis stepped in. "Connie, this is Janie — Greg's PA. Janie, this is Connie — Greg's wife."

Connie smiled warmly at the new arrival. "Janie, how lovely to meet you. I've heard a lot about you. Greg's an insufferable pig at times, isn't he?" she laughed.

The tall blonde looked coolly at Connie and said, "Oh, he's not bad. I've heard a lot about you, too."

"He didn't tell me you were coming. Is it about work?"

"Yes. It's a last-minute thing. Once I heard about the party, I thought it would be easier for me to come down here and sort it out with him."

Connie looked baffled but remained polite. "Can I offer you a drink? Something to eat? Where are you staying?"

"I'd love a double espresso. And I haven't booked anywhere to stay yet."

"Stay here! We've plenty of room. I'll take you up to a guest room and you can come down for your coffee when you've had a chance to freshen up. Greg will probably be back by then."

CHAPTER
TWENTY-SIX

"Throttle back. Point the nose to the right . . . gently."
Henry talked Abi through the approach to the mouth of
the cave that led to Atlantic House's secret boathouse.

"That's it . . . easy does it."

"I have done this before, Poppa."

"Yes, I know. But *Abi's Gale* handles a bit differently
to the *Dorothy*. Now throttle back a bit and aim for
that wall there, then we'll turn the corner."

Abi beamed with pleasure at the thrill of driving her
own boat into the cave. She only wished she had a few
spectators, but part of the boathouse's purpose was to
prevent arrivals and departures being observed. They
slowly motored into the cave and up towards the
man-made jetty.

Henry donned a battered blue cotton cap. "Well
done, Abi. We'll make a seaman of you yet."

Greg, barefooted in his shorts, scrambled out into
the thigh-deep water and up the semi-submerged
slipway. He caught the rope one-handed and held it
until Abi arrived to secure it to the metal ring
embedded in the concrete floor. "Well done, Skip!" He
mock saluted her.

It took them a while to wipe the boat down and make her safe next to the *Dorothy*. Abi was beaming with excitement. "She's the best present I've ever had, Dad. Thank you so much." She grabbed him in a bear hug. "And the party tonight is going to make this the best day of my whole life!"

Henry smiled indulgently at his beautiful grand-daughter. "Tell you what, if we're clever and sneaky, we might get out of here and over to The Bungalow before the rest of the family catch us. That way we can have a celebratory hot chocolate together."

"Personally," said Greg, "I could use a Scotch." He put his arm round Abi. "Next year I can take you for a proper drink in the pub, but for now, hot chocolate will have to do."

She laughed and kissed his tanned stubbly cheek. "Thanks, Daddy. This really is the best birthday ever!"

The three of them climbed the stairs and made a dash for The Bungalow without being seen.

When they finally rolled up to Atlantic House after their celebratory hot chocolate, with a dash of Scotch for the men, they found a hive of activity and a very miffed Connie. She was in the hall, surrounded by balloons.

"There you bloody are! Where the hell have you been? Have you eaten? If you're hungry you'll have to ask Janie to make you a cheese sandwich. She's just clearing ours up, so you'd better get in quick."

"Who's Janie?" asked Abi, as Greg and Henry gasped "Janie!" in unison.

"Hii!" Janie was standing in the door of the kitchen, brandishing a sharp knife. "I make a mean cheese and pickle if you want some?"

Greg felt his legs turning to liquid beneath him. His eyes swivelled from Janie to Connie and back again.

Henry, doing his utmost to conceal his fury, stepped forward. "Welcome, Janie," he said, in a not altogether welcoming voice. "This is a surprise."

"A good one, I hope?" she giggled mischievously. "I've got some paperwork that Greg wanted me to bring down."

"You have?" Greg was finding it hard to breathe and talk at the same time.

"Yes. We discussed it yesterday. Remember?"

Greg shook his head then nodded it in confusion.

"OK, who wants a sandwich?" said Janie, turning back to the kitchen.

"How did the boat go?" Connie asked Abi. "I was watching you zipping across the bay."

Greg and Henry remained in the hall, watching as the women disappeared into the kitchen. Greg was feeling as if he'd been the victim of a hit-and-run accident. Henry was staring at him, his colour rising ominously.

"I want a word with you," he hissed. "In the study."

Greg blinked and looked at his father-in-law's deadly serious face. He did as he was told.

"Here, drink this." Henry passed a glass of Scotch over, before waving Greg to a seat and sinking down in a chair himself.

"Thank you," said Greg meekly.

"What the devil do you think you're doing, inviting her here?" Henry's voice was controlled, but the fury in his tone was unmistakable. "And, before you say a word, bear in mind that I already know the answer."

Greg sipped the Scotch to buy some time. Henry was no fool in business or in private. How much did he know? How did he know? Greg took another, larger mouthful of his drink.

"I don't know."

"Oh yes you do."

Greg looked at his hand, clasping the glass. "I didn't ask her down. There is no urgent paperwork."

"Then why is she here?"

"I don't know!" He looked up with horrified eyes.

"You're having an affair with her, aren't you?" Recognising a rhetorical question, Greg didn't bother with an answer.

"Aren't you?" thundered Henry.

Greg simply nodded his miserable head.

"She's not your first mistress, I take it?"

Greg looked away, his averted eyes speaking volumes.

"You bastard!" Henry's voice was icy with contempt. "You're an utter fool. How could you jeopardise the happiness of your wife, your daughter — not to mention risking your position in the company! What were you thinking?"

"I'm sorry." Greg rubbed his eyes with the fingers of his good hand and started to weep. "I'm so . . . so . . . sorry."

"Sorry you did it, or sorry you were found out?"

"I was going to end it after the holidays."

"Were you? And how would you be able to resist Janie in the office? Have her sacked? Bring in a younger, blonder model?"

"Nooo," Greg wailed.

Henry stood up and went to the door.

Greg was scared. "What are you going to do?"

Henry looked at him contemptuously. "I'm going to make sure my granddaughter and my daughter are going to have the best party this house has ever seen. As for you, keep out of my way, keep your hands off Janie, and try to behave like a decent husband and father."

Greg relaxed a little. "You're not going to tell them?"

Henry could not conceal his disgust. "Thinking of your own skin as usual? You really are a complete shit. I will deal with you when I've had a chance to think about things. In the meantime, remember: I will be watching your every move."

Greg avoided Janie for the rest of the afternoon and took to his bedroom in need of sanctuary. He couldn't think straight. His mind kept going round and round in circles, like a dog chasing its tail, until he felt sick and giddy. Why was Janie here? How did Henry know? Would Henry tell Connie? What would Abi think? Where would he go? What would he do? And back to the beginning again.

He lay on the bed, curled up like a baby and wept. Some time later there was a tentative knock at the door. He lay rigid. Another pint of adrenalin squirted into his system, tensing his muscles in readiness to flee. He heard a man's voice.

"Greg? Are you awake? It's Francis. Can I come in?"

Greg got to his feet and opened the door a crack to check that Francis was on his own. He was.

Francis took in the broken, red-eyed mess that was now sitting on the edge of the bed, sobbing.

"Now, now, old man," said Francis, embarrassed. "Why did you ask her to come here?"

"I didn't," Greg howled. "She's here uninvited. Make her go. Tell her I'm not well. Tell Connie I need her. Tell her I can't come to the party. Tell her I've got a virus or something."

Francis stood firm. "No one suspects a thing. Janie has gone down to the beach with Belinda to set up washing lines and fairy lights or something. Connie is supervising them."

Greg groaned and flopped back into the foetal position.

"You can get through tonight. Then tomorrow you'll have to have a serious talk with Janie and finish it. That'll be the end, and no one need be any the wiser."

"But you don't understand," moaned Greg. "Henry knows about Janie. He's going to tell Connie and that'll be goodbye Greg. No family, no job, nothing."

Francis pursed his lips and studied his hands. "Well, you should have thought about that before."

"I'll never do it again. Ever. Connie must believe that. I can't lose her." He wept louder.

"She knows nothing — yet. But she will if you carry on like this. Look at you: crying like a baby! Grow up, Greg, and face the music. Show them you're a man who has erred but who loves his family."

300

Greg sat up, irked. "Like you, you mean? You pious little butter-wouldn't-melt git! Bringing the buxom Belinda down here for you to ogle? You've got some nerve, telling me how to behave."

Francis took a step nearer to Greg and without warning punched him hard on the nose. "Don't you ever speak to me that way again. Now, get yourself up and in the shower. Have a shave and behave like a husband and father should!"

With that, Francis turned and slammed the door behind him.

Greg staggered to the bathroom and looked at his swollen nose. No blood, but the blow had made his eyes sting even more than the tears.

He took in his reflection. Broken arm in its dingy plaster, grey scattered through the once luxurious hair on his chest, and the hint of a pot belly hanging over his shorts.

He turned on the cold tap of the basin and splashed his face. He spoke to himself: "Gregory, mate, you've been in some tight corners before and come out fine. This is just another. Get through tonight and by tomorrow you will have come up with a plan. You are not going to lose everything you have. You're a winner, Greggy boy. A winner."

The assembled throng stood at the bottom of the stairs watching as Abi made her descent, dressed as a shimmering pink mermaid. Belinda had sewn scallop shells to the cups of a pink halter-neck bikini and had scattered sequins and seed pearls all over them. Abi's midriff was bare and from her hips to her toes she was clad in a tight pink shiny lycra side-split skirt, again smothered in sequins. At the back, a frothy train of sparkling pink net billowed over each step. Her long hair had been tonged into rippling waves. A circlet of tiny shells formed her crown.

"Ta-dah!" she laughed, holding out her arms and posing.

Connie was holding her camera. "Smile!" The flash lit Abi's face like a film star.

"Mum, Dad, I want a picture with you both. Belinda, would you take it?"

"I'll take it." Janie had stepped in and taken the camera from Connie.

"Thanks, Janie." Connie smiled and took Greg's hand as they posed with Abi.

"Hey, Dad. You smell nice!" Abi sniffed appreciatively. "You look pretty hot too!"

"Doesn't he?" said Connie, smiling at him and touching his cheek tenderly. She leaned in to kiss him. "Love you."

Greg's eyes flicked towards Janie, who looked as if she had neither seen nor heard anything. He glanced at Henry, who was busy whispering to Dorothy, and then he spotted Francis, who was giving him a discreet thumbs-up.

There was a loud pop from the drawing room as a champagne bottle was opened, followed by the sound of Jem laughing and apologising. "Oops! Went off a bit early. Sorry."

302

Henry walked to the drawing room. "I told you I was going to give you the signal!"

"I know. Soz and all that! I'm not trained in this." He held the foaming bottle.

"Get it in some glasses, Jem. It won't do us any good on the carpet."

"Yes, Poppa."

Henry took centre stage and held out a hand for Dorothy to join him as all the family, along with Janie, Belinda and Emily, stood round in a semi-circle.

"Friends and family," said Henry, "we are here tonight to celebrate Abi's birthday. Before her guests start to arrive on the beach, I thought we'd take a moment together to raise our glasses and toast our Abigail."

"Abigail!" They all said as one, and drank.

Henry waved his arms to quiet the chatter. "I have another important announcement to make." He put his arm round Dorothy's waist. "Dorothy and I have been together for more than forty happy years. She is my best friend and the love of my life. What I have to tell you now may come as a shock, but you are all old enough to accept and understand." He took a deep breath and looked over at Connie and Pru. "Your mummy and I fell in love with each other so quickly that we didn't have time to make things legal. We set up home and had you girls, but we never actually got married."

The room was silent. Connie and Pru looked stunned. "So the other day, I took Dorothy ring-shopping. I have in my pocket the diamond she has always deserved." He turned to Dorothy, taking a small box from his jacket pocket. "Darling, I know this might seem a bit sudden . . ." He smiled at his own joke. ". . . But would you do me the honour of becoming my wife?"

Dorothy held out her hand and he slipped the large and perfect solitaire diamond ring she had chosen on to the third finger of her left hand. She kissed him tenderly on the lips and said, "I'll need some time to think about it . . . Oh, OK. You're a silly old fool, but who else would have you?"

Connie and Pru went to their parents and hugged them tearfully, full of questions, while Francis called out, "Three cheers for Henry and Dorothy — hip-hip . . ."

Belinda, unnoticed, slid out into the hall and sat on the bottom step of the stairs, her heart breaking.

CHAPTER
TWENTY-SEVEN

After the big announcement, Abi, Jem and Emily walked across the garden and down to the beach to greet the first arrivals.

Francis took Greg into the kitchen on the pretext of needing him to help with the food.

"Here, have one of these." Francis handed his brother-in-law a large glass of punch. Greg downed it in three gulps and held the empty tumbler out for another. As Francis ladled the punch into the glass he looked at Greg closely. His skin was pale and his hands were shaking slightly. His breathing was more like panting. "Are you OK?"

"Of course I'm not bloody OK. I feel as if I'm about to have a heart attack. My life has turned into a living nightmare."

"You're doing fine. Just keep smiling and stay by Connie's side. Don't give Janie a chance to get you on your own."

He looked gratefully at Francis. "Thank you for punching me on the nose. You brought me to my senses."

"Any time. It doesn't look bruised."

"It was a bit red, but I told Connie I had a cold coming on and she covered it with some makeup. How's your hand?"

"Sore. I've never hit anyone before."

They looked at each other and chuckled. "This is the closest we've ever been, Francis," said Greg. "I don't know what I'd have done without you."

They fell into an awkward embrace, Greg's plastered arm grazing the painful knuckles of Francis's hand.

Pru and Connie were in the drawing room with their parents. Henry and Dorothy were on one of the sofas and the girls were sitting on the floor by their feet.

"When you launched into your speech, I thought you were going to tell us that one of you was about to die," said Pru, shaking her father's knee in mock anger.

"Me too," said Connie. "It made the rest sound so trivial in comparison! Why on earth did you leave it so long to tell us the truth? Why didn't you just get married? Why keep it a secret? We wouldn't have minded."

Dorothy shrugged her shoulders. "We told everyone we'd eloped, and that was that really . . ." she finished lamely.

"I don't understand," persisted Connie. "Why did you *pretend* you'd eloped? Why didn't you just elope?"

Dorothy looked at Henry for help. He had already warned her not to tell the girls about Susan.

"Silliness on my part. It seemed an innocent white lie at the time. A bit of fun. But once everyone considered us married, it became impossible to tell the truth."

Pru frowned. "I still don't get it. That was so stupid of you."

Henry looked at his elder daughter and admired her reasoning. He felt very uncomfortable in persisting with the fictitious story. But what choice did he have? Luckily, Connie unwittingly came to the rescue.

She got to her feet. "So when are you going to get married? You've had a long enough engagement."

Again, Dorothy looked to Henry for a lead.

"We'll sort something out in good time. Let's get Abi's party on the road first, shall we?"

"We're not allowed to stay too long because we're considered old and uncool," said Connie.

"Speak for yourself," said Pru, standing up and shrugging on a new black leather jacket over her skinny jeans. "Francis and I are going to dance the night away."

Belinda had slipped back to Dairy Cottage to repair her tear-stained makeup. When she was done, she formed her lips into one of her well-practised over-bright smiles and went in search of Francis. When she found him, serving punch to an ill-looking Greg, she asked for a glass herself.

"It's nice. But not enough oomph," she proclaimed.

"There's almost half a bottle of vodka in there," said Francis. "That's plenty. I don't want the kids getting drunk."

"Fat chance of that. It's as weak as tea!" said Belinda. "Greg, can you manage to take down a couple of bowls of salad with your broken arm?"

"Yes, ma'am."

"Good. Francis, you take the big tub of chilli, and I'll be down with the punch in a minute."

She watched as the two men did as they were asked. When they were out of sight, she found the rest of the bottle of vodka, a bottle of Cointreau and some tequila, and poured them all into the big punch bowl.

Down on the cooling sand, the sun was slipping towards the horizon and the sea was at its lowest ebb. Music from Merlin's Mobile Disco was setting the party mood and the first of the guests were chatting and laughing with Abi. Belinda had designed a large party zone, marked out as a square by bamboo canes pushed upright into the sand. She had tied washing line all around the tops and on to that had looped balloons and fairy lights. Along one side of the square was Merlin's disco. He had a laptop, decks, huge speakers, lights and a bubble machine going. Opposite him on the other side of the square was Pearl's ice-cream caravan and the long buffet table, now holding the chilli and salads.

Belinda found Greg and Francis and ordered them back to the house to get the rest of the food. She went over to Merlin. "Have you got a microphone in case of speeches?"

Merlin picked a hand mic up and twirled it like a gunslinger. "Sure do, beautiful Belinda with the big bosoms."

She really wasn't in the mood. "Merlin, you are a moron."

308

Abi came running up to her. "Where are the pink skirts? All the girls want to wear one."

"In those black plastic bags under the food table. There's a bag of blue Neptune crowns for the boys too."

Abi kissed her. "You're a star!" And dashed off.

Half an hour later most of the guests had arrived and Merlin's music was hitting the spot. A mixture of seventies classics and the latest dance music got all the partygoers moving.

Merlin watched Pru as she sat at the edge of the throng, nursing a glass of wine. It brought back memories of the party on the beach in Newquay all those years ago, when he'd spotted her sitting apart from the crowd, aloof, contained.

He rolled a cigarette and cued up a couple of very long tracks to play on his laptop, then he went and sat next to her.

She looked at him and shuffled to the other end of the rock she was sitting on.

"Like old times, eh?" he said, lighting his cigarette. The loose strands of tobacco lit up like dry tinder.

She glanced at him again and then turned back to watch the dancers.

"It was at a party like this that we first got together, remember?"

"Hmm." She still wouldn't look at him.

He blew some smoke rings into the air and asked, "How about a dance?"

Now she did look at him. "With you?"

"Yep. I don't see anyone else asking." He looked around him and side to side. "Do you?"

Pru couldn't help but laugh. "No thanks." She got up, leaving Merlin looking pleased with himself, and wandered down to the sea, slipping her sandals off and enjoying the cold water on them in the warmth of the evening.

The painful memories came flooding back.

After their first night together, he disappeared for ten days. She hung about near Atlantic House and the beach, refusing to join the family on trips into Trevay or Plymouth.

Her mother soon grew annoyed with this state of affairs. "I would like to spend some time with you, Prudence. If you won't join us on our trips out, you *will* at least help me run some errands." Dorothy passed her daughter a lengthy shopping list just as Connie walked by. "Constance?"

"Yes, Mum."

"Why is your sister mooning about, refusing to leave the house?"

"She's fallen in luurve."

Dorothy sniffed. "Oh, is that all. A holiday romance. Who is the boy?"

Pru looked daggers at her sister, who blithely continued: "She met him at that beach party in Newquay. He's called Merlin and he's an odd-job man in the winter and a lifeguard in the summer."

Pru shouted at Connie, "He's not an odd-job man! He's a labouring builder. There's a difference, you know."

"No there isn't." Connie stuck her tongue out.

310

"You're just jealous because you fancy him yourself!" snapped Pru.

Connie blushed furiously.

Dorothy stepped in. "Whatever he is, don't tell your father." She gathered up her handbag and car keys. "Come along, Pru. Stop brooding about young Lochinvar and come push a trolley round the supermarket with me."

Sullenly and speaking in words never more than one syllable in length, she did the shopping, packed it into her mother's car, unpacked it into the larder and fridge, then, as soon as was humanly possible, she escaped out of the house and back down to the beach.

It was late in the day by this time and the young families were packing up to leave. A few hardy stalwarts were starting to light small portable barbecues. Pru walked miserably down to the waves, her head hanging low, her hands stuffed into the pockets of her shorts. Feeling the prickle of tears, she angrily wiped her eyes on the sleeve of her sweatshirt. On the wind came a man's voice calling her name:

"Pru! Pru!"

Looking up, she saw him about fifty metres away, running towards her, his blond curls streaming behind him: Merlin. She stopped walking, not knowing whether she should run to meet him. Instead, she opened her arms. When he got to her, he lifted her off her feet and spun her around. Finally he put her down and looked into her soul.

"Hello, Prudence Carew."

"Hello, Merlin Pengelly."

"Have you missed me?"

"No."

"Yes you have. A little bird tells me you've been moping about down here since I last saw you."

"Who told you that?"

"Him." Merlin pointed up the beach to the lifeguards' hut. A young man in lifeguard red shorts and windcheater put his binoculars down and gave a thumbs-up.

Pru blushed. Had she been so obviously pining for the last ten days? Merlin took her hand and kissed it. "I've got news for you. I've swapped from Newquay to work this beach for the rest of the summer. I am now your personal lifeguard."

"Come on, Pru, you know we were good."

Merlin had sidled up to Pru and snaked a hand around her waist.

"What about a kiss, for old times' sake?"

"No. You were a bastard to me. You broke my heart."

"And you broke mine when you refused to speak to me."

"Merlin, I want to thank you. Because of you, I am the woman I am today: strong, successful, some would say a ball-breaker — and it's all down to you. I vowed that never again would I let my guard down to another human being. Not even my husband — until this holiday. It's only now that I realise how much I love Francis. So, no, I don't want to dance with you or kiss you, Merlin."

312

Merlin threw his cigarette butt on the sand and stamped it out with his flip-flop. "Plenty more fish in the sea, Pru. Plenty more fish in the sea." And he returned to his job as DJ.

There's nothing sadder than an old hippy on the pull, thought Pru as she watched him go.

Janie was dancing very sexily in a silk mini dress with no bra to keep her firm breasts in place and a tiny thong which was noticeable every time she wiggled her hips. She'd made certain she was dressed as provocatively as possible in order to show Greg what he was missing. As she snapped her head to one side, making her long hair flow Beyoncé style, she caught Merlin's eye and gave him her most sultry smile. He cued up a few more tracks, back to back, and stepped out from behind his decks to join her on the dance floor.

Giving it all he had he threw what he imagined were some impressive shapes and shouted above the noise: "Hi! I love your picture."

She pulled a face that made her cheeks dimple. "Huh?"

"I said, I love your picture."

"What picture?"

"The one I'm going to take of you lying in my bed."

She stopped dead and thought about slapping his face. But then she saw Greg watching her, so she pulled Merlin close and kissed him as passionately as she could. Thrilled that his new chat-up line was having

313

such a positive effect, Merlin enthusiastically kissed her back.

Greg was behind the buffet table serving dollops of chilli to Abi's friends. He had seen the whole thing.

"Janie seems to be getting on well with that idiot plumber."

The sound of Henry's voice in his ear made Greg jump, causing him to spill an ugly splat of mince on top of the vegetarian sausages.

Henry patted his shoulder. "I'm watching you — don't forget."

Belinda appeared with another bowl of punch. "Oh, what's this on the vegan bangers? The veggies won't eat them now."

"They're not exactly flying into people's mouths," Greg responded drily.

Belinda ignored him. Setting the punch bowl down, she turned to Henry. "Great party! And a double celebration! Fancy you and Dorothy not being married!" She elbowed him in the ribs. "Saucy!"

Henry looked down at the sand, embarrassed. "Ah well . . . you know how it goes. These things happen."

"Yes. We all have our skeletons." She picked up a sausage and munched on it. "So why didn't you get married in the first place?"

Henry was forced to repeat the lie about eloping.

"Sounds daft to me. I mean, there was nothing to stop you nipping off and getting married at any time, was there?"

The sound of Stevie Wonder blasted from Merlin's disco.

314

"Ooh. I love this one. Would you have a dance with me?" she asked Henry.

Relieved that she'd changed the subject, Henry agreed and led her on to the dance floor. Taking her in an elegant hold, he asked: "Can you cha-cha?"

"Yes! My mother loved dancing. She taught me all the ballroom stuff."

"Here we go then. Cha-cha one, two . . ."

And they were off. Soon, the crowd stood back and allowed the couple the entire dance space. When they finally came to a flamboyant end, they were rewarded with tremendous applause. Henry held Belinda's hand while she curtsied and blew kisses, then escorted her off the floor.

"Your mother taught you well," he said, puffing a little from the exertion.

"Thank you." Belinda ran a hand through her damp hair. "She was a good teacher."

"Was she a dance teacher?"

"Nothing so provincial!" Belinda laughed. "No, she danced in the theatre. She was a part-time model too. But when she met my father, she was a Bunny Girl."

Henry stood still for a moment before recovering himself. "Really? What was her name?"

"Susie Taylor." Belinda stopped smiling and looked him dead in the eye. "Hello, Daddy."

CHAPTER
TWENTY-EIGHT

It was the night of Henry's twenty-eighth birthday and he was walking into the glamorous Playboy Club on London's Park Lane. Where else would a young man want to be in 1968?

"Want a drink, H?" James was at the bar and shouting across the music.

"Large Scotch," Henry shouted back. He stood watching the Bunny Girls as they circulated with full drinks trays, dispensing the glasses with the famous Bunny dip: a move where the girls backed towards the table and handed the drinks gracefully with a small reverse knee bend, preventing, Henry thought, their plentiful breasts from spilling out of their costumes.

The girls looked incredible. Very classy, very sexy and unlike any woman Henry had ever seen in the flesh.

"Here you are, old man. Cheers." James appeared beside him. Henry took the glass and raised it. "To us!" They each took a good swig. "How long have you been a member here?" Henry asked.

"Pa gave me membership when I was twenty-five. Pretty cool, eh? Ma doesn't know. She doesn't know Pa joined either." He laughed. "Some things are best kept secret! Fancy playing the tables?"

"I don't know how. And I don't have enough cash."

"My treat — come on."

In the casino room, James got them both settled at a roulette table. The croupier, another Bunny Girl, was watching as the ball bounced into number 17. Henry, fascinated, watched as she pushed a huge pile of chips to the winner and collected all the losing bets. She must have a brain like a calculator, he thought. James slapped a handful of mixed chips in front of him. "There's a hundred there. Happy birthday."

"Thanks. What do I do?"

Following James's example, he placed a bet: one five-pound chip on number 28, his age. It came up. The croupier Bunny smiled and pushed him his winnings. "Well done, sir," she said, giving him a radiant smile.

"Beginner's luck," James said scornfully. James ordered them each another drink and together they played the table until James ran out of money and Henry felt he might run out of luck. When he cashed the chips in, he had enough to pay James back his hundred and treat him to dinner in the club's dining room.

It was two in the morning by the time they spilled out on to Park Lane. Standing outside was a girl in a shiny red PVC coat, short enough to reveal shapely knees and black wet-look boots. It was the croupier Bunny.

"Hello again," said Henry. "Looking for a cab?"

"Oh, hello." She smiled, her gorgeous lips framing perfect teeth. "Yes."

"Which way are you going?" he asked.

"West, Shepherd's Bush."

"What a coincidence — I'm going that way too." Henry stood on James's toe to stop him from contradicting. "Would you care to share a cab?"

She hesitated for a moment before replying, "Bunnies aren't supposed to fraternise with customers, you know . . . But that would be very kind. Thank you."

James insisted that they take the first cab and waved them off. Henry couldn't believe his luck, having her all to himself. She told him her name was Susan Taylor, she was twenty-four and a model. The Playboy thing was a bit of fun, though it did give her a regular income.

Henry did his best to impress her, telling how he had only recently returned from America, having completed a business course at Harvard. His father had stumped up the cash, all part of grooming him to run the family firm.

"What is the family firm?" she asked.

"You probably won't have heard of it: Carew Family Board Games? To be honest, I barely scraped through my final exams. I fell in love with sailing while I was out there and instead of knuckling down to my studies I was off to Cape Cod at every opportunity, mucking about in boats."

The taxi came to a halt. "This is me," she said, waiting for him to open the door for her. As she jumped out, she offered a pound note as her contribution to the fare. Henry refused it.

"Absolutely not. My pleasure. Good night."

A week or two later, Henry was walking along Oxford Street, heading towards Selfridges to buy his mother some perfume for her birthday, when he saw a bright-red PVC coat coming towards him. It was raining and the wearer had her head hidden by a smart umbrella. He looked at the feet and saw black wet-look boots. As they drew closer, he called, "Susan?"

The brolly shifted and Susan's face was revealed.

"Hello." He smiled, offering his hand.

She accepted his invitation to coffee in Selfridges café and later helped him choose his mother's perfume. "Would you care to have dinner with me one night?" he asked, holding the heavy shop door open for her.

"I'd love to. Tomorrow is my night off. Is that too soon?"

"Not at all," he beamed. They arranged to meet at an Italian restaurant on Kensington High Street.

It wasn't long before she had moved into his rented cottage in Battersea. Henry was head over heels in love. Susan was beautiful; he never tired of looking at her. He loved to take her shopping and would buy her any outfit she wanted. When they walked down the King's Road together, arm in arm, Henry was on cloud nine. He saw the way other men looked at her and found it hard to believe that he had found someone like her, who actually wanted him too.

The sixties may have been drawing to a close, but London was still swinging, and Henry and Susan made the most of what it had to offer. They would hit the town with James, often with a pretty girlfriend in tow, and life became one long round of parties and cocktails.

But their lifestyle took its toll on Henry's bank balance. Eventually there was nothing for it but to bite the bullet and ask his father for more money.

"If you are to take over the running of the family firm, then you need to exercise some restraint, Henry. Learn to economise and cut your coat according to your cloth!" said his father sternly.

"Does that mean you're not going to give me a loan?" Henry was furious. The company was doing well and he knew his father could afford it.

"Correct."

"Fine. In that case, you can find someone else to take over the family firm. I only came back here for your sake — I should have stayed in New England and pursued my own dreams. In fact, I think that's exactly what I will do. I still have friends in Cape Cod; I'll have no problem getting a job there. To hell with you and your board games!" Henry raged.

"Henry, don't be so childish!"

But it was too late. To his father's dismay, Henry accepted an offer to skipper a yacht from Boston down to the Carolinas for the summer.

And his father wasn't the only one who was less than happy about the arrangement. Susan was horrified when Henry told her what he'd done.

"What about me?" she wailed.

"You can come with me, darling."

"And leave the Playboy Club? And what about my modelling?"

320

He put his arms round her waist and drew her to him. Closing his eyes, he buried his face in the scent of her hair and murmured, "I can't live without you."

She pulled away from him. "Then don't go."

"But it's all arranged. Wait till you get there — you'll love it. And we can get you a job over there."

"Doing what?"

"We'll need a ship's cook."

"I'm a dancer and a model and I have a good job at the Playboy Club. If you think I am going to spend the next six months scraping a living as a *cook*, cooped up in a tiny cabin, you are very much mistaken."

Before Henry knew what was happening, the row had escalated, culminating in Susan walking out.

When she came back, two days later, she found Henry hung over and unshaven with red-rimmed eyes. He was pathetically pleased to see her.

However, when he tried to kiss her, his mouth still reeking of stale alcohol, she pushed him away.

"I've come to collect my things."

"What?"

"You heard." She walked quickly to the bedroom.

"You can't." He chased after her. "We're going to America."

"You are. Not me." She pulled out a bag and started packing.

"I won't go, then. I'll cancel it, forget the whole thing." Henry was aware of the desperation in his voice, but couldn't help himself.

He grabbed her hand and she shook him off. "It's too late. I've met someone else."

Her words hit Henry like a bucket of ice-cold water.

"In two days? Who is it? I thought you loved me." In a panic, he followed her to the bathroom where she was gathering up her cosmetics and potions. "Who is it? You must tell me."

"That's none of your business, Henry. All you need to know is that we're finished."

And with that, she was gone.

Henry was devastated. Unable to turn to his father for advice, he rang James. Should he plead with her? Haunt the Playboy Club until she agreed to come back to him? Follow her and find out who this other man was?

"No!" said James. "Forget her. Go to America and wipe her from your mind. She's not worth it."

Two weeks after Susan had walked out, Henry stepped on a BOAC Super VC-10 jet, bound for Boston. For the next six months he would be skipper of a sixty-foot luxury yacht called *The Goblin*.

If he hadn't been heartbroken, he would have enjoyed the job . . . and the company of some of the beautiful women on board.

It was late June by the time they returned to Boston after several weeks spent cruising around Cape Cod, Nantucket and Martha's Vineyard. Henry stepped off the boat and headed for the harbour master's office to collect the post. There was a letter and a packet. He opened the packet first. It was a limited edition travelling set of Snakes and Ladders, a gift from his parents, with a note sending their love and hoping he'd be home soon. He smiled fondly and resolved to drop them a line.

He turned to the letter. He recognised the handwriting immediately: it was from Susan. He tore it open. She said she'd missed him and longed to be with him, if only he would still have her. She apologised with all her heart for hurting him and swore that she would never hurt him again.

Henry ran to the nearest phone and rang her straight away. Amid many tearful "I love you's", he promised to send a ticket the following day.

She was coming back to him.

He was at the airport when her plane landed. The moment Susan appeared, he enveloped her in his arms.

"I'm never going to let you go again," he whispered into her soft hair. "I love you, Susan."

She clung to him in return and found his lips.

"And this is our cabin." Henry opened the door with a flourish, stepping aside so she could see the tiny space with its sofa, table and shower/loo.

"Where do we sleep?" she said quietly, looking around.

He laughed. "The sofa and table turn into a double bed. Look —" With practised ease he demonstrated how to open out the bed, and then threw himself on it.

She climbed in beside him. He hadn't made love to anyone since losing her. And now she was back. In his arms and on his bed.

"I've missed you," she whispered. Then she wriggled free for a moment and, leaning over the edge of the bed, opened her vanity case. Inside were her Bunny ears. "A little souvenir from home," she giggled.

He kissed her. "Oh, Susan, I've missed you more than I thought I could miss anybody. Now put those bloody ears on and take everything else off!"

It all worked out very well and on a romantic spur-of-the-moment impulse, during a stopover in Nantucket, they stood in front of the town clerk and were married with the crew as witnesses and guests. Now she was Mrs Henry Carew.

By September they were back in Boston. One of his old Harvard friends had loaned them a one-bedroom apartment in the city, and Henry got a job teaching rich city kids how to sail dinghies. Susan was picking up a little modelling here and there. They weren't making a fortune, but they scraped by.

Then one day Henry picked up the telephone and heard a voice from the past: James.

"Hello, my old mate! I just blew in across the pond and fancied looking up my old mucker! How the devil are you?"

It turned out James was planning to be in Boston for a few months, maybe longer. His millionaire father had set him up with his own business as an art dealer, and he was planning to open a North American office, maybe pick up a Jackson Pollock that was being offered at auction, look up some old contacts, as well as scouting around the various galleries and visiting wealthy private clients to drum up business.

The moment James landed, the three of them hit the town. It was just like old times, as if their friendship had never been interrupted.

Susan's birthday fell during the second month of James's stay. Henry had arranged a surprise trip to Vermont, but as soon as they got there, Susan was very sick. The celebratory dinner had to be abandoned: she felt so ill she couldn't eat a thing. Next morning they walked to the drug store and asked the pharmacist to recommend something for an upset stomach.

"Is it possible you're pregnant, ma'am?" he asked.

"No," she replied. Then, "I don't think so."

"Well, ma'am, maybe you should see your doctor. In the meantime, try these."

As soon as they had paid for the indigestion remedy and left the shop, Henry asked her: "Pregnant? Do you think you might be?"

"Maybe. I don't know."

Henry did a small jig on the pavement. "That's what it is! You're having a baby! You're having a baby! We're going to be parents! Oh, I'm going to be the happiest dad in the world!"

On their return to Boston, Susan made an appointment with the doctor. Henry fidgeted restlessly in the waiting room.

"Well? What did he say?"

"You're going to be a daddy."

He hugged her. "When?"

"Early June."

"June! We'd better start cutting back on nights out and luxuries so we can save up for —"

"Yes. OK," she said wanly. "Excuse me, I think I'm going to be sick."

"Well done, old man!" said James, slapping his back and handing him an expensive Cuban cigar. "Looks as if you're going to be well and truly settled — wife, family and all that. Can't say it's for me — I'm planning on remaining footloose and fancy-free. Far too many pretty ladies needing my attention!"

Henry laughed; James relished his playboy reputation and certainly seemed to have the necessary bank balance to support the lifestyle. With a child on the way, Henry was feeling less assured about his own finances. Much as he loved sailing, his family's welfare came first. If they returned to England, provided his father could be persuaded to welcome him back into the fold, they could look forward to a secure future. His mother would see to it that Susan and the baby had all the support they needed. Henry resolved to write to the old man, set things in motion. But just in case the answer was unfavourable, he decided to say nothing to Susan for the time being.

Within a week he had his reply.

His father rang him at the sailing school, ecstatic at the prospect of the prodigal son's return; he even agreed to pay their plane fare home. The afternoon's lessons had been cancelled due to bad weather, so after handing in his resignation Henry set off for home, eager to deliver the good news. He was so excited, he ran into the apartment, not even stopping to take his coat off.

Sue wasn't in the kitchen or the living room. Hearing sounds coming from the bedroom, he opened the door.

Susan had her back to him. Apart from her Bunny ears, she was naked. And she was sitting astride the similarly naked body of his best friend, James.

In that split second Henry didn't know whether to drag his wife off the creep and smash his face in, or walk away. It was too much to take in.

"You bastard!!" cried Henry, lunging towards the bed.

"Steady on, old man. Take it easy," said James, leaping up.

"How long has this been going on?" It was a struggle to force the question out — his throat was so constricted with grief it felt as if he was being strangled.

Susan, hastily pulling the covers up to hide her naked body, said nothing. It was James who answered.

"Look, mate, I know how it looks, but you can't blame me — she's the one who made all the running, practically threw herself at me. I mean, what do you expect when you pick a Bunny Girl for a wife?"

"You utter shit!" spat Susan, her face twisted with hatred.

"Ah, but I'm a rich shit, aren't I?" said James, scooping up his clothes and putting them on. "You've been after my money since the beginning. Remember when she left you, Henry, back in London? It was for me. Course, once she realised she wasn't going to part me from my cash, she went running back to you. Only she's not too keen on living in poky little cabins and one-bedroom apartments, having to get by on a sailor's salary, so ever since I showed up in Boston she's been all over me."

Henry couldn't speak. He felt as if it were all some terrible nightmare, that it couldn't really be happening.

"I'm sorry, mate," said James. He reached out a hand, but Henry slapped it away. "Yeah, you're right. I've behaved like a shit. But believe me, you're better off without this one." James gestured towards Susan as if she were nothing.

Henry and Susan looked at each other in silence as James walked out of the room and let himself out of the apartment. Henry felt as if his heart had been ripped out and smashed into a million pieces. Finally he spoke.

"How could you? You're carrying my —" His veins turned to ice as the awful possibility hit him. Voice sinking to a barely audible whisper, he asked her, "Is it my baby?"

Susan shook her head and shrugged her shoulders, before turning her back on him and putting her clothes on.

"But you . . . Why . . ." Henry shook his head in disbelief. "You're despicable," he said, his strength returning. "I'm going out for an hour. When I come back, I want you and all your things gone. I never want to see or hear from you again."

"You can't throw me out on to the street. Where am I supposed —"

Henry gave a mirthless laugh, "Oh, I'm sure a resourceful girl like you will come up with something. Perhaps your wealthy boyfriend will have you back. You'll never get another penny from me, I swear it."

Slamming the door behind him, Henry stormed out. He walked and walked, not knowing where he was going, until he walked into a bar, and there he stayed till the owner threw him out. He couldn't believe that his best friend and his wife had betrayed him. Well, they could both go to hell. That gold-digging slut would never get another penny of his money as long as he lived. After the way she'd lied to him, telling him she loved him, telling him she was having his baby. He didn't know what to believe any more; it was as if their whole marriage had been a lie.

All Henry wanted to do was to go back to England and start again. Forget about Susan and James and the whole goddamn business. When he'd sobered up, he phoned his father and told him everything. Within hours he had wired him the fare and Henry was on his way home.

CHAPTER
TWENTY-NINE

As Henry looked into Belinda's tearful face, he could feel the past crashing into his present. "I'm not certain that I am your father."

"That's not true, is it? You told her you didn't want a baby, you threw her out."

"No, no . . . I never —"

"As soon as she was pregnant, you abandoned her, penniless, on the other side of the Atlantic."

"No!" Henry felt the anger rising. "No! I would never have done that. I wanted a baby. I wanted you." He looked around to see if anyone had noticed the change in him. "We need to talk somewhere else."

"Right here is fine. After all, I *am* family." Belinda was sobbing now. "Why did you leave us to have another family?"

Looking at her properly for the first time, Henry could see that there was something of the Carew about her. In her eyes and in her brow. He reached out to her, wrapped his arms around her and held her close. "Are you really my daughter?" There was hope rather than doubt in his voice.

The sobbing Belinda clung to him. "Yes."

Henry's voice quavered. "I've waited a long time to hold you."

On the dance floor, Belinda's doctored punch was loosening all inhibitions. Jem and Abi were having the time of their lives. Merlin had once again returned to his job of DJ, reluctantly letting the gorgeous Janie go. He looked around to see if she was still dancing, but she had left the floor and vanished.

She was hunting down Greg.

Greg, now that Henry seemed absorbed in something Belinda was saying, was hunting down Janie.

Eventually he saw her walking around the outer edge of the party. Catching up with her, he took her arm and steered her away from the lights and into the deepening dark of the beach. Furtively he glanced around to see if anyone had spotted them leaving. The coast was clear.

He held her tight. "Oh my God. I've missed you!" He inhaled her beautiful but forbidden scent. "What were you thinking of, coming here? Now Henry knows about us."

Janie's eyes lit up. "Good. You can tell Connie and Abi, then we can be together." She kissed him hard.

When he surfaced he said, "It'll be tough. Neither of us will have a job. I shan't have a home. We'll have only our love to keep us warm." He moved in for another kiss but she held him at bay.

"What do you mean?"

"Henry will sack us both and Connie will take me to the cleaners. We'll be poor but together. Quite romantic, actually."

He kissed her again, slipping his hand under her skirt and grasping a smooth firm buttock.

Pru, who had yet to rejoin the party, was cooling her feet at the water's edge. In the gloom she could make out two figures in a passionate embrace. A few more steps and she knew their identity.

Unable to believe what she was seeing, she called out, "Greg? Is that you?"

The two figures broke apart and the girl — Pru let out a gasp as she saw the mane of blonde hair and realised that it was Janie — hurriedly pulled her dress down. Covering his face with his hands, her cheating rat of a brother-in-law turned tail and ran into the dark.

Gathering her senses, Pru hot-footed it back to the party.

Connie was trying to follow Jem as he showed her his limited skills at street dancing. She was enjoying herself immensely. Very tiddly, giggling and spinning wildly, while Jem was attempting to catch her when she looked as if she might fall. Dorothy was dancing elegantly with a group of teenage girls who were in complete awe of her. Merlin was sharing a couple of long spliffs with Pearl and her boyfriend, and the music was really rocking. The perfect night for the perfect party.

Pru walked straight over to Connie and urgently touched her arm.

"Con, I need to talk to you, right away."

Connie, three sheets to the wind by this stage, shrugged off her sister. "I'm dancing, why don't you join us? Your wonderful son has been showing me how to 'bust some moves'!"

"Stop behaving like an overgrown teenager," Pru snapped. "This is important."

"Oh, for God's sake, loosen up for once. You're always bringing everybody down. What's your problem? Can't you stand to see anybody else enjoying themselves? Always trying to ruin my fun, always spoiling things."

"At least I'm not making a drunken exhibition of myself while my husband shoves his hand down his secretary's knickers!"

Slightly stoned as he was, Merlin hadn't noticed that the music was coming to an end and he didn't have the next track ready. In the short silence, Pru's words rang out loud and clear.

"Ooops," said Merlin, savouring the moment.

Pru's words washed over Connie like a bucket of cold water. "What did you say?"

"You heard. I've just caught that so-called perfect husband of yours up to no good with that floozy of a secretary. I'm pretty sure she wasn't taking dictation!"

A cold anger rose up in Connie. "You nasty, jealous cow. You've always wanted to ruin everything, always muscling in and taking things that were rightfully mine. You hate to see me happy, don't you?" she screeched.

"You're just a pathetic little whinger, too scared to do anything for yourself and always playing the victim. Well, you got your own back, didn't you? Destroyed the one thing that really meant something to me, knowing

333

it would break my heart! I loved Merlin," countered Pru.

"Oh, here we go again, still bleating on about bloody Merlin!"

"You saw that I was happy, and because you were a selfish little madam, you threw yourself at Merlin, knowing that he was my boyfriend and that I was in love. I knew it when he took me to the fuggee hole and a pair of your knickers fell at my feet when he shook the quilt out for me to lie on. I knew they were yours because I'd bought them for your birthday! You did it on purpose, to hurt me." Pru was crying now, something she hadn't done for a long time.

"Since when did you ever care about my feelings? Whenever I had something, you did your best to spoil it or take it away from me — I hate you!" Connie, too, was now in tears. She lunged at her sister, but both women were stopped dead in their tracks by a girl's anguished scream.

"Stop it, stop it, stop it!!" Staggering from the punch that Belinda had made, Abi pushed her way through the dancers to get to them. "How could you! In front of everybody. And saying those horrible things about Daddy! I hate you both. You're so selfish, neither of you care about anyone else but yourselves. This is my birthday and you're ruining it!" She screamed again at the top of her voice. "I'm sick of both of you — the party's over!" And with that, she ran off.

"Abi, darling, come back!" Connie shouted. She started to run after her, but tripped and fell, landing on her knees in the sand. Jem shot past her, calling Abi's name. When Connie looked to see where they'd gone, Abi had been swallowed up by the darkness.

Hearing the commotion, Dorothy rushed over.

"What's going on?" she demanded.

"We've upset Abi," said Pru, deflated and ashamed. "She's run off."

Henry and Belinda had appeared and were helping Connie to her feet.

"Where's Greg?" said Henry.

"The last time I saw him, he was down by the water with that secretary of his," said Pru.

"Shut up!" screeched Connie, putting her hands over her ears, her mascara running towards her chin. "Shut up. Stop saying these horrible lies. Just because Merlin fancied me more than you. Greg loves me and would never ever be unfaithful to me."

"Never mind Greg," said Dorothy, "he can take care of himself. It's Abi I'm worried about."

Francis was directing Merlin and some of the boys to shine the disco lights in the direction Abi had run to, but they weren't powerful enough to illuminate much beyond the party zone.

Everyone was calling Abi's name. Some of the drunken teenagers thought it was all a joke, until Henry barked at them to shut up or else no one would be able to hear if Abi was calling for help.

A few minutes later Jem ran back, chest heaving, barely able to get the words out: "Has she come back, Poppa?" Grim-faced, Henry shook his head. "I ran down to the seashore, right to the cliffs and then all the way along, calling and calling, but I couldn't see her."

"Maybe she's gone back to the house," said Pru.

"Wherever she's gone, we need to find her," said Francis.

"All she had on was that flimsy mermaid costume, it's not safe for her to be running around in the cold and dark," said Dorothy, her arms around a sobbing Connie.

Everyone looked to Henry. He strained to see beyond the lines of fairy lights. It was pitch-black out there. She could have stumbled from the cliff path in the dark, fallen on the rocks. If they didn't find her soon, she might get caught by the turning tide. He beckoned Francis and Jem and instructed them to get a search party together. Pearl and her boyfriend set off to find some torches. Merlin was ordering people to go and turn their car headlights on to light up the night and help the search.

The only thing that mattered now was to find Abi.

Blinded by tears, Abi had run to the seashore, then across the shallows to the sanctuary of the cliffs. All she could think of was to hide in the darkness and leave the ruins of her birthday behind her. She stubbed her toe on a boulder and fell forward into black space before landing in a rock pool. Limpet shells rasped against her cheek. Scrabbling to stand up, she put her hand to her face and felt the sting of blood. An agonising pain shot up her foot and Abi realised that she must have hurt her ankle badly when she fell. When she tentatively tried to put weight on it, an excruciating pain shot through her and she felt as if she would pass out.

336

Sinking to her knees, Abi began to crawl. It took her a moment to realise that the dark opening ahead of her was the entrance to the cave that led to the undercliff boathouse of Atlantic House. She crawled inside, in utter agony, and collapsed on the damp sand. Then she started to call for help.

All she heard in return was silence, broken only by the wash of the tide.

Shivering with pain and fear, Abi began to sob.

"Here, drink this." Dorothy poured hot coffee for Pru and Constance, who were rapidly sobering up.

The search parties were out combing the cliffs and seashore with torches; occasionally the sound of them shouting Abi's name could be heard through the open windows.

Henry had insisted that Connie go back to wait at the house in case she came home. Pru and Dorothy had gone with her. The two sisters had barely spoken since they left the beach.

"Where on earth is Greg?" asked Dorothy.

"We don't know, he seems to have disappeared," said Pru.

"Pru says that she saw Greg . . . with Janie, his secretary. She says they were snogging," Connie told her mother. "That's what caused the row at the party. That's why Abi ran off like she did. And it's all because of Pru."

Henry, who had just entered the kitchen in time to hear Connie's outburst, laid a hand on her shoulder and said sadly, "I'm afraid that what your sister told you was true."

"Daddy?" Connie searched her father's face, and found only his steady, truthful gaze.

"I learned about it a few days ago, but couldn't decide what to do. I left it too long, and now this . . . I'm so sorry, Connie. Your husband has behaved like a shit, and I've let you down. I should have had Pru's courage and . . ."

"Shhh, dear," said Dorothy, placing a hand on his arm. "This isn't the time."

Connie's face crumpled and she put her head in her hands. "Oh God, I can't deal with this right now, not with Abi out there, missing. I just want her back. Nothing else matters." Great, heaving sobs wracked her body.

Pru reached out and put her arms around her sister, pulling her close.

No one knew what to say. In the silence they heard something heavy banging down the stairs. Connie leapt up. "Abi!" She ran to the door and stopped when she saw Janie, dragging a suitcase behind her.

"What were you doing with my husband?" demanded Connie, blocking her exit.

Janie laughed. "What do you think? Playing Twister?"

Connie slapped her across the face. "That's from me," she said. Then she stamped on Janie's sandalled foot. "And that's from my daughter."

Suddenly appalled at what she'd done, Connie stood back. In a quiet voice she said, "Shame on you. Get out."

Clutching a hand to her face, Janie limped to the front door. As she stepped outside, she threw over her shoulder: "No wonder he wants to leave you — what a ghastly family you are!" She closed the door with a bang before Connie could get to her.

Pru entered the hallway. "Did you hurt her, Con?"

"I think so."

"Good."

Arm in arm they went back to the kitchen to wait for news.

It was some time later when they heard footsteps on the terrace. Belinda had come back to report on progress, or the lack of it. The search parties had covered the beach and the cliff path, but there was no sign of Abi. Henry and Dorothy had gone back to The Bungalow to make more phonecalls and drum up some more volunteers.

Connie started to cry again. "Perhaps she's walked into the sea and drowned. We must call the coastguard and the police."

"I'll get on to them." Belinda rubbed Connie's shoulder and went to use the phone in the study.

Connie watched her go. "She's been so kind. Whereas —"

There was a crash. They looked up to see a drunken Greg staggering through the French windows.

"Greg! Where have you been?"

Greg swayed slightly, obviously the worse for wear. "Connie, love, you're everything to me," he slurred. "She means noth —"

"Never mind that now, you bastard. Abi's missing. Our little girl's missing," Connie screamed at him. "It's been almost two hours now. Francis and the others have been out looking all that time and they can't find her."

Abi was frightened. The pain was getting worse as the effects of the alcohol wore off. The cold was seeping into her very bones, and the slightest movement of her ankle made her feel as if she would be sick or pass out. She had given up calling for help. No one would hear her over the sound of the sea.

She could see the tide had changed and was starting to come in, but it would be a while yet before it crept into the cave. A sudden flare of lightning lit the night. She looked at the luminous dial on her new watch and counted the seconds before the thunder. Twenty. So if five seconds counted for a mile that meant it was about four miles away. Her grandfather had taught her that.

It was almost one in the morning. Over two hours had passed since she left the party. Were they looking for her? But even if they were, how would they know she was here?

Another bolt of lightning. This time more than twenty seconds passed before she heard the thunder. Good, she thought, the storm was moving away.

Hurry up and come, she pleaded, hugging herself to try and stop the shivering. *Please, Daddy, hurry up.*

When Belinda returned to the kitchen, Connie and Pru had been joined by Francis, Henry and Dorothy. Greg

340

had taken a flask of coffee and insisted on going out to look for Abi; though they doubted he was in any condition to be of much use, the others were so glad to see him go they offered no objection.

"The coastguard are on their way," announced Belinda.

Henry looked at her and smiled. "Thank you."

Belinda suddenly remembered her own child. "Where's Emily?" she asked Francis, clutching a worried hand at her throat. "I thought she was with you."

"Jem's taken her back to Dairy Cottage," said Francis. "I asked him to wait with her there until you get home."

Belinda was relieved. "Thank you. How lovely it is to be among family."

Henry gave her a warning look.

"Can I tell them?" she asked him.

He shook his head with a frown.

"Tell them what?" asked Dorothy, eager to take everybody's minds off the awful wait for news of Abi. Until the coastguard arrived, there was little they could do for the time being.

"Well . . ." Belinda stood with her hands folded in front of her. Henry groaned and looked at his feet. "This will come as a big surprise, but it's happy news. For me, anyway."

She had an audience now.

"You see," she looked at Pru and Connie, "I'm your half sister."

You could have heard a feather land.

Dorothy turned to Henry, a horrified expression on her face. "Is she Susan's?"

Belinda smiled. "Yes, I am Susan's — although everyone always called her Susie."

"Is she alive?" asked Dorothy urgently.

Belinda's eyes swam, "No. I told you, remember? She died last year."

"I don't understand," said Pru. "Who is Susan?"

CHAPTER
THIRTY

Henry sat with his head in his hands as Belinda told her story.

Pru looked at her father. "Is this all true?" A loud crack of thunder broke right over Atlantic House.

Henry didn't move. "Susan had been seeing someone else. When I found out, we had a terrible row. She led me to believe the baby wasn't mine."

According to Belinda, Susan had stayed in Boston picking up the odd modelling job until she'd earned enough money for the air fare home. She knew she couldn't afford the hospital bills if her baby was born in America. Back home in the UK, she'd decided to bring up her daughter alone, afraid that if she approached Henry for money he would drag her through the divorce courts and try to win custody of the child purely to spite her. For a while, she'd returned to modelling; she'd even found Belinda some baby modelling jobs. Returning to the Playboy Club wasn't an option; the life of a Bunny was not one that could incorporate children. Instead, Susan had to rely on whatever financial help she could get from a string of wealthy boyfriends, some of them married, none of them interested in commitment.

"Mum never had any trouble meeting men. Hanging on to them was a different matter. I think she always had unrealistic expectations."

Pru frowned. "What makes you so sure Henry is your father and not one of your mother's boyfriends?"

"When my mother was dying, she told me everything." Tears rolling down her cheeks, Belinda turned to Henry: "She missed you. When I was growing up, she would never tell me about my father, but after she had the stroke it all came out. I found her marriage certificate amongst her papers and asked her about it." Defiantly she looked Pru in the eye: "My mum may have been a bit promiscuous, but she wasn't a liar — and I'm willing to take a DNA test to prove it."

Someone knocked loudly on the front door. Francis went to answer it. On the doorstep were two police officers. One a burly man of about thirty and the other a woman in her twenties. Francis ushered them into the drawing room.

The male officer, who introduced himself as Nick, questioned them about the events that had led up to Abi's disappearance while the female officer made notes. When they were done, she asked for a photograph of Abi and immediately took off back to the station to get the details circulated.

"The coastguards have been alerted and are coordinating search efforts," explained Nick. "But the weather's not helping. The Met Office have issued a severe gale warning — there's a storm front moving in towards Land's End and we're going to be in for a battering over the next few hours."

344

As if on cue, a fork of lightning lit up the garden and a boom of thunder rolled overhead.

Connie, her face distorted with anguish, leapt up. "My daughter's out there in this — it's no use us just sitting here. We need to find her."

Pru and Dorothy both reached out to her, wrapping their arms around her.

"This may seem obvious," said Nick, "but have you searched the house from top to bottom? Is it possible she could be hiding in here somewhere?"

"We looked in every room," said Dorothy.

"Did you check under beds? In wardrobes? The attic? Kids that age, when they get upset —"

"Let's go and check," said Francis, waving for Nick to follow him.

Connie and Pru were left with their parents and Belinda.

"So now we know why you two never married," said Pru in a dull voice. "You were already married . . . with a family. "Did you know all the time, Mum?"

"Yes," said Dorothy. "Or rather, I knew about Susan. Neither of us knew about you, Belinda. If we had, things would have been very different. Henry and I might never have got together . . ." She clasped her hands together. "But we can't change the past. It's how we deal with the future that's important. Our first priority is to find Abi. The rest we'll deal with as we come to it."

Francis and Nick returned. Everyone looked at them expectantly. Francis shook his head. "Nothing," he said.

"Any outbuildings? Garden shed, greenhouse? Any neighbours she might have gone to? With all that thunder and lightning going on outside, she'll have tried to seek shelter. Can you think where she —"

"We've already checked The Bungalow," said Henry.

"Jem's at Dairy Cottage, so we'd know if she was there," said Francis.

"There's the garage and my greenhouse," said Dorothy.

"And the smuggler's cave," said Pru.

"Oh God, please don't let her be down there," gasped Connie.

"There's only one way to find out," said Belinda decisively.

"I'm coming with you!" Connie leapt up to follow.

"Wait for me," said Pru.

The rain lashed at the three sisters as they hurried along the path, following the beam of Belinda's torch. All three felt a lurch of hope when the thin ray of light hit the fortified door and they saw that it was ajar. They shoved aside the heavy door and ran into the stone room: the stacks of old furniture and garden equipment were illuminated by the light coming from the stairs leading down to the boathouse. Abi must have turned them on when she came in.

They made their way down the steps as quickly as they could. The sound of waves breaking against the cave walls below drowned out their voices. The tide must have come in a long way.

As they reached the last step and turned to enter the cavern, they saw Greg struggling to untie *Abi's Gale* from its moorings with his one good hand.

"Greg, what are you doing?" shouted Connie. "You can't go out in this!"

Greg looked up. "I'm going to find Abi."

"Don't be ridiculous," said Pru. "Look at you — you're in no fit state."

Belinda stepped forward and tried to take the rope from Greg's hand. He whipped it away determinedly, all sign of his earlier drunkenness gone.

"Get out of my way! I have to find my daughter."

"The police and the coastguards are out there looking for her," said Belinda. "There's nothing you —"

Ignoring her, Greg turned the key in the ignition and the boat's engine spluttered into life. As he took his eyes off Belinda to turn the boat around, she leapt wildly and landed on her knees on the slippery-planked bottom. "I'm coming with you," she said. "There's no way you can manage with one hand."

Barely able to hear her above the roar of the engine and the crashing of the waves, Greg nodded his assent.

Leaving Connie and Prudence shouting after them on the small jetty, Belinda and Greg set off down the cavern towards the sea. The waves were rolling in on large unbreaking peaks, tossing the rubber hull of the boat as if it were a toy.

"I'm scared, Greg," cried Belinda. "Please. Turn us round. Go back."

Greg had struggled out of his sling and was trying to use his broken arm to grip the wheel for extra leverage as he circumnavigated the bend in the cave.

Suddenly they could see the ocean, black and angry against the swirl of dark clouds scudding over a waning moon.

And then a voice cried out:

"Daddy! Help! I'm here."

As the navigation lights illuminated the cave wall to their right, they saw Abi, clinging to a tiny ledge about half a metre above the maelstrom. Unable to walk on into the cave and up to the house, she had been overcome by the tide as it poured into the cave. She had climbed the rocks as high as she could with her damaged ankle, but the effort had left her exhausted.

"Daddy, I'm so frightened. Help me."

"I'm coming, Abi!" yelled Greg. "I'll try to get underneath you. Be ready to jump when I tell you to."

She nodded. Terrified, wet through, her teeth chattering from cold and shock, it was all she could do to cling on.

Belinda joined Greg at the wheel. He yelled instructions in her ear, guiding her to steer the boat out of the cave and into the open sea so they'd have space in which to turn. Battling against the wind, and with the rain whipping into her face and eyes, Belinda wrestled with the wheel while Greg controlled the throttle. It was all she could do to hold the boat steady. The moment there was a lull between waves, Greg pushed the throttle forward, sending the boat back into the cave.

"Get ready, Abi," he yelled. Guiding Belinda's hand to the throttle, he told her, "Hold tight, keep her steady — whatever you do, don't let go." And then he moved into position to catch Abi, bracing his broken arm against the bar to steady himself while he held out his good hand to the stricken Abi.

"One, two, three . . ." he shouted. "JUMP!"

As he said the word, another flash of lightning split the sky, blinding them.

Greg and Belinda could hear nothing above the waves and the wind and the engine, but they knew Abi hadn't landed in the boat. They would have felt the weight of her landing.

It took a moment for their vision to adjust. When they looked up to the rock ledge, now on their left, they saw that it was empty. Greg immediately reached over and turned the engine off. If Abi was in the water, she would be in danger from the twin propellers.

Belinda looked at him, horror etched on her face. "Dear God, where is she?"

"Shut up and listen," Greg barked.

There was a faint splutter to their right. Two pairs of eyes scanned the water and spotted Abi's slight frame, her arm reaching out towards them.

"Abi!" cried Greg.

She tried to speak, but a large wave crashed over her, sending her down.

"Abi!" Kicking off his shoes, Greg dived into the freezing water.

Belinda could only watch helplessly as Greg swam towards the place they'd last seen Abi.

The waves were getting stronger all the time. With only one good arm, Greg was struggling, unable to keep himself above the surface, spluttering and choking as the sea flooded his mouth and eyes. Desperately Belinda looked around for something that would help. Grabbing one of the boat's ropes, she hurled it towards Abi.

It fell just short of Abi's reach and she disappeared under another wave. Belinda scanned the raging foam, willing her to reappear. As soon as she did, she threw the rope again, shouting, "Catch, Abi!"

This time it landed within her reach and she caught the rope. Belinda hauled on the rope as hard as she could, dragging the girl towards the boat. As soon as Abi was alongside, she leaned over and grabbed her. Abi was too weak to haul herself up, so Belinda had to hang on for dear life with the waves lifting the boat high and then plummeting down. Just as she thought her strength would give out, the RIB suddenly tilted at an angle that allowed Abi to pull herself into the safety of the boat.

"Daddy, Daddy," she sobbed. "Where's my daddy?"

Belinda looked frantically out into the waves, but in the foaming and crashing water, she could see no sign of Greg.

For what seemed like an age they desperately scanned the water for signs of Abi's father. The tide was ripping in with a vengeance now, forcing *Abi's Gale* against the jagged walls of the cave.

Belinda was the first to realise it was hopeless. "We need to get out of here, Abi. There's nothing more we can do. We must save ourselves." She had to roar above the storm surge to be heard.

"No, no. We must find him. We must." Abi was still desperately scanning the water. "I'm not leaving without my daddy."

"But look, the water's going into the cave. I bet if we go back to the jetty we'll find him there. Come on, Abi, help me get the boat back."

Belinda hoped she was right and that Greg had swum to safety. If not, they would have to trust to the coastguards to find him.

As the boat pulled into its mooring, an anxious Connie and Pru fell on Abi and held her tightly. Pru had grabbed a warm blanket from the *Dorothy* and she wrapped it around her niece.

"Where's Greg?" said Connie.

Belinda shook her head. When Connie saw the look on her face, she started to wail.

CHAPTER
THIRTY-ONE

As the women staggered up the stone steps to safety they were met by a police officer on his way down.

Belinda grabbed him. "He's still down there."

"Who?" answered the police officer.

"Abi's father. He tried to save her life."

"Is there anyone else unaccounted for?" Belinda shook her head. "OK, I'll radio for back-up."

Belinda turned to go back to the cave but the policeman grabbed her.

"Let me go — he's still down there. We have to find him."

"We will," he said, turning her and walking her back out to the garden. "You've done your bit, love. Now go indoors and get warm. There's nothing more you can do here."

The moment she saw Abi, Dorothy ran to her and hugged her tight. "Oh, thank God you're safe!" she cried, leading her towards the Aga. "You poor thing, you're soaked to the skin. We have to get you into some warm things."

Henry moved towards them but was intercepted by Nick the policeman. "There's an ambulance on the way," he said. "They'll take the young lady to hospital, check her over for injuries, hypothermia and water inhalation." Noticing that Belinda was soaked as well, he said, "You'd better go in for a check-up too."

"Oh, Daddy," sobbed Connie, "Greg is missing. He jumped in to try and save Abi and now they can't find him — I think he is dead."

Belinda opened her arms and Connie, her whole body shuddering, collapsed into her embrace. Pru went to them, wrapping her arms around them both.

Connie and Pru sat huddled together in the waiting room of A&E while the doctors examined Abi and Belinda.

Pru had got them hot tea from the vending machine and they wrapped their hands around the warm cups, grateful for the heat.

"I could do with something stronger," said Connie.

"Shame Dad isn't here, he's normally got a hip flask, hasn't he?" Pru replied.

"Oh, I think Mum might have put a stop to all that when they discovered his high blood pressure."

"Shame."

"Quite."

The two sisters looked at each other and shared a smile of mutual understanding.

"Con, listen. There's something I want to say —"

Connie interrupted: "No, let me speak first. There's something I need to get off my chest, something I should have said a long time ago." She looked into Pru's eyes. "I really, really regret hurting you. You were right, I knew what I was doing when I slept with Merlin. I was selfish and jealous and I just wanted to get back at you."

"Oh, Con." Pru held her sister's hand tightly. "We've both been so stupid. All these years, at war with each other — and over that moron. Yes, it was an awful thing to do, but I know I was an awful sister to you." She swiped away her tears. "I should have been grateful to you — I might never have found Francis otherwise. And look at what a treasure I found in him! I've been lucky."

"Unlike me and Greg." Connie shook her head sadly. "Deep down, I've always suspected something was amiss, all those furtive phone calls at odd hours, the weekends away, the suspect purchases on his credit card. I had my suspicions all along, but I kept telling myself what a good husband he was. And a good father . . . there's no denying he worships Abi. Oh God, Pru — do you think he's dead? It will destroy Abi if —"

"I don't know, Con. I just don't know. I promise you though, whatever happens, we'll get through this. I'm going to start acting like the big sister I should have been all along."

"Actually, you're not the big sister any more," said Connie, smiling through her tears.

Pru looked blank for a moment, then gasped. "Crikey, I'd almost forgotten about Belinda."

"Mrs Wilson?"

At the sound of the doctor's voice, the two women jumped up. "My daughter — is she going to be all right?" asked Connie.

354

"Well, she's had a nasty shock and she's obviously very distressed about her father. Physically, we need to monitor her lungs for any side-effects of salt-water aspiration — sometimes victims of near-drowning can suffer a delayed reaction, so we'll keep her under observation for a couple of days just to be on the safe side. Other than that, she has a scrape on her face and a broken ankle, but she should make a full recovery."

"Will it be OK if I stay here too, Doctor?"

"Yes, of course." He looked over his shoulder as Belinda emerged from A&E. "Fortunately your friend didn't inhale any water, so she's free to go."

"Actually," said Pru, "she's not our friend. She's our sister."

It was 5.32 a.m. when the lifeboat crew recovered Greg's lifeless body from the sea. The police liaison officer who'd been sent to Atlantic House to keep vigil with the family broke the news. Henry insisted it would be he that would drive to the hospital to tell Constance and Abi the dreadful news on the following morning.

The next few days passed in a blur. While Connie stayed at the hospital with Abi, Henry did his best to deal with the funeral arrangements and the police inquiry. Francis and Dorothy held the fort at Atlantic House, cooking family meals and seeing everyone was looked after.

They were just sitting down to dinner one evening, with Francis busying himself handing out bowls and plates, when Dorothy paused, serving spoon in hand,

and announced: "You know, Francis, I never quite understood your appeal — till now."

Francis stood, nonplussed, deciding to say nothing until he was sure what turn the conversation was going to take.

"Mummy . . ." said Pru, a warning in her voice.

"It's all right, dear, I just want Francis to know that I am delighted and proud to have him as my son-in-law. Now, pass me those wine glasses, would you?"

"Hear, hear!" Francis felt the pressure of Pru's hand on his leg. He looked at her and smiled. "Mum's right, you know. I don't know what any of us would do without you."

He blinked and looked at his wife's smiling face. "It's what husbands do, isn't it?"

After the dinner, while Jem took Emily to watch television in the rumpus room, Henry, Dorothy, Francis, Pru and Belinda remained around the kitchen table, and the topic of conversation returned to the subject of Susan.

"There's one thing I still don't understand," said Henry. "When your mother told you about me, when you found out who I was, why didn't you just call me?"

"It was all too much to take in. I'd been through a lot already — Brett ending our marriage, Mum's stroke — all within the space of a couple of months. When I found the marriage certificate and wedding photos amongst her things, I was devastated. I'd always thought I was Howard's daughter."

"Howard?"

"He was Mum's boyfriend when I was little. They were together for quite a while. It was Howard who set her up with the flat in Pevensey Bay, but he was married so he never actually lived with us. He used to bring me presents and I'd call him 'Daddy'. I suppose I wanted a daddy like all the other kids had, and he never corrected me or anything so I sort of assumed it was true.

"After Mum told me the truth, I looked you up on Google. It was so strange to see your face. I sat looking at my face in the mirror, trying to see if there was a resemblance. I thought about writing to you, or phoning you up. But . . . well, you'd abandoned Mum, walked out on us. I'd just been abandoned by Brett, I couldn't face dealing with more rejection. All the same, I couldn't let it rest, I had to know what you were like . . . what your other family was like, the one you'd walked out on us for. So I left Eastbourne and rented a house near the Carew factory. Then I met Francis at the school and discovered he was your son-in-law."

"How did you find that out?"

"School-gate gossip. Anyway, once I'd found you, Francis, it felt as if destiny was taking a hand."

Pru shifted uncomfortably in her seat.

Belinda turned to her. "I'm sorry, Pru. I may have looked as if I was making a play for Frankie. It's just that he is such a kind person and I was at a bit of a low ebb. Lonely. Can you understand?"

Pru reached out and touched Francis on the arm. "Turns out I needed a wake-up call. I'd lost sight of what a good man I had."

357

"I don't want to hurt your feelings, Belinda," said Dorothy, "but how can you be sure that Henry's your father and not this James fellow?"

"I'd be happy to take a DNA test."

Dorothy snorted indignantly: "We are *not* the Jeremy Kyle show."

Ignoring his wife, Henry announced, "That will not be necessary. As far as I am concerned I am your father, Belinda. And Emily." She looked at him. "Would you do me the honour of becoming my second granddaughter?"

Second tragic drowning at cursed beach house, said the headline in the local paper.

It has been confirmed that a man in his forties has tragically drowned in the old smugglers' cave beneath historic Atlantic House on Treviscum Bay. The victim lost his life trying to rescue his teenage daughter, who had been trapped on a narrow ledge of the cave by the rising tide. By horrible coincidence, the tragedy happened on the anniversary of a previous drowning at the same location: fourteen-year-old Claire Clovelly perished in August 1978 after hiding in the cave following a family argument. Her heart-broken family never returned to the house, which remained abandoned for ten years until it was sold to the current owners.

A horrible trick of fate — or is there something more at work? Local legend has it that a dying smuggler placed a curse on Atlantic House after he was stabbed and left to drown in the cave by the owner, Sir Rupert Trelawney. Sir Rupert was subsequently arrested but released without charge following the intervention of his wealthy friends, who created an alibi for him. He went on to become Member of Parliament for the county, but had served only a month when he was found dead, apparently of a broken neck, at the foot of the stone steps leading down to the smugglers' cave.

Greg's funeral service was held in Trevay Church.

It was a simple service, touchingly conducted by the Vicar of Trevay, Louise.

Henry paid tribute to Greg's selfless heroism in trying to save his beloved daughter. Abi, still on crutches, insisted on paying her own tribute. Supported by her grandfather and mother, she said simply, "He was the best dad in the world," before placing a small but beautifully crafted model sailing boat on his coffin.

CHAPTER
THIRTY-TWO

Snow was falling gently on the churchyard, muffling the footsteps of the small wedding party.

Henry was looking very handsome in a handmade tweed suit woven in the softest of heathery green wool. His black suede waistcoat, snow-white shirt and paisley cravat were Dorothy's choice.

The bride, wearing an Alice Temperley lace wedding dress in a subtle cream that brought out the colour of her skin and eyes, was carrying a bouquet of mistletoe.

The Reverend Louise was waiting for them at the ancient door of Trevay Church.

"Welcome, welcome, on this happiest of days!" she said, a huge smile creasing her face.

The bride and groom walked down the aisle together, with Emily and Abi as bridesmaids.

The congregation was small. Pru and Francis. Connie and Jem. And Belinda, of course.

The months since Greg's death had been difficult for Connie. Her main focus had been Abi. Painful as Greg's betrayal had been, Connie was careful to avoid all mention of it. Abi didn't need to hear about his failings; it was better to let her remember the father she'd loved as a hero. And for all that he had been a philanderer and a lousy husband, there was no questioning his devotion to Abi. So Connie kept her feelings to herself — except on those occasions when she ran to her sisters for support, and vented the hurt and rage she couldn't acknowledge when Abi was around.

As her parents exchanged their vows, Connie bowed her head when it came to the line about forsaking all others. She could still recall her own wedding day, still hear Greg's voice intoning that vow. Living without him was hard, but living with the truth was harder.

It required an act of will, but Connie pushed all the negativity away. This was a special day — and one to celebrate. It wasn't every day you got to go to your own parents' wedding, after all.

The wedding breakfast at the Starfish Hotel was a low-key but convivial affair. Photos were taken and Dorothy flashed her new wedding ring and the diamond engagement ring. The waiters fussed about with champagne and lobsters; and the cake, when it was carried through the dining room, drew applause from the other diners. Simple and elegant, it was two-tiered with intricate lacy icing with a bride and groom on the top.

Henry stood and hushed the party.

"Before my wife and I cut this cake, we both want to express our gratitude that you are all here today. To have my children and grandchildren here is the greatest gift of all." His voice broke a little and he coughed lightly. "The last few months have been a difficult time for all of us here. For Connie and Abi especially, losing a husband and father. But I think we can all say that the last few months have brought our family closer together. And I know that we are all looking forward to getting to know the new members of our family all the better." His voice caught as he looked at Belinda and Emily.

"This may seem an odd choice of timing on my part, but I would like to take this opportunity to make an announcement regarding my plans for the family business." He paused and looked down at the new gold band on his left hand. "My wife and I have been to see our lawyer. In addition to drawing up a will, we have made certain arrangements that will be set in motion with immediate effect. As of today, Carew Family Board Games is no longer in my name: I have transferred ownership to Pru, Connie and Belinda. The three of them must run it as they see fit as joint chief executives."

Pru and Connie looked at each other in shock. "But, Daddy," said Pru, "I have a job. And Connie and Belinda have no experience of running a company."

"Thanks for the vote of confidence," snapped Connie, dangerously veering back into old territory.

"She's right, though," said Belinda.

"Hey, don't start ganging up on me, just because I'm the youngest."

Dorothy quietened the three of them with a loud "Shhhh".

"If I may continue," said Henry. "In my final act as chief executive, I took the liberty of appointing a new company secretary. He is an excellent organiser who can be trusted to keep a keen eye on the balance sheet and to ensure that the company sticks to its budget." He turned to Francis: "After managing Pru for eighteen years, my boy, I think you'll find the company a piece of cake."

"What?!" spluttered Francis. "But —"

"We'll need to recruit a new MD, of course," continued Henry, ignoring the interruption, "but as joint chief executives, the future of the company is in your hands."

He turned his gaze to his grandchildren.

"Jem, Abi and Emily — when this lot are retired, the company passes to you. If anyone wants to sell the company in the meantime, it has to be a unanimous decision between you all. The will states this most particularly. Do you all understand?"

He looked around at his family, who nodded solemnly. "Good." He picked up his glass of champagne. "And now I want to make a toast. To my family, and in particular, to my long-suffering new wife, Dorothy. I love you all." He raised the glass: "Here's to us!"

Epilogue

Five Years Later

The estate agent placed her clipboard on the worn slate steps of the porch while she found the key to the ancient, silvered oak door.

"It's a marvellous old key, look." She showed it to Mr and Mrs Brigham and their two young daughters.

"Is it a smuggler's key?" asked the youngest.

"Grow up," said her sister. "Smugglers are made up."

"They are not! Are they, Mummy?"

Her mother, ignoring them, was anxiously watching as Danielle Hawkes of Trish Hawkes & Daughter Property Agents, put the old key in the lock.

"The door is a bit stiff. It hasn't been used much ..." Danielle grunted as she pushed her hip against the solid wood and turned the key. "Oof ... there we are."

The door swung open to reveal an impressive oak-panelled hall with light spilling into it from the open door of the grand drawing room.

The family walked through the hall and stopped in front of the windows and the breathtaking view over

Treviscum Bay and the rolling breakers of the Atlantic beyond.

"Welcome to Atlantic House," said Danielle.

Mr and Mrs Brigham looked at each other and smiled. Inwardly, Danielle was smiling too at the prospect of a lucrative sale. The place had been standing empty for several years, following a tragic accident in the cave below. A man had drowned, and the daughter whose life he'd saved wouldn't go near the house after that, so the family had abandoned the place.

"Come and have a look around," she urged. "The previous owner did a great deal of renovation work, but sadly the plumbing has leaked badly and there is some water damage to fix. Let's start upstairs."

The two little girls raced ahead of them. "I want this yellow room," squealed the older girl.

"I saw it first. I want it," said the younger.

"Go and find another one. This is mine."

The little sister stomped off and opened a door at random. It led to a beautiful blue room with double-aspect windows looking out on to the beach and sea.

"This is my one then," she shouted down the corridor. "It's much better than yours."

Her elder sister came running. When she saw the blue room she stamped her foot. "No. This is my room. The other one will suit you 'cos you're little."

"That's not fair."

"'Tis."

"'Tisn't!"

"Shut up, you two!" shouted their father sternly. "Mummy and I need to think!"

Danielle opened the door of the master bedroom with a flourish. "And this would be your room . . ."

Every Time We Say Goodbye

Colette Caddle

It hasn't always been easy, but Marianne has worked hard to give her children a secure and loving home. But then comes the news that changes everything: her husband has been found dead and her future is uncertain.

As Marianne struggles to move on, the past keeps drawing her back. For Dominic Thompson was not the man everyone thought he was. In spite of everything, though, she's not quite ready to believe the worst of him, and she is determined to discover the truth.

Now, even in her darkest moments, there is one thing Marianne can hold on to: a love that has always seen her through . . .

ISBN 978-0-7531-9190-3 (hb)
ISBN 978-0-7531-9191-0 (pb)

Who Needs Mr Darcy?

Jean Burnett

Mr Wickham turned out to be a disappointing husband in many ways, the most notable being his early demise on the battlefield of Waterloo. And so Lydia Wickham, née Bennet, must make her fortune independently. A lesser woman, without Lydia's natural ability to flirt uproariously on the dance floor and cheat seamlessly at the card table, would swoon in the wake of a dashing highwayman, a corrupt banker and even an amorous royal or two. But on the hunt for a marriage that will make her rich, there's nothing that Lydia won't turn her hand to.

ISBN 978-0-7531-9164-4 (hb)
ISBN 978-0-7531-9165-1 (pb)